SEND

SEND

PATTY BLOUNT

sourcebooks

Cover design by Richard Deas
Cover photos © Josef Kubicek/iStockphoto; cuppacam/iStockphoto; joseasreyes/123RF

Published by Sourcebooks Fire, an imprint of Sourcebooks, Inc.
P.O. Box 4410, Naperville, Illinois 60567-4410
(630) 961-3900
Fax: (630) 961-2168
teenfire.sourcebooks.com

Library of Congress Cataloging-in-Publication data is on file with the publisher.

Printed and bound in the United States of America.
BG 10 9 8 7 6 5 4 3 2 1

For my mom, Marie Moreno (1941–2012),

who first showed me the magic that lives in books

CHAPTER 1

Starting Again...Again

A punch to the jaw wasn't how I imagined starting my first day at another new school, but fate had a warped sense of humor.

As a big jock pinned a skinny nerd to the dusty hood of a Civic, I wondered how I, a guy famous for *causing* a tragedy, was now the only person around to prevent one. I scanned the parking lot, but it was deserted except for the two guys locked in a tense clinch and me. If I'd left a minute later or gotten stuck at one more traffic light, I could have been just another kid on the cafeteria line, hearing the buzz. "Hey, did you hear about the fight in the parking lot this morning?" Instead, I was the skinny kid's only hope.

Can you say "ironic"? an annoying voice asked in my mind. *Suppose you plan to swoop in and save this kid or something.*

On a rising tide of panic, I realized I had no other choice. The skinny kid looked ready to pee his pants.

The voice in my head snorted. *You're an idiot.*

I rolled my eyes but didn't bother saying anything out loud. Engaging the voice in conversation only amped up its determination to annoy the crap out of me.

You have two options, the voice said. *Do something or do nothing.*

Yeah. Thanks for that probing insight. With a loud sigh, I cursed my luck and the god who took such perverted delight in twisting it. I guess suffering the kind of trauma I had probably caused some mental health issues.

Probably?

Okay, I amended with an eye roll, definitely some mental health issues. As long as I didn't actually listen to a thing the voice told me to do, I wasn't technically crazy, right? I didn't need *help,* especially the kind that comes from a little white pill or, worse, a mandatory hospital stay. I had it under control.

Dude, be smart. You break up this fight, you're making an enemy, and you can't afford that, not if you want to keep your secret. Just ignore it.

For most people, the little voice in their heads was the voice of reason, a conscience or something. But mine was more like a mirror that reflected the things about me I wished nobody could ever see. He said to ignore it because he knew I'd want to more than anything else in the world.

Because he knew I *couldn't.*

"You're a loser, Dellerman! Always were, always will be."

Cruel words, words I'd heard—worse—words I'd used dozens of times struck the kid called Dellerman, making him flinch.

I grabbed the door handle.

Don't do it, man.

Save your breath. We both already knew that I would. I lived with one kid's blood on my hands. I couldn't handle one more.

The jock was built like some prehistoric caveman, all protruding facial bones and muscle. Lots of muscle. He hauled Dellerman off the Civic's hood by the kid's shirt and shook him. The tendons in Dellerman's thin neck popped into view as he struggled. I opened my car door, rehearsing how I'd tell my parents why we'd have to move *again* after what I was about to do.

You think saving this one is gonna make up for the one you killed?

The words pounded a stake through my heart. I shook it off with a don't-you-get-it laugh. I was hoping to save three, not one. Forgiveness was too much to ask for, and I understood that. But maybe a bit of mercy wasn't. If I did enough good things, maybe I wouldn't spend eternity barbecuing over an open pit in hell. Sure, I didn't want to see this Dellerman kid beaten up, but I also hoped to spare the caveman from the regrets that kicked my ass every damn day.

The caveman would probably not understand my decision to butt in. Okay, he *definitely* wouldn't understand. But eventually, everybody looks back on the stuff they used to do and winces. For most people, that regret doesn't set in until some milestone birthday, but for me, it happened when I was thirteen and a judge sentenced me to nine months in juvenile detention. I'd regretted a lot of stuff since then.

"I'm saving us all," I said, too loud. Captain Caveman spun at the sound of my voice as I shoved out of my car. He appraised me but didn't release Dellerman. He wasn't as tall as me; I knew he was considering his chances. He didn't know they weren't very good.

"Who the hell are you?"

I shrugged. "Don't worry about it. Just leave the kid alone and I'll leave you alone."

He taunted me with lips curled into a mocking grin and a bring-it-on wiggle of his fingers. "Oh, I'm not worried about *you*."

He should have been worried. If he had a brain, he'd have been terrified. According to the state of New Jersey, I was dangerous, a menace to the society it had removed me from for nearly a year.

He threw a punch that I easily blocked. I heard running footsteps behind me and spun. A security guard and a teacher were coming for us. I also saw something else.

A girl. Staring at me from the front seat of a black pickup.

Dude, duck. The warning came a second too late, which he'd probably planned.

The fist that connected with my face clinched it for me. God was bullied as a kid.

First rule of engagement: never turn your back on a threat.

I was on my hands and knees on the grassy median that divided the parking lot, my head thick and curdled from being sucker punched, but even that wasn't enough to silence the voice.

When I look inside me for the voice, I see me but yet…not *me*, not exactly. More like a version of me, the me I used to be at thirteen. All gangly limbs, big feet, and bad skin. I call him Kenny and try to keep him bound to a dark, empty corner of my mind. If I could find a way to gag him too, I'd be psyched. As hard as I fight to forgive myself for what I did to Liam Murphy, Kenny fights as hard to make sure I *can't.* I figure he's just one more part of God's Wrath Plan I'd put in motion five years earlier when I was thirteen.

"Shut up," I told him, out loud.

"What?"

That wasn't Kenny's voice. I forced my head up. My eyes blurred and finally focused on three worried faces, four if I counted the one that existed only in my mind. And I didn't.

Like I care.

I squinted up at the most beautiful girl I thought I'd ever seen. I was having trouble focusing on anything but her face.

"What happened?" the teacher had asked. My stomach pitched when I got a clear look at him. He wasn't a teacher. He was Mr. Morris, the freakin' principal. He was the reason I was at school so early. We had an appointment before first period.

Dude, Kenny chuckled. *You're so doomed.*

"Jeff Dean was going to beat up Brandon Dellerman, but this guy jumped out of his car, walked right up between them, and stopped them. Jeff hit him when he wasn't looking."

Her words somehow penetrated the thick swamp that still choked my thoughts. She saw me jump out of my car? She saw me step between them? If she saw all that, why the hell didn't *she* try to stop them? She was a girl. She would have been safe from the caveman, and I would still be the nameless new guy.

You don't know that for sure.

True, I was forced to admit. But still. Breaking up fights before the first bell wasn't the best way to stay invisible.

The girl turned back to me and asked with a taunting grin, "You okay?"

Hatred, waves of it, rolled over me, pulling me under. She'd stood there, cool and blond and…and…fucking perfect, watching, just watching. She could have stopped it, could have helped. Instead, she'd done nothing. Damn, she was beautiful, like ice in sunlight. Her eyes, a cold blue with black rims, mocked me from behind trendy wire frames. Gold hair spilled around her face, but there was nothing, nothing but the cold. I hated her, hated her down to my bone marrow for what she'd made me do, what she'd made me risk. Mostly, I hated her because she had no idea.

"I'm fine." I scrambled to my feet, my face hot.

"Mr. Ellison, I want you to go straight inside and see the nurse," the principal said. "Our appointment can wait until after."

Mr. Morris knew about my record. That's why he wanted to talk to me. There was no reason why that meeting couldn't take place. My head and face ached, but I'd live. I opened my mouth to tell him so, but he turned to the cold blond.

"Miss Murphy, show Mr. Ellison to the nurse's office and then come see me. I want to hear *exactly* what went on here." The principal turned to address other students now gathering around to watch.

I groaned, but it wasn't at the bark of laughter from inside my head or Miss Murphy's huff of annoyance. It was her name. Of course, it would be Murphy. I turned my eyes to heaven and cursed again. I'd met a Murphy at every school I'd attended, just one more daily reminder of the kid I'd killed.

My face heated as Miss Murphy continued glaring.

"You're shaking." She put her hands on me, eyes narrowed, searching me up and down for signs of serious injury, but it wasn't concern I saw in her eyes.

It looked a lot like satisfaction.

Fuck this. Fuck *her*. As I shoved past, I got a good whiff of her, and my mind blanked on everything except how freakin' good she smelled. She smelled like the beach. Tropical fruit or something exotic. Like sunblock lotion. I loved the beach. Of all the things I'd missed during the months I'd spent in juvenile detention, summer on the water headed the list. Long Island had tons of beaches, another reason I was determined to not mess up this time. Holtsville was the fourth or fifth town we'd tried since I'd killed Liam Murphy.

I wanted to stay here.

Liam killed himself, Kenny corrected, and I sneered.

See, Kenny thinks he's playing me. A few minutes ago, he's making digs that I killed Liam and now it's "Liam killed himself." If I say "up," he says "down." That's what he does. Since the first night I spent locked up, he waterboards my soul. Relentlessly. I knew his game now, so I didn't reply. I couldn't. Not out loud anyway. I was having such a great first day of school; talking to myself would have made it just perfect. Come to think of it, ruining my first day at another new school was probably Kenny's plan all along.

Yeah. I live to serve.

"I'm fine." I shrugged. "Just got the breath knocked out of me."

Miss Murphy's eyebrows shot to her hairline. "Yeah, well, Jeff Dean will be telling a totally different story."

My vision reddened at her taunt. "Oh, I'm sure you'll set everybody straight, since you saw the whole damn thing." I heard her suck in air. Good. I guess nobody ever talked to Voyeur Barbie like that before. I scanned the parking lot's trimmed lawn, tree-lined borders, and rows of parking spots but saw no sign of the caveman. "What happened to him anyway?"

"Security hauled him inside while you were out." Brandon Dellerman answered with a jerk of his thumb toward the building.

I drew myself up to my full height, all six feet three inches of it. "I wasn't *out.* I was just, uh, catching my breath."

Miss Murphy's smirk warned me she didn't buy it.

"Come on. Nurse's office is this way."

Brandon put out an arm, tried to steady me. I took a step, stopped, waited for him to let go.

"Uh, you sure you're okay?"

I grinned down at him. He was like a foot shorter than me. Even if I wasn't okay, I doubted he'd survive the 220-pound impact if I fell on him.

"I should be asking you that."

He let go of me, shrugged, turned red. "I'm okay. Thanks. For helping and stuff. I'm, uh, Brandon. Brandon Dellerman."

"Yeah, hi. Daniel. Dan."

Liar.

Kenny, it's not a lie. That's my name now.

You keep telling yourself that, Danielle.

I ignored Kenny. I ignored Miss Murphy, but she was determined to obey the principal's order. As she led me down the first corridor, she shot me a look so cold I was willing to bet it could freeze a nuclear explosion mid-mushroom cloud and still have enough power left over for the fires of hell.

In my mind, Kenny gasped. I braced for his usual spiteful comment, but it never came. *That* was a first—a profound moment in our history. Because Kenny exists purely to torment me, letting an opportunity go could only mean one thing. He had bigger, more painful retribution planned for later.

Inside the nurse's office, I was anxious to be rid of my escorts so I could talk to Kenny and manage the situation. "Well, we're here." I didn't bother to thank Miss Murphy and quickly turned to Brandon. "Brandon, watch your back. That Jeff Dean guy is dangerous."

The office looked the same as all of the other nurse's offices at all the other schools I'd attended. Posters hung on every wall, warning me to "Drive Responsibly," "Say No to Drugs," and "Pause to Think" before I acted. Another one said this was a "Bully-Free Zone."

I paused to appreciate the irony.

Brandon ducked his head, shaking strands of greasy, colorless hair in front of his eyes, but I could see the fear in them and something else. Something that looked like defeat.

"If you want, I'll give you a ride home after school. Just in case."

Ah, ah, ah. Kenny waved a finger in my head. *Did you forget? You're not allowed to be alone with kids, remember?*

I gritted my teeth and wished I could forget. Even for just a minute.

Brandon's face paled, his acne standing out in sharp relief. "I'll have my car tomorrow."

I blinked. I figured Brandon for a freshman, but he was at least a junior if he had a car. "Offer's good anytime."

Brandon stared at me, his eyes awed. Nodded.

An older woman, like my mother's age, maybe older, approached me wearing scrubs and glasses on the tip of her nose, carrying a folder in her hands. A name tag pinned to her shirt said she was Mrs. Rawlins. She tossed the folder to a desk, grabbed a square packet, and squinted at my jaw. "Daniel

Ellison? Wanna tell me what happened to your face?" She tore open the packet, dabbed a gauze pad on my chin, and a hot belt of pain lashed at me.

"Jeff Dean," Brandon answered for me.

The nurse frowned and nodded, requiring no further explanation. I guess I underestimated Dean's reputation. My breath hissed past my lips when she rolled a brown-tipped cotton swab over my chin.

"This could use some stitches."

No way. My eyes snapped to hers. "Steri-Strips are fine."

Her eyebrows lifted. "I take it you've seen your share of emergency rooms."

Something like that.

"Your shirt's all bloody. Why don't you use that room to change into your gym shirt?" Mrs. Rawlins indicated the door behind her, where another poster warned me to wash my hands during flu season.

The scars. Jesus, the scars. I can't take off my shirt. Shame congealed the blood in my veins.

"You two. Out. Get to class." Mrs. Rawlins had to have noticed the horror on my face.

I knew without looking that the blond was gone. I didn't smell the beach anymore, and I felt cold.

"Have a seat, Mr. Ellison." Mrs. Rawlins indicated a row of chairs by her desk. "Let's call your mom and have her pick you up."

Oh, not a chance. I moved to a chair, taking my sweet time, and planned my next lie.

CHAPTER 2

Sure. Fine. Whatever.

"Well, Mr. Ellison, you've had a hell of a first day so far, haven't you?"

I resisted the great urge to roll my eyes. Mr. Morris was the king of understatement.

"What did Mrs. Rawlins say?"

"That I'm fine." That was only partially a lie. Mrs. Rawlins's exact words were "As long as it doesn't get infected and you don't have a concussion, you should be fine." Whatever. She'd sent me on my way with homework and an ice pack.

He picked up the phone, raising thick caterpillar eyebrows. "Really? When I call to confirm that, she's going to say *fine*?"

Busted.

Oh, good. Kenny was back to normal. "Okay, okay. She thinks my face needs a few stitches, but I told her Steri-Strips were fine. Then she insisted I call my mother."

"Did you?"

I nodded. "Yeah. This," I said with a wave of my hand under my chin, "is nothing compared—" Abruptly, I shut up. I didn't want to discuss my whole juvenile detention record.

The principal's hand came up at that, and his eyes drilled through me. "Mr. Ellison, I know all about your history." He tapped the file folder open before him, and I squirmed. Was this guy a mind reader or something?

Doubt that. Kenny's tone dripped with scorn.

"And I appreciate how Mrs. Rawlins must have embarrassed you, but we are required to notify your parents in a situation like this."

I sighed. "Yes, sir."

He regarded me over the thick folder spread on a cluttered desk. It reminded me of something my grandfather always says about cluttered desks being a sign of genius, and I choked on a laugh. The crumbs from a bagel or muffin sprinkled over memos marked with the school district's logo told me what he'd done first that morning. A pile of bright blue wristbands tumbled out of a torn plastic bag on the corner. I wondered what cause blue represented lately. Steam curled from the Styrofoam coffee cup beside his phone, and a homemade pencil holder was close to bursting with the array of writing implements jammed inside it. Beside it, a Slinky toy sat abandoned and bored.

Mr. Morris was a hands-on principal. This would not be a good thing for me, and I let the dread spread.

He smiled, tight-lipped. "Your…ah…crime is a matter of public record, and you're listed under both of your names."

True.

"I can't lie if I'm asked about your, ah, record. Which means I can't guarantee your secret can be kept."

Also true.

"I advise you to not call attention to yourself. The less conspicuous you are, the less likely your secret will be discovered."

I glared at him. "Mr. Morris, was I supposed to let that kid get beat up?"

Mr. Morris held up both hands. "Mr. Ellison, you're not in any trouble. Julie Murphy and Brandon Dellerman told me what happened. How you stopped the fight. You did the right thing. I've given Jeffrey Dean in-school suspension for picking the fight."

Julie. Her name was Julie. Pretty name. I still hated her. I frowned and blurted, "It wouldn't have been a fight, sir. It would have been a bloodbath." I'd seen hatred in Jeff's eyes.

He held up a hand. "Agreed. I'm *glad* you were there this morning. Brandon would have been seriously injured had you not been there to look out for him. But I'm worried about *you*."

My eyebrows shot into my hairline.

"You'll need to look out for yourself. I can't be everywhere, and you've made an enemy before classes even began."

I nodded with a sigh. I suppose if the risk grew too dangerous, my family could always flee. Again.

"Okay, some other items." He reached for a blue bracelet, tossed it to me. "I want you to wear this."

I glanced at the slogan. *Stand Up to Bullying.* I grimaced, my jaw throbbing as I slipped the wristband over my hand.

"We've got a whole series of events planned to prevent school violence. I expect not only your cooperation but your enthusiastic support of these programs, seeing as you're *reformed* now."

Bro, I'm gonna kick his ass.

With a hand slapped to his shoulder, I kept Kenny pinned down. It's the first test, Kenny. Do not make me fail it.

"Is that all, sir?"

"Almost. Mr. Walsh, our gym teacher, is anxious to meet you. He, ah, knows the truth. I thought it was prudent to keep him informed if you're going to change in the locker room and shower and such."

The shame burned too bright, and I couldn't sit there for one more minute, listening to this bull. "I'm not a pervert, Mr. Morris."

Dick, Kenny muttered. *So much for carefully reviewing our case.*

For once, Kenny and I agreed on something. At least Mr. Morris had the grace to blush.

"No, no, I understand that, but you know how it is. The board, the PTA, a lot of people are concerned that I'm letting a, ah, juvenile delinquent...into their school."

I gripped the armrest of my chair and stared at my feet while Kenny raged inside me. I knew damn well Mr. Morris was going to say something else. I also knew he had no choice but to let me in. You can't break the law and not learn a little something about it in the process. I was thirteen when I broke the law and had to endure a New Jersey court adjudication of delinquency—a legal term for saying I was found guilty. Even though I was a minor, my record is considered *protected,* not sealed, which is why my parents suggested changing our names. My parents also insisted I talk to the principal myself. I wasn't sure if that was because the whole story had made the news or because Liam's family kept threatening me. I agreed. Really, what choice did I have? I was willing to wear the blue bracelet for a chance to finish school, but come on! Locker room supervision?

Please.

After I counted to ten—twice—I looked up. "Mr. Morris, can I say something?" At his nod, I continued, "I was thirteen years old when I did what I did. But I didn't rape anybody. I didn't peer up girls' skirts. I didn't sell pictures to pedophiles, and I sure as hell didn't want anybody to *die*."

Dude. Kenny let out a low whistle. *You tell him.*

"Life has been hell for my whole family, and changing my name seems to be helping. I promise you I'm not about to screw that up."

Mr. Morris's eyes darted around his desk. "Yes. Well. Good. That's, uh, good. See that you keep that promise, Mr. Ellison. You'd better get moving. The bell's about to ring."

I pressed the ice pack Mrs. Rawlins gave me to my jaw and fled, the principal's words replaying in my head: "You've made an enemy."

True. But Brandon Dellerman was the first friend I'd made since my release from juvie.

I might like it here.

Yeah. Me too.

My eyes snapped to Kenny's, but he'd retreated deep into the corner of my mind, where he'd set up his own room. I heard him flip on his stereo and mashed my teeth together.

He knows how much I hate rap.

I strode through the corridors, shoes squeaking on the fresh wax coating over the linoleum. The school was packed with hundreds of kids who avoided me like I was infected with something contagious. This was a good thing.

Kenny's fury did an effective job of masking the pain on my chin. I found my locker, dumped my bag inside, and kept only a three-subject notebook. According to my schedule, my first class wasn't homeroom but public speaking, an elective I had for only the first half of the school year.

I found the classroom, skidded to a stop when I saw Jeff Dean sitting in the first seat near the window.

Oh my God, seriously? You really are cursed.

Curious looks bounced from him to me and then stayed glued on me when I folded myself into an available seat at the back of the room just as the second bell rang. Great. Word had already gotten around. I didn't make eye contact with anybody. Kenny moaned in my mind, and I flinched.

Come on, man, public speaking? What were you thinking?

It sounded fun at the time. But now the thought of standing up and speaking in front of all these strangers had me sweating.

Someone could recognize us. New York is next door to New Jersey, you know.

Kenny had a point. It had been five years, but news of my detention in New Jersey could certainly have reached eastern Long Island, which was another reason for the name change. My heart pounded, and I tried to control it with deep breathing when it hit me.

Her scent.

Julie Murphy smelled like some exotic tropical place—it was full out the most amazing thing I've ever smelled. I looked up, leaned in, and breathed deeply before I remembered I hated her.

"Hey. Doesn't look so bad." She took the seat beside me, dropped an enormous purse to the floor, and jerked her chin at the ice pack I had pressed to my face. "Chin up." She grinned at her own joke.

There was a long pause while I stared, trying to make sense out of Julie Murphy's Barbie Doll looks and steely heart. I expected a great smile. I found full lips pulled into a mocking grin instead. I expected clear blue eyes that twinkled. I found ice blue eyes staring back at me, hard, bored, and disinterested. There was a deep line between her eyebrows, and I wondered how many hours of frowning it had taken to carve that into someone so young.

I managed to string together two words. "I'll live."

Kenny chortled in my mind, and I wished I could kick him physically instead of just mentally. *Yeah. Public speaking. Now I get it.*

Her shoulders lifted in a careless shrug. "Oh well. Maybe next time."

I shot her a dirty look. If that was supposed to be funny, I didn't get the joke. Before I could press the issue, she'd turned her head away from me to greet some girls who'd sat in the next row.

Dude, you pissed her off. Apologize.

Hell no. She should apologize to me. You know what? Forget it and just go back to where you came from.

I come from you.

I gripped my head, wondering if Kenny would ooze out of my ears if I squeezed it hard enough. The teacher arrived and shut the door with a firm click.

"Okay, settle down, people."

He had a big voice, deep and resonant—totally unexpected from the compact body that made him look younger than he was.

"I'm Mr. Williams. This is my tenth year teaching this course, so you guys are an anniversary for me, I guess." His grin was corny. I heard the girls sitting beside Julie Murphy snicker.

"You know my name, but I don't know any of yours, so let's go around the room, shall we? Names and the reason why you decided to take my course. Let's start…here." He indicated the window side of the room, eliciting groans from the six students who occupied those desks. But a sharp knock on the door bought them a few more minutes. Mr. Williams opened the door, took a slip of paper from an aide, and shook his head with a frown. "Really, Mr. Dean? The term has hardly begun and yet you're expected in the ISS classroom."

The class seemed to gasp in unison as Jeff collected his stuff, glaring at me on his way to the door. I sank lower in my seat when all eyes turned to me.

"Okay, okay, show's over. I believe this row was to go first." The students in the row near the window moaned again.

My poor heart pounded again. Everyone would remember me now that they'd seen Jeff's glare of death aimed my way. What would I say? How much could I safely divulge? I rehearsed and revised and repeated and suddenly realized I'd missed the first ten students. Mr. Williams was up to the trio of girls beside Julie. The curly-haired brunette was Lisa, the girl with the ponytail behind her was Morgan, and the cheerleader-type behind her was Ashley.

Finally, it was *her* turn.

"I'm, uh, Julie Murphy, and I'm here because I want to be, like, a psychologist or, um, something like that."

Then it was my turn. "Um. Yeah." What the hell's my name today? Shit. "I'm, um, I'm Daniel Ellison. I'm taking this class because I want to be a lawyer."

My knees bounced under the desk. Two dozen pairs of eyes burned into me and panic choked me.

"What happened to your face?" Mr. Williams asked.

The morning's events played back in my mind, and my temper surged.

"That asshole took a cheap shot." I jerked my thumb toward the door.

The class let out a collective oh. Mr. Williams shook his head. "There are plenty of alternatives to the word *asshole*, Mr. Ellison. Should I make you write them all down?"

Kenny doubled over, giggling.

"No, sir. Sorry," I mumbled.

And then he looked to the guy sitting behind me.

"Paul Oliva. No freakin' idea."

The class erupted, and I was forgotten…by everyone *except* Julie Murphy, judging by the way she kept looking at me.

I liked Mr. Williams, liked the class even though I was terrified of speaking in public, and liked Lisa and Paul. Morgan and Ashley, on the other hand, were nothing but airheads, an observation I shared with Paul twenty minutes after our speech class ended when we met in the locker room to change for gym. He let out a loud laugh at that.

"Hey, all we have to do is look at them. I can handle that much." Paul whipped his shirt over his head, stuffed it in his locker. "Can you imagine how their speech project is gonna go? It won't matter what topic they pick. Every speech they make will sound like it aired on the CW." He let his wrists dangle, fluttered his eyelids, and spoke with a falsetto. "Health care is, like, really important and stuff? So, we all have to, like, you know, really pull together and just, like, do it, for real, you know?" When he pretended to toss imaginary long hair over his shoulder, I clutched my sides, laughing so hard it hurt.

The bell rang.

"Shit. We're gonna be late."

When Paul looked pointedly at the shirt I was still wearing, I paled. I wasn't taking off my shirt in front of anybody. "Meet you up there." I angled my body into my locker, dropped my pants.

"Okay."

Thank God. I watched him head down the row of lockers and turn the corner.

Dude, you know you can't get away with this for long, right?

Yes, Kenny, I'm aware. I let my head fall against a locker with a sigh. I tugged on my shorts, stuffed my jeans into the locker, finally pulled my shirt over my head, and heard a loud gasp.

I spun, smacking an elbow against my locker door, found Paul back in the main aisle, his face frozen in shock, blue eyes bulging.

"What the fu—"

"Forget it," I warned, tugging my gym shirt over my head to hide the scars that crossed my torso like a relief map.

"What happened to you?"

"I said forget it." I slammed my locker and left him there, mouth still gaping.

The day ended. Finally. Fortunately, it appeared I had no more classes with the temper-challenged Jeff Dean. I did, however, have two periods in common with Julie Murphy. Speech class and lunch. I even had one class with Brandon—calculus. I was pretty good at math, but Brandon ran circles around me. Math was my final period, so I reminded Brandon again I'd be happy to drive him home.

"Nice." His face lit up when he saw my car, and I beamed.

"Yeah, thanks. It's new." My parents surprised me with the blue Ford Edge on my eighteenth birthday in April. I was a year older than my classmates—yet another secret I was trying to keep hidden. I put the car in gear, headed west out of the parking lot.

He lifted a shoulder, huffed out half a laugh. "My mom said I could drive her minivan to school once a week. Stay on sixteen until you hit Blue Point Road, then turn left. My dad's got the cool car. Mustang."

My eyebrows lifted as I stopped for a light. "Sweet. Does he let you drive it?"

"Only with him in it, so taking it to school is probably not gonna happen."

I laughed. "Yeah, probably not." I saw Blue Point Road and got into the left turn lane. "This it?"

"Yeah. Go right on Circle Court. My house is that beige one with the red shutters."

I pulled to the curb, hit the button to unlock the doors, and waited while he collected his books.

"So, um, thanks for, you know, everything."

"Yeah, no problem. See you tomorrow."

I waited for Brandon to unlock his front door before I pulled a three-point turn. I had to wait for the school bus belching to a stop midway down the street. A glimpse of blond hair had my stomach flipping. Julie Murphy, hauling the biggest purse I'd ever seen over one shoulder, left the bus and headed up the walk of the house next to Brandon's, a mirror replica in gray. My nose twitched. I remembered how good she smelled. I tracked every motion, every toss of her hair, every move of those long legs. She must have felt my eyes on her because she suddenly turned and glared right at me before she disappeared inside.

Weird.

Probably nothing, I assured Kenny, wishing I believed it.

"There. How's that?"

"Um. Pretty good actually. It doesn't hurt as much anymore."

And it didn't. When you're wounded, a mother's touch held magic. Before my sentence, I hated when my mother kissed me good night. Bandaged my knees. Ruffled my hair. I thought I was way too old, too cool. When I was in juvie, I missed all that mushy mom stuff, so now I allowed myself a moment to sink into it. I gingerly touched her handiwork—the fresh bandage over the swelling in my jaw.

My mother ruffled my hair, and I grinned, a stab of love piercing my heart. "Don't look so surprised, Dan. There are lots of things I'm good at, you know."

Another stab of pain. Every time she called me by that name, it hurt. But we'd agreed.

I hissed in a breath and touched my chin. It really did feel better. Over my eighteen years, I'd given my mother plenty of opportunities to hone her first-aid skills while I learned to operate the huge body I'd developed. Walking with size fourteen feet while the rest of you was still puny wasn't as easy as it sounded. I often wondered why she still bothered after I ruined this family. I'd let her down, but she'd never turned her back on me. She'd fought like a demon to have me transferred to a safer detention center and petitioned the courts to reduce my sentence. I knew I didn't deserve her, but damn it, I was glad I had her.

"Danny. Look at me."

Gray eyes, eyes I'd inherited, stared up at me. There were lines around them now. Lines I'd put there.

"I love you, always will."

My eyes slid shut when Kenny's voice spoke louder.

No. She won't.

"What you did doesn't change that," she said.

Yeah. It does.

"When you're hurt, I'll always take care of you."

No, she won't. She can't. Because she doesn't know.

Her arms came around me and squeezed. Mom didn't know about Kenny. If she did, she'd be lobbying to get me a bed in a mental hospital. The court-appointed therapist I was forced to see once a week didn't know either.

Nobody knew. Nobody could ever know that I saw, heard, and talked to a version of myself, frozen forever at thirteen.

Yeah, but I know.

I don't know *why* or *how* Kenny came to be. I think he's always been there...part of me. But his first appearance *outside* of my head happened when I got jumped in juvie. I thought I was delirious. Until he pointed out my attackers' weaknesses and I got away, bloodied and concussed, but got away. I don't know why he saved me. He hates me. He gets perverse thrills from kicking me when I'm already down. He won't go away. He continues to torment me, and I've been out of juvie for years.

Torment you? I'm a gift.

Yeah? Can I exchange you for something that fits?

Okay, I'm a blessing.

You're a fucking curse. A loud sigh leaked from my lips, and my mother pulled away.

"Tell me about the rest of your day. How did it go with the new name?"

"It was good." The note of incredulity in my voice did not slip past my sharp mother unnoticed.

"You're surprised?"

"Yeah. It's…well, almost too good, I guess. I keep waiting for the other shoe to drop, you know?"

Mom snapped the first-aid kit closed and stuffed it back inside its home in one of the kitchen cabinets.

She loved this room. When we moved here, the expression on her face when she saw the huge sunshine-yellow kitchen with the glass-front cabinets, U-shaped granite countertops, and six-burner stove was like a kid's in a candy store.

Or a kid's on his first day out of juvenile detention.

When she reached over to stir the vat of spaghetti sauce simmering on the stove, I grabbed some plates and started setting the table on the far side of the long room, anticipating the meal ahead. Garlic, oregano, sausage, and meatballs. My stomach let out a rumble. Spaghetti in juvie was a gelatinous mass covered with something closer to ketchup than *gravy*, as my grandfather called it.

My mother tore off a hunk of Italian bread, dipped it into the pot, and handed it to me, holding her hand under it to catch the drips. I devoured it in a single bite, scorching my tongue and throat. I shut my eyes and moaned. God, that was good.

"After word got out about the fight, the kids mostly avoided me, nothing new there," I said when I could talk. My mother was stirring the sauce again. "But there's this girl—"

The spoon clattered to the stove.

"A girl? What girl? Is she pretty?" Mom grinned and waggled her eyebrows, then leaned across a gleaming counter to hang on every one of my words. I laughed, even though my face got hot.

"No, Mom, it's nothing like that. She, um. Well, she's how this happened." I indicated my bandage. "She saw everything but didn't do anything. She just *watched*." The fury washed over me just remembering how she recited everything that had happened with complete indifference.

My mother just kept grinning. "Give her a chance. Maybe she's just shy."

Yeah. Sure.

My mother was one of those irritating glass-half-full people. Always thought everything was going to work out for the best. I shook my head and put flatware beside the plates I'd arranged.

"Hey. You're short a place setting."

I clenched my jaw, flinching at the pain it induced. "Mom, you know he won't—"

"Daniel."

Murderer.

Shut up! I screamed silently.

"He'll come around. Just give it time."

Time? I snorted out a laugh. "Mom, it's been years. Pop's not getting any younger and neither am I." I turned away. I couldn't talk about this anymore.

"Danny, honey." She put out a hand to stop me, but I shrugged it off. "Danny. Wait."

I ignored her, stalked out of the kitchen, but Mom could be stubborn when she had to be. She chased me through the dining room we hardly ever used, into the family room, and out to the foyer, where abstract Pier One art hung in place of family photos. Those were all upstairs, where no one could see them and figure out we were a family of liars. I had one foot on the steps that led to the second floor when she shouted. "Damn it, *Kenny*. I said wait."

I froze for a moment, one foot still raised. Then I whirled to stare at my mother, stunned. It was against the rules, my parents' rules. We'd agreed never to use my real name. I wasn't Kenny anymore. That name belonged to the voice in my head. And to my grandfather because I was named after him. Now I was Daniel Ellison, a name I chose because Daniel meant *God is my judge* and Ellison came from the prayer, *Kyrie Eleison*.

Lord, have mercy.

Kind of unrealistic, expecting anyone to show me mercy after what I did, but like I said, it was my parents' idea. After people found out who I was and what I had done...well, it was another reason why we had moved a bunch of times.

"I know your grandfather's hurting you, and I don't know why, I swear. He doesn't talk much to me either. But he lives here too, and he is always welcome at the dinner table, no matter who isn't talking to who." She climbed two steps so she could look me in the eye, put her hands on my shoulders, and squeezed. "He'll come around. I promise you he will. Just keep the door open, okay?" Her hand moved to my cheek. "For me? Please."

Sudden stinging behind my eyes compelled me to squeeze them shut. I nodded. How could I not do whatever she asked of me after all I'd done?

"Oh God. What's wrong? What happened?"

My father was home, his face a study in terror.

"It's fine. Everything's fine, hon." Mom hurried to him, put a soothing hand to his chest. "Danny's had a so-so day."

When she pointed to my bandaged chin, his eyes popped, so I walked back down the steps and returned to the kitchen to start the story from the beginning.

CHAPTER 3

It's Official: My Life Sucks

The next day, the sun was hot enough to pull heat waves off the asphalt. I followed the road that snaked into the parking lot, trapped behind a lost parent confused by the drop-off procedure. I found a spot near the same grassy median where I face-planted yesterday, finally noticing the decent property this school had. Plenty of parking, places to walk without risking life and limb, air-conditioned classrooms. This school even had a pool. I thought about the high school I would have attended back home in New Jersey. That building dated back to the seventies. No air-conditioning. No pool. This place was so much better, and I was glad to—

Abruptly sick, I killed the engine, scanning the lot for trouble. It was a habit now, born during my stay at the Monmouth County Detention Center, and it had saved my neck more than once.

Kenny's loud sigh echoed in my head. *Dude. Nobody's looking to get the jump on you. You're safe.*

I snorted out a laugh. Yeah, right. Safe.

Hey, I told you to stay out of that fight. Don't blame me if the whole new identity thing falls apart.

Yep. That you did. I acknowledged with a tight frown. How could a voice in my own head know so little about me? Better question, why did I care what a voice in my head thought? All I knew was that I couldn't live with any more guilt. It was like I swallowed a slow-moving poison that was killing me a cell at a time. You'd think the voice that knew what I was thinking would know that or something.

Boohoo.

Why are you here, Kenny? I'm not in juvie anymore. I don't need you.

I lumbered out of the car and aimed the key chain remote to lock it.

He was suddenly standing right there, blocking my way.

Yeah, you do. He jerked his chin over my shoulder.

I followed his gaze, saw Julie talking to Jeff a few rows down beside the same tricked-out black pickup truck. My teeth clenched. What the hell did she see in this guy? Okay, so he was popular and on the football team. And he was good looking, if the way all the girls' eyes tracked his every move was any indication.

Heh. Like lookin' in a mirror.

I do not look like that.

Whatever you say, man.

Julie was mad; I saw the crease in her forehead from here. She put a hand on Jeff's chest, said something I couldn't hear, and my hands clenched. She shook her head and turned to walk away, but Jeff grabbed her arm, swung her back around with a loud "Hey! I'm not done!"

I sprinted toward them before Julie's hair resettled.

Bad idea, dude! Kenny shouted in my head, but I tuned him out.

"Let go of me." She twisted out of his grasp, gave him a little shove that did nothing but enrage Jeff more.

"Shut your mouth and listen to me." He grabbed her again.

"Get your hands off me!"

I was already there, prying him off Julie and pinning him to the hood of the black truck. He broke my hold, spun to face me, but my other hand was already fisted. I cocked it back, made sure he saw it. "She said take your hands off her."

"New guy." Jeff pushed the words through teeth clenched tight enough to leave impressions in metal. "You hot for me or something? Every time I turn around, you're in my face."

I scoffed, ignored his feeble attempt to rile me. "Maybe that's because your face is always where it shouldn't be."

He shook my hand off. "My face? You're the one stickin' his nose into my business. Back off or—"

"Or what? Huh, Dean? What do you think you're gonna do?" I smiled the kind of cold grin I'd perfected in detention, the kind of smile that confused my opponents, and God knew I had a lot of them over the years.

"I said I was sorry, Jeff," Julie said. "Please. Just let it go."

He glanced from her to me, his body still angled toward mine. With one last glare at Julie, he stood down, stepped away, and flung up his hands. "Okay, fine. I'll stay out of it if you do me a favor. Don't get between me and Brandon anymore. And you," he said and punched a finger at me. "You don't know who you're dealing with."

"Yeah, yeah, yeah." I wasn't intimidated. *Intimidating* was six kids in men's bodies glaring at you in the common area of a juvenile hall while the guards' backs were turned. I wasn't afraid. *Afraid* was six kids in men's bodies coming for you in the dark. Jeff was about as tough as a loaf of white bread. He stalked off, shooting glares over his shoulder every few feet. I held my stance until he was out of sight.

"You okay?" I asked Julie, who stared at me with a mixture of fear and surprise etched on her face.

"Perfect," she said with a big fake grin after she stared for a whole minute. She readjusted the huge bag on her shoulder and took a step toward the school building. "I had it, you know. You didn't need to—"

"Butt in?" I snapped, my voice tight.

Her eyes darted to mine, hurt, then shifted away. She had on different glasses today, and these frames really called attention to her eyes.

Oh, hell.

I walked away, then walked back. "Look, I'm sorry." A quick glance at her face told me she was confused. Confused was better than hurt. I could work with confused. "I just don't get what you see in that guy."

You and me both, man.

"Wait." She put her hand on my arm, and my arm twitched. "You think...me and Jeff...oh God, no!"

"You're not seeing him? You're not his girlfriend?" My stomach tightened at the thought. Or maybe that was just Kenny.

She wrinkled her face. "No. What made you think that?"

"Oh, I don't know. Maybe I got it from you watching him while he got ready to tear the limbs off Brandon? Yeah. That had to be it." I took off walking again.

Back the hell off, man. Kenny warned me with a light love tap to my head that made me stumble a step.

Julie caught up to me. "We dated for like a month back in freshman year. Now he's with my friend, Colleen. He drives me to school once in a while because he lives around the block. So, uh, where the hell did you come from? When Jeff stopped me, I looked around for help and didn't see a soul."

That stopped me in mid-stride. I whirled to confront her. "Let me get this straight. Jeff goes after Brandon and that was just fine. But when Jeff comes after you, you expect someone to help you? Have I got this right?"

She met my gaze, her face carefully arranged to look neutral, but I caught the muscle twitching in her jaw. "Look, you're new here. You don't know the whole story with Jeff and Brandon, okay?"

"What, and you do?"

"Yes. And unlike you, I don't think Jeff is entirely wrong here. Also unlike you, I mind my own business. Except for yesterday."

"I'll remember that next time I see him hassling you," I snapped and strode off, but she was right behind me.

"Hey, wait!" Her tug on my arm barely penetrated my anger. "I appreciate what you did. But you don't know Jeff. I do. He's got some problems. He'll deal with them. I know how to handle him, so just stay out of this, okay?"

I stared at her for a good thirty seconds, processing her words. Was Jeff really that bad? Whatever. I wiped sweaty hands down my jeans. Crap, I left my phone in my car. I started walking in the opposite direction, Julie on my heels.

"Nice." She jerked her head toward my car, looking up at me from under her eyelashes. I spent a thought-scattering minute wondering if that was how she looked when she was kissed. "I'm curious. What was it doing in front of my house yesterday? Did you follow me home or something?"

I jerked, slammed my head on the doorframe as I reached in for my phone. I hoped she didn't notice my knees buckle. "I'm not a stalker, Julie. I didn't follow you. All I did was take Brandon Dellerman home. I don't hurt women, so you don't have to be afraid of me."

"Jeez, obsess much?" Her mocking grin widened. "I was just asking."

"I gotta go." I locked the car again.

"So, go," she mouthed with exaggerated slowness. With a flip of her hair, she walked away, and when I closed my eyes, I swore I was on the beach.

Hmm. Weird. I thought she was his girlfriend.

Yeah, it *was* weird. Maybe they're not over each other. No. Don't even go there.

Why not, man? She likes us.

Kenny. Give it a rest. I don't like *her*.

Really?

I stared at him, my jaw hanging. You—*you* like her, don't you? That explained a lot.

Kenny wouldn't look at me and kept walking. I hurried to catch up and pressed him again. Come on, admit it. You like her.

He turned on me as we walked through the main doors. *I'm not telling you anything. You'll just use it to hurt me. You always do.*

I...I don't. I don't hurt you. I just want you to leave me alone.

You don't get it, genius. I can't.

Oh, I get it, Kenny. Nine months in juvie wasn't enough. Getting carved up like a Thanksgiving turkey wasn't enough. Watching Mom and Dad ostracized and harassed wasn't enough.

Too upset to think straight, I continued out loud. "You're here to haunt me for the rest of my fucking life. I get it. Believe me, I get it, so just answer the damn question already. People are staring. Do you like her or not?" A chubby girl shut her locker and looked at me funny. I held up my cell phone and touched an ear hidden by too-long hair, hoping she'd believe I had a Bluetooth.

I did not.

The terms of my reduced sentence stipulated my cell phone had no online access. No texting. No web surfing. No pictures. I'm pretty sure I was the only guy in America who used his cell phone only to make calls.

The bell rang, and Kenny ran to his corner, slammed the door without answering me. I could hear him, muttering, shuffling around. I pounded on the door, demanding a response, but he was silent.

Looks like Julie was going to be a problem.

A big one.

First period. I was nearly late. I had to stop at my locker and regroup after my encounter with Julie. What the hell was between her and Jeff? She seemed like an okay girl when she wasn't intentionally pissing me off. What was she doing with him?

Dude, you heard her. They're not dating.

Yeah, I'd heard her. So if they weren't dating, what was that argument about? I dropped my backpack and slid behind my desk, trying to ignore the biting pain in my chin that was somehow worse today than yesterday. Jeff was already in his seat near the window, and Julie was already in the seat beside mine. I cursed under my breath when the desk shifted a few inches, the screech making me clench my jaw, ratcheting the pain up to maximum. Julie's head swiveled to me, the line between her eyebrows flashing once while I cradled my head, watching her from under my lashes.

Her black plastic glasses caught my eye again. As my gaze traveled over her curves, I realized the glasses matched her outfit—tight black pants ending high on her calves, with a skimpy white T-shirt that revealed glimpses of a smooth belly if she moved in just the right way. My mouth fell open. Black-and-white sandals showed off a toe ring. She looked up at me from under a curtain of gold hair, blue eyes crinkling at the corners.

Busted.

Kenny laughed when my face got hot.

"That looks a lot worse than it did yesterday."

I glared. "Feels worse too."

She made a face. "Aw. Poor little you."

It sounded like she was making fun of me. I swore if she told me to keep my chin up again, I would have to extend a finger.

Kenny choked. *Oh, please. Like Saint Daniel even has a middle finger.*

Okay, maybe I wouldn't, but I would really want to. Kenny was about to retort, but luckily, the teacher walked in at that moment.

"Okay, people, settle down. Settle down." Mr. Williams hurried to the head of the class. "Starting here, everybody count off one to four and then repeat. Go."

He tapped the guy sitting to my right, who dutifully said "One."

By the time the count went up one aisle and down the next, I was a three.

"Okay, grab your gear and stand up. I want the ones over here by the door, twos here in this row, threes in the back of the room, and fours by the window. Move."

Desks screeched on linoleum. Laughing and chattering, we mixed. I noted with a mix of interest and annoyance that Julie was also a three.

We settled in the back of the room and watched, amused, as Paul Oliva and Lisa McKenna traded their spots with the two girls in our group and made their way to us. The girls joined the other half of their clique at the window and squealed. At the same time.

I rolled my eyes.

"Yeah. Tell me about it." Paul caught me and nodded. "I figured they'd be dead weight anyway."

I laughed. No doubt he was right.

My eyes roamed, looking for something that made this classroom different from myriad others I've been in since I got out of juvie. The same chalkboards, the same desks, the same sounds and smells. Another Murphy.

This Murphy was staring at me.

"What?" I challenged her.

Her eyes narrowed, and she shrugged. "Nothing. You just look familiar."

Irrational panic exploded in me, and I had to run.

Easy! This time, Kenny pinned me in my seat. *Don't be an idiot.*

With every ounce of strength I had, I stayed put. He was right. Damn it, I hated it when Kenny was right. My father constantly reminded me to stop acting like a guilty man, which was hard to do when *murderer* is branded over your heart like Hawthorne's *Scarlet Letter*.

I'd killed a child—not with a gun or a knife or my hands but with words and technology. There were no degrees of guilt. You're either guilty or you're not—and I am.

Julie stared at me as Mr. Williams again called for our attention, but my mind was still spinning. Maybe she'd recognized me. Maybe she was related to the same Murphys. Oh God. Maybe her brother was Liam. How could I find out without divulging that I was the one who'd killed him? I was pretty sure Liam had no sisters. The only relatives ever in court were his parents. Hell, I didn't even know his name until after I…until *after*, when it was all over the news. No. No, it couldn't be true. I'd gone to a school with hundreds of other kids in a New Jersey beach town, and it was there where I'd teased and taunted little Liam. If he had a sister, what would she be doing in a school in a town a hundred miles away? No, I was being paranoid, that's all. The odds were just too great to imagine.

Maybe, but that's just the kind of luck you have.

True that.

I kept sneaking glances at her. She didn't look familiar. Just as I breathed in relief, Kenny hit me with this: *Think about it, genius. All the memories, the heartbreak. They probably moved away to escape it all, start over. You know, like you did.*

I cursed Kenny out loud, but nobody noticed. I hadn't thought about that. Of course, that was likely. I needed to stay far away from Julie until I could be sure. My parents would know about Liam's family. They'd had to file a restraining order against his father.

"Okay, guys, here's the plan. Working in teams of four, you'll reach into this hat, pick a bill congress is considering passing, research it, and then present your stance on it—pro or con. The goal is to win support for your position, so even though you are working in quads, you will present to the entire class with the goal of winning their votes." Mr. Williams approached our group. "Miss Murphy, any idea why this assignment is a good idea?"

Julie's eyes popped. "Uh. No."

Mr. Williams turned to Paul. "Mr. Oliva?"

Paul shrugged.

"Mr. Ellison?"

I swallowed. "Um. Well. I guess because persuading others to see your point of view is an important skill for someone who wants to be a lawyer?"

Mr. Williams inclined his head. "One of them." To the rest of the class, he continued, "The ability not merely to speak but to speak eloquently under pressure cannot be overstated. Just ask former president Bush."

The class snickered.

"In this assignment, you'll learn how to prepare your facts and respond to attempts to derail your progress." He clapped his hands. "Okay, examples. *Roe v. Wade*, legalizing marijuana use." He ignored the hoots that rang out across the class at that one and tossed a pile of handouts to the student in the first desk, who passed them along. "Here's the rubric. Now decide who picks."

Noise levels rose as the groups complied.

I turned to Paul, who looked at me in horror. "Not me."

Julie's glacial eyes were still stuck on me. With a lift of my eyebrow, I dared her.

"You pick."

She shook her head.

"Fine. I'll pick the damn law out of the hat."

I should have known better than to tempt fate. I gulped when I unfolded the slip of paper and read it.

The Good Samaritan Laws.

My life sucked.

Oh, man. This is hilarious, Kenny said. I shot him a glare.

Sweating, I tapped one of the girls in the group beside ours. "Wanna trade laws?"

The girl, hot in a common way with the same hairstyle, same clothes as the other girls, exchanged a glance with her teammates. "What law did you pick?"

"Good Samaritan Laws."

The girl stared at me, a bit frightened. "No, thanks. We got the health care reform bill." She smiled brightly as she turned back to her friends.

Paul choked back a laugh and caught my eye. "I should play the lottery or something." His smile faded, and he jerked his chin toward Julie. "What's with her?"

She sat frozen, her eyes glassy and fixed on the description of the law printed on our handout, now clutched so tightly in her hand the paper crinkled under the pressure. My own anxiety faded in comparison.

She's upset, man. Find out why.

Screw that.

When Kenny's eyes—which I suppose were my eyes—narrowed, I caved in. "Julie, you okay?"

She jerked like I'd slapped her. "Yeah. Fine."

Kenny nudged me again. *Fix it, make it better.*

I laughed and hastily covered it with a cough. Kenny was not a fixer. He was a breaker. Kenny liked Julie, but I didn't. Could my life get any weirder?

"You don't look fine. You look sad. Something wrong with this law?"

She speared me with a look so cold I swore I could see my breath as I exhaled.

We still had twenty-five minutes of class left. Lisa scooted her chair to the computers that lined the rear wall of the classroom and Googled the law I'd picked. The screen showed four million hits. Four million.

"Hey. Earth to Dan." Lisa snapped her fingers in front of my face. "How about making yourself useful?"

"Um. Yeah. Sure. Just thinking."

"Freakin' blonds," Lisa muttered.

I rolled my eyes. The blond was on my mind but not for the reason Lisa suspected. Julie watched but did nothing while her boyfriend almost broke a freshman into pieces. Didn't even open a cell phone. How could somebody do that?

"Here. Start taking notes." Lisa tapped the monitor in front of us.

I clicked a pen, grabbed my notebook, and did what I was told. We learned Good Samaritan laws varied from state to state and existed primarily to prevent rescuers from being held liable for injury or illness that resulted from the rescue itself. In some states, these laws also included a "duty to rescue," making it illegal to do nothing while witnessing someone in danger.

"This is a ridiculous law."

My eyes snapped to Julie's. "Yeah, I guess it's ridiculous to help people who need it."

She shrugged, refusing to meet my gaze. "No. Just, well, ridiculous to force people to help. What if you get hurt too? Or maybe you just, I don't know, freeze up? Can't think of what to do, so you do nothing? What then? You go to jail because you panic under pressure?"

Lisa, Paul, and a few other people stared at Julie, who was totally unaware that her voice was quivering. Her eyes shimmered, and it was hard to miss she was on the verge of tears. But that didn't stop me.

"When you stand by and watch someone beaten up just because you think he's a…a dork, then, yes, maybe you should go to jail."

Her eyes popped, and she whispered, "That's enough."

Oh, I was just getting started. "I wonder how many other kids you've watched Jeff smack around. This some kind of sport to you?"

She leaped up so quickly her chair fell over. "Go to hell," she muttered, swinging her enormous purse over her shoulder and running from the classroom. Two dozen eyes stared at her back. Then two dozen pairs of eyes swung to me, full of "Oh, shits" and "What the hells."

You jerk, Kenny screamed. *You made her cry. You made her fucking cry.* In my head, his raging was so loud I wished I could climb out of my skin to escape.

Okay. Okay, you win. I'll find her and apologize. Knock it off.

The destruction in my head stopped. My eyes slid closed in blessed relief only to fly open when I felt a tap on the back of my head.

Kenny stood in front of me, hands on his skinny hips. *Make it good. You know I'll be watching.*

So much for staying away from Julie.

CHAPTER 4
Watching Like It's MTV

On my way to my third-period class, I spotted Julie at her locker. Kenny pushed me to catch up. I smelled the beach again, and it pissed me off. Kenny's crush on Julie was going to kill me. First, I hated her. Second, she hated me back. Third, I didn't date. Ever. Two reasons for that: first, I didn't know how long we'd be staying in a particular town, and secondly, nobody could get to know me, really know me, because I couldn't share anything about myself. Anything that was true at least.

You want me quiet? Then fix this. He slammed the door to his room and rattled my teeth. I pressed a hand to my aching jaw.

"Hey."

Annoyance flashed across her face.

Say something, man. She's not happy.

"Okay. Look, I'm sorry."

She scoffed and rolled her eyes.

"No. Really, I am. I didn't mean to upset you."

"Yeah, you did." She took a few steps, whirled, and stalked back to me. "You think I'm an idiot, right? An airhead or something? Cheerleader Barbie?" She pushed at her blond hair like it offended her.

I hid a grin. Airheads had been the sum total of my assessment of the girls in our speech class but not Julie. She caught my grin and misinterpreted it.

"From the first second you saw me, I knew you were thinking I was the biggest bitch in the world because I didn't help."

Okay. She was right. I looked at the floor. "Still. It was mean to hit you with that in class."

She shook her head, lip curled into a sneer. "You're unbelievable. You won't even try to deny it."

I lifted my palms. "Why deny something that's true?" And then I got mad all over again. "Tell me how you could do it. I sat in my car for five damn minutes, waiting for someone—anyone—to stop Jeff so I wouldn't have to do it myself. You were there the whole time. Just watching."

Her eyes turned arctic, and her body tensed. "I may have been there. But if you think I get off on seeing kids bleed, you're just sick. You were there, you broke up the fight, so what exactly is the big deal here? You break a nail or something?" She did a little dance with her hands waving in the air.

Grinding my teeth, I ignored the last part of her attack. "You were watching the whole thing like it was MTV."

She slapped a hand to my chest, tried to shove me back a step. "Stop it. I was staring, but I wasn't *watching*." Her eyes glared with outrage.

"Oh, that clears it all up."

"You don't understand."

"No, you're right about that. I don't understand at all." I took a step forward, and she took a step back, pressed against the lockers. "Enlighten me. Tell me what you were staring at but not *watching*."

Knock that crap off, man. She's not a threat. Stop trying to intimidate her.

I'm not!

You are.

I could see myself reflected in her glasses. She pressed her lips together, swallowing hard, and a new wave of self-disgust washed over me. Kenny was right. I'd scared her. I took a step back, put some space between Julie and me.

"I…I can't. You'll think I'm crazy," she finally said.

A laugh escaped my lips before I mashed them together. "Crazy's kind of a relative term for me."

She stared blankly, and I didn't bother to explain it. "I wasn't seeing Jeff and Brandon. It…it just reminded me of…something else. From when I was in eighth grade." She shut her eyes, shivered.

Leave her alone, man. No more. Kenny squeezed my arm in warning. *You're not the only one with scars.*

I ignored him. "So you're saying you had a flashback? You…froze up?" She'd said the same thing in class, and I hadn't believed her.

She nodded, waiting for me to say something more, something less jerky. But I had nothing. She stiffened, and her eyes went back to full cold. She took a step away.

"Wait." I found my voice. "Okay. If this assignment bothers you this much, maybe we can go to Mr. Williams this afternoon and, like, pick again or something."

Julie shook her head. "No, it was a long time ago. I think it's time I finally did something." She showed me that patented mocking grin. "I'm sure you'll agree."

I lifted a shoulder. Who was I to judge how long it should take to heal from a trauma? "I mean it. I'm sorry."

Slowly, she nodded. "Good. Thanks. I was starting to think you were a bigger bully than Jeff and—"

My blood boiled over at her words. I slammed a palm against the locker next to her and stalked off, bowling through a trio of kids in my way.

Jesus, dude! Are you crazy? All you had to do was apologize, but you totally messed things up. You scared the hell out of her. She'll never talk to us again.

Good.

Who needs her.

CHAPTER 5

Racking Up the Points

At lunch, I'd spotted Brandon at his locker in the south corridor. I stopped at a water fountain, watching from under my lashes as he swapped books. He hunched down into himself like that cloaked him in invisibility or something. A chubby girl at the next locker edged away like he had an infectious disease. He gave no sign that he cared or even noticed until she slammed her locker and walked away. His eyes tracked her for a few seconds, and even from across the hall, I could see his pain.

Don't bother. It won't help.

I don't know what you're talking about, Kenny.

Oh, please. You can't lie to yourself, bro. Kenny tapped his temple.

I ignored him and followed Brandon down the hall, watching him sidestep the foot that tried to trip him and dodge the hand that tried to knock the books out of his arms. The corridor was a battlefield. No, it was a hunting ground, and Brandon was in season.

Dude, if you help him, you become him. Get it? You'll be hated.

Hated.

I considered that. With a grandfather who wouldn't talk to me, a gang of childhood friends who abandoned me, it was pretty clear I already was hated. What was a few more names on such a long list?

Kenny made a sound of disgust. *You are so slow. Come on, man, see the light!* He threw his hands in the air. *If they hate you, they will target you. They will look for the things that can trip you up. And they'll find them. Jeff Dean is already sniffing.*

My hands clenched into fists. Damn it! Why was this so hard? Anybody could see Brandon was suffering. Anybody who bothered to actually look, that is. Five years back, I'd have been one of the people sticking out his foot as the kid passed me. A flush of repulsion passed over me, and my skin crawled. I wasn't proud of my past.

It's risky, man. Too risky for someone so into hiding his identity.

I shrugged. Yes, it was a risk, but I still had my new name. Making friends with one kid wasn't going to out me unless everybody found out I also have a record. I followed Brandon into the lunch line. I grabbed a tray, piled on two cellophane-wrapped sandwiches, a Snapple, and an apple, purposely jostled a kid with that let's-get-Brandon gleam in his eye I'd already come to recognize, and paid for my meal.

Brandon didn't notice me until I sat beside him at a table in the center of the room. Center tables were like the *Titanic*'s steerage section. Cool kids had their far corner tables already reserved. I felt their eyes on me as I screwed off the cap of my juice. "Hey, Brandon. Mind if I join you?"

He peered at me through strands of greasy, colorless hair and shrugged. "It's your reputation."

"I don't have a reputation. I just got here."

He bit the corner off a square slice of what masqueraded as pizza here. "Yeah, that's my point. Eating with me isn't going to help."

"Do I look worried?" I unwrapped a sandwich, bit halfway through the first triangle, and spoke with my mouth full. "I don't know anybody here but you and figured you're better than eating by myself."

He laughed once, a rasp of air that held no humor. "Yeah, well, that's a first. I've been eating alone since seventh, no...sixth grade."

"That really blows."

Another laugh, this time with sound. "Yeah, tell me about it." He nibbled another piece of his pizza. "So, what's up with you and Dean? Heard you broke up another fight."

Told ya so.

Ouch. I winced. "Uh, you heard about that, huh? It wasn't a fight. Just an argument. I tried to help. What the hell is his problem with you anyway?"

Brandon shrugged. "I exist."

I finished the first sandwich and started on the second. "You never did anything to him?"

Brandon made no response except for the shadow that passed over his face and watched me eat. "You always eat sandwiches in, like, four bites?"

I shot him a look and waved my hand, encouraging him to answer my question.

"Fine. I stole his girlfriend once."

The hand about to tip the Snapple to my mouth froze, mid-flight. Brandon grinned. "Gotcha," he said.

I laughed and hated myself for believing Brandon couldn't possibly win any girl from Jeff. People nearby stared at me for laughing. I glared back.

Yeah. I'm laughing. I'm eating lunch with Brandon Dellerman, and I'm laughing. Assholes.

"Seriously, what's his problem?"

Brandon sighed and stared down at his grease-stained paper plate. "We…uh…used to be friends. When we were little. Then Jeff's mom died, and he's…well, let's just say he didn't handle it well."

I tried to imagine it. My own mother's death. Immediately, my chest tightened, and my lunch soured. Too much. Way too much. "I don't think anybody could handle that well."

Brandon shrugged. "Yeah, well, he blames me. Like I killed her or something. He's been pissed off at me ever since her funeral."

I angled my head, waited for him to confirm or deny. "You didn't have anything to do with her—"

Brandon's eyes darted to mine, huge and hurt. "No way, man! She had, like, cancer or something."

I was totally lost now. Why would Jeff hold Brandon accountable for his mother's natural death?

Dick, do I need to remind you there are two sides to every story? Maybe you should ask Jeff what his problem is.

Jeff's an idiot. I don't need his version.

Yeah. You do.

I wanted to ignore Kenny's insistence but was too curious. Just when I was about to press Brandon for more details, I noticed the way his hands shook, so I quickly changed the subject. "So, what is there to do in this town? You don't have a skate park. I checked."

"You skateboard?"

"No. In-line." In-line skating helped me maintain my ice-skating skills when I couldn't get near a rink. I hadn't been near a rink in years. "I play hockey."

Brandon nodded. "I'm not into sports. I just play a lot of video games."

At last. Common ground, neutral territory. We spent the last fifteen minutes of the lunch period exchanging tips on *Assassin's Creed*, *Call of Duty*, and *Madden NFL*. I'd had to intimidate one brave soul who dared to throw something at Brandon as we made our way to the recycling bins. He immediately backed off and even apologized.

Smart kid.

When the bell rang and Brandon took off with a grin—a real one this time—I figured maybe whatever coolness I had by virtue of going hand to hand with Jeff (and living to tell about it) might rub off on him.

Want a medal?

You know, you were quiet during lunch. I like you a hell of a lot better like that.

Yeah, yeah, yeah. I missed you too. You're wasting your time with Brandon.

I was being nice.

Kenny rolled his eyes—my eyes—whatever. *You're not just being nice to him. You're trying to save him. You're only doing it for maximum points.*

I blinked. You don't know what you're talking about.

Really, man? 'Cause it seems to me you're hoping there's a scorecard somewhere. You kill one, you save one, you're off the hook. Hate to break this to you, but I don't think that's how it works.

No. No, you're wrong. I tried to argue, but Kenny was done. He slammed the door to his cave, jacked up his stereo.

Drowning Pool's "Bodies."

Awesome.

CHAPTER 6

Big Scary Things

The days piled up, one on top of the other, the way they do when you fall into a routine. September bled into October with warm days, but the air lost that heavy wetness that made you feel like you were trying to breathe underwater.

I liked it. In fact, I loved the ordinariness of it. I got up, went to school, came home, worked out or did some yard work, studied a little, and then tumbled into bed. Repeat playlist.

Dude, you talk to yourself. Not so ordinary.

Okay, I acknowledged Kenny with a tight frown as I flipped out the sheets squished in a ball at the foot of my bed. So I talked to myself. That was a bit out of the ordinary for some people, though not for me. I'd made friends. Lisa, Paul, and Brandon. Definitely outside of the ordinary. I'd started driving Brandon to and from school on the days I didn't have to stay later for the SAT prep course I attended. Brandon was funny once he actually opened his mouth and talked. Lisa and Paul, the other half of my speech project team, had invited me to practice sessions at their houses. I'd drop Brandon off, meet the team, and we'd practice the rebuttals, the rapid-fire questions, and our opening statements when we weren't just hanging out.

And then there was Julie.

I'd apologized to her, but it wasn't enough. She continued her ice-queen treatment of me. When we worked on the speech project, she sat beside Lisa and addressed me only when she had to. We had the same lunch period, but she always walked right past me and sat with two girls: Colleen and Beth. She didn't like me—I got that—and I was fine with it, except for one thing.

It was the way she looked at me.

I'd already talked to my parents about her name, but they dismissed it as coincidence. My dad said he thought Liam was an only child. Julie couldn't be the same Murphy. Still, there was something about the way she always seemed to be wherever I was, the way her cold blue eyes bored through me. It had me spinning horrible alternatives to explain it. If she wasn't a sister, then maybe she was a cousin? Whatever it was, I couldn't shake the sense that somehow Julie Murphy *knew* me.

I was sure of it and fucking terrified.

So I tolerated her treatment, even encouraged it. When Paul and Lisa couldn't make our speech practice dates, I manufactured excuses to avoid being alone with Julie. When I did have to speak to her, I was deliberately rude. Kenny wasn't exactly helping my cause.

You're a dick.

"Jesus, Kenny, shut up!" I yelled out loud. I was alone in my room and able to indulge Kenny. Uh, myself, I mean.

Look at her, man! Why would you want to avoid that?

"Give it a rest. We cannot be together under any circumstances. None. Zero. Get it through your head."

Why? he yelled back, and my eyes crossed. *Give me one good reason.*

"It's too damned risky."

I want her.

I laughed. I couldn't help it. Kenny was thirteen. Life was easy when you were thirteen. "She's not a puppy, Kenny."

I know. I still want her.

"Yeah, well, you can't just go around taking whatever you want whenever you want it."

She wants us too.

I turned to stare at him, sitting beside me on the double bed that took up most of my room. Besides the bed, the only other furniture in the room was a desk and a tall dresser, but I did have shelves and shelves of books on whatever wall space was left over. No computer though. I wasn't allowed. That and my game system were downstairs in our family room because my online privileges were always supervised. "You're delirious." Julie and I tolerated each other for the sake of our speech class project, but that was it. Julie wanted me? No. No way. If this was how Julie expressed her interest in a guy, I'd pass.

He bounced on my bed. *Okay. Think about it. In speech class, she sits on the edge of her chair when we talk. And when she has a question, she lets Paul and Lisa answer it first but uses our answer instead.*

I gaped at him, not sure what surprised me more—that he kept using the word *our*, that he was right, or that I hadn't noticed any of this before. "So, let's suppose you're right—"

I am.

"And I'm not saying you are. It doesn't change anything, Kenny. It's still too risky to get involved." I tugged the sheets over me.

Bullshit! All you do is risk this deep dark secret of yours. You shouldn't have broken up that fight. You shouldn't have gotten chummy with Brandon. You didn't listen to me either time and now Jeff Dean is gunning for you. The one thing you should do you won't because it's risky? Gimme a break.

He picked up the hockey puck I kept on the desk next to my bed and looked like he was going to heave it through my window for a long moment. It was from the last game I was allowed to play. I used it as a paperweight now.

Instead, he sighed and flipped the puck over in his hands.

I remember this game.

One long finger traced the contours of the puck. Funny, I never noticed Kenny's hands were the same size mine are now.

Us versus Freehold High School. We won in a shootout.

I smiled. It had been a hell of a game. I hadn't played since, and I suddenly realized how much I missed being on skates. At thirteen years old, walking with size fourteen feet presented some challenges, but on skates, I was a thing of awe. And then I remembered that night in the detention center when I'd finally listened to Kenny and let him loose. I remembered the carnage. I took the puck out of his hands, put it back on my pile of papers. "It's too dangerous, Kenny. I'm six-three. I'd probably end up killing somebody. Again."

So is this how it's always gonna be? He waved his hand between us. *No girlfriend. No sports. Nothing?*

I spread my arms, palms up. "It *has* to be. Living as Daniel Ellison is working, Kenny. Nobody's throwing rocks through the window or slashing the tires on Mom's car. It's working."

Your name is Kenneth James Mele. You should be proud of that, not trying to hide it.

I shook my head. I was named Kenneth after my grandfather and James for my father. "I'm not hiding it. I'm protecting it. And that's why I can't be with Julie, Kenny. We can't be friends. Friends talk to each other about themselves. What could I tell her that isn't part of the lie?"

You lie to people all the time. How is this different?

"Because it is." I lifted my hands, let them fall. "I don't like lying to everyone, Kenny." I shook my head. "It's one thing to keep everybody safe. It's a whole different thing to lie to Julie just so she'll go out with me."

Then tell her the truth.

"No!" A noise in the hall had my head whipping toward my door, but it was still closed. "I can't tell anyone the truth. If it comes out, it starts all over again." I stared up at the ceiling. "Kenny, I can't do that to them anymore. I can't expect them to keep packing up and moving away every time I get a death threat."

You're eighteen. You can live on your own now. Move out.

"And do what exactly? Do you really believe there's a huge demand for convicted—oh, wait, pardon me—*adjudicated* juveniles with no diplomas?" In the state of New Jersey, the technical term was "adjudicated juvenile," but "convicted" worked just as well.

It's been five years, man. You can get your juvenile record expunged now. Do it so we can move on.

I scoffed, shook my head. Move on. Yeah, right. My dad's been bugging me about doing that. Juvenile records, okay, sure, but the...the other part was harder to hide. So why bother?

Come on, man! Do something. Fight back! He stood up and took a swipe at me. Kenny may have existed only in my mind, but don't be fooled. When he hit me, I felt it.

I lay back down on my bed and said nothing out loud. I'd been fighting since I was Kenny's age. Every day, I fought, even though I knew it was a lost cause. So instead, I fought for the things I could still get. A high school diploma. Maybe a degree. But friends? A girlfriend?

No. I punched my pillow and closed my eyes, but it was a long time before sleep took me.

"What makes you think that, Dan?"

I gave Dr. Philips half a laugh and shook my head. "I think the question should be 'What *doesn't* make me think this,' don't you?"

I was so damn tired of Dr. P.'s question. I'd been seeing a version of her, answering a version of the same question every Friday for about five years now, and nothing changed. Not one damn thing. I was still crazy. I skirted the issue by telling her all about Julie Murphy, disguising Kenny's interest in her as my own. She'd just asked me if I felt there was no potential for a future together, and I'd said, "Well, duh."

"She thinks I'm Dan Ellison, defender of the bullied, saver of lives. Letting anybody see the, uh, 'real me—'" I made air quotes and took in a breath to finish my thought, but Dr. P. held up a hand.

"Hold it. Let me interrupt you there. You said 'the real me.' What does that mean? Who is the real you?"

Careful, bro. She's got a straitjacket in your size.

I shifted, stared at my fingernails. "A bully. A murderer. A…and worse."

"I heard you used to play hockey," Dr. P. changed the subject.

We were good at it.

"Yeah." I laughed once. "We were good."

"We?" Dr. P.'s ears prickled at the plural word. "Who's *we*?"

Crap. "Just me and my friends." I covered the slip with a shrug. "But I can't do things like hockey anymore."

"Why can't you do those things?"

"Kind of defeats the whole changing my name thing, doesn't it? If I keep the same friends and do the same things, Liam's dad can find us again and—"

No, man. We won't let him get anywhere near Mom or Dad.

A shiver ran down my back on hairy spider legs. Jack Murphy was crazier than I was. The thought made me cringe. He'd vaulted over the bar and nearly choked me during my sentencing hearing, shouting threats and obscenities at me, my parents, my attorney, even the judge. We'd packed up and moved from the only house I'd known the day of my release when he showed up at the front door, along with half our neighborhood, carrying a baseball bat. Just one more thing to add to my list of sins.

"Is this about Liam's father or about the girl?"

I raked my hands through my hair and rubbed the throbbing spot at the back of my head, but it did no good. None of this mattered! I wanted to tear the hair from my scalp. I sucked in a big breath and returned to my seat, the cushy recliner opposite Dr. P.

"Look, it doesn't matter who I hang out with. I'm lying to them. All of them. And the more we hang out and talk, the more people seem to like me—I mean, the me they think I am."

"You don't like lying?"

I thought about that for a minute. I knew lying was wrong. Immoral even. But I was doing it for the best of reasons. It was so easy to believe that made it right.

"I do and I don't." I spread out my hands. "See, the thing is it's *working*. All that crap didn't follow us to this town. I don't worry about my mother out alone or about my father losing business or Jack Murphy ringing the doorbell to bury a bullet in my brain."

"Dan, you're not a *good* bad person and you're not even a *bad* good person. You're normal, flawed just like everybody else. Does that make sense?"

Kenny groaned in my mind.

She shifted in her chair, crossed her legs, adjusted her glasses.

She waited a moment and asked, "Dan, what do you think makes a person good?"

Her voice held no humor, though she still smiled. I wasn't sure where she was going with this, but I propped my ankle on my knee and thought about it. My mother—she was good. My dad. Brandon. They were all good.

"Good people," I began, "do good things. Bad people do bad things."

An eyebrow arched at me, and Dr. Philips angled her head. "That's very simplistic, don't you think?"

I lifted a shoulder. It wasn't simple, not at all. "It should be."

Dr. Philips waved her hand, indicating I should continue. "Tell me…what's an example of a bad thing?"

Without hesitation, I replied, "Killing someone."

"Okay, now let's consider the reverse, say, the driver of a car involved in an accident that kills his passenger. Is he now a bad person because of this?"

"Well, no, of course not, but—"

"What about if that driver had, say, fallen asleep at the wheel? Is he bad now?"

Yes! He should have stopped at a motel if he was so tired. Well, wait. Maybe he didn't realize how tired he was. Hell. "He made a mistake."

Dr. P. pointed a finger at me. "You got it. He made a mistake. It doesn't mean he's a bad person."

My temper surged at the moralizing tone in her words. "Okay, look. I know where you're going with this." I waved my hands. "Everybody makes mistakes. Yes, sometimes killing someone isn't bad. Doesn't make it good either."

Dr. Philips nodded.

"Dan, people aren't *just* good or *just* bad at their most fundamental level. Everybody, every one of us, has the potential for both."

Oh.

Hell no.

This…this wasn't what I wanted to hear. I slumped lower in my seat. I couldn't look at Dr. P. I knew there was bad in me, had known it for years. I could *see* it, and its name was Kenny. And that was why I kept him a secret. When she gasped and uncrossed her legs to lean toward me and take my hand, I sort of had to look at her. "I think you've misunderstood me, Dan. I'm saying you're not bad and never were. You did something that wasn't so nice, but neither was it evil, so I wonder why you persist in believing yourself to be."

Her words and the Hallmark tone that carried them twisted my lips into a sneer. "Not so nice? Really? Dr. Philips, the judge didn't sentence me to nine months in juvenile detention because I broke the 'not so nice' law. He did it because I did something so…despicable," I said as my sneer spread. "He wanted me off the streets to protect people."

Dr. Philips peered over her glasses and smiled. "Again, overly simplistic. Dan, the truth is the crime you committed *was* malicious and you deserved to be punished," she said and ignored my wince. "I won't argue that. However, I think your sentence was overly harsh. But your judge wanted to send a message."

Irony, Kenny sang.

Pop always said the same thing. There were no laws against posting pictures of kids wearing Scooby-Doo underwear online, so I was charged with the next best thing—distributing kiddie porn. And then I thought of the scars on my chest.

Message delivered.

"But you have to remember Liam committed suicide. He was twelve years old. All you did was post a picture of him. I'd say his response was excessive, which makes me believe he had a lot of other problems."

Thinking about that made me frown. "So, you're saying I shouldn't feel guilty for what I did."

Dr. Philips rocked her head from side to side. "No. What you did was just one more problem for Liam in a life of so many. He reached his limit. You do feel guilty, and I think that's a very good thing, but you must put it into the proper perspective. You shouldn't feel so guilty that you believe you don't deserve happiness in your life or, indeed, that you don't deserve a life at all."

I laughed, a short, humorless sound. "Pretty sure Liam's family would say I don't."

She didn't bother replying.

Great. Did that mean I was right?

"Okay. Our hour is almost up. I'd like to suggest something. Think of it as homework, give it some active thought." She grinned and winked. "There are big differences between men and women, and I'm not talking about the physical ones."

I ignored Kenny's evil little snicker.

"I'm talking about the emotional ones. Women like to talk about problems, analyze their feelings, but men find little value in it."

I grinned at the irony. "True."

"You're a man, Dan, with a problem you need to fix because it's the way you were designed. Changing your name gave you a way to do that. And it worked for a while at least. Now you have a new problem, specifically finding ways to permit some happiness in your life. Think of the ways you can fix *this* problem, and we'll pick up with that next week, okay?"

Dr. Philips stood, and I shook her hand. As I left her office, my brow creased in thought.

You have to tell Julie the truth. Kenny started in as soon as I started the car.

No. No way in hell was I about to put Mom and Dad through all that again. I thought of the mums my mother planted. Planting flowers meant she wanted to stay. She liked it here.

I would not ruin that.

CHAPTER 7
Sweeter Than You Look

Dr. Philips's homework assignment was all I thought about on my way home. Crap. It made sense in a warped sort of way. I was a fixer. A repair man. The image of me in a tool belt made me roll my eyes. I hid a smile at the bottom of the Italian ice I'd just bought. Cake batter. Yum.

Since we'd moved to Holtsville, I'd driven past Ralph's Italian Ices every day. I'd never stopped at the always-crowded store, but I did today because an enormous sign said it was the last day of the season and I didn't want to miss out. So I sat at a rickety picnic table while summer hung on by its thumbs, slurping my cake-flavored ice, imagining how I could fix all the crap in my life.

Pop. He was a tough one. He didn't talk to me. I didn't know why. He'd talked to me in juvie, so it had nothing to do with my crime. It wasn't until later, after I was released and we'd had to move a bunch of times—

Yahtzee.

I couldn't believe I hadn't put this together before. He must be tired of all the moving. He'd been living with us since I was about nine, after Gram died. They'd lived apart for a long time before that. I don't know if they were divorced or not. Every time I'd ask, my mother would whisk me out of the room. I knew Pop wasn't an easy man to get along with. He and Dad fought. A lot. But when I was little, we were tight. When Dad sent me to my room, Pop was the one who talked me out of all the "You'll be sorry" fantasies I plotted while I was mopping my tears. After I...after my arrest, Pop was the one who hired a second lawyer because the first one only wanted me to plead guilty.

Pop had gone nuclear. Fired the guy on the spot, said we'd take our chances in court. I was terrified. "Trust me." He'd winked and grinned, and I had trusted him. We went to court with a second lawyer. After my sentencing, Pop held my hand as the bailiffs handed me off to juvenile detention and visited as often as it was allowed. I wasn't just scared; I was fucking terrified. He warned me, said I had to lose that "Wake me up 'cause I'm having a nightmare" look or they'd pass me around like an appetizer.

He was right.

It was nearly Halloween by the time I was released. They'd had a welcome home party for me. Mom, Dad, and Pop. None of my friends came. Probably because they were no longer my friends. Kenny was there, though, sitting right next to Pop and freaking me way the hell out. It was all okay though. Nothing mattered. I was out. I was home. My family hadn't left me there to rot like I'd so often worried. We ate all my favorite foods and talked about school. I'd missed a lot. Half of the previous term plus two months of the current one. I was anxious to get back to my friends, my teammates, even though none of them had ever called or visited.

"Buddy—" My father's face tightened, and his voice held the same tone it always did when he had bad news to deliver. I'd braced for it. I knew after what I'd done, I wouldn't be allowed to play hockey or return to school, but before he could say the words, glass exploded all over us. Something hit me hard from my right, and suddenly, I was on the floor. I'd fought against the heavy weight pinning me there. My mother's screams echoed in my ears. My dad had run to the front door, wrenched it open, and from my vantage point on the floor under my grandfather's arm, I'd seen a small crowd of kids in front of our house.

They were shouting that they didn't want a deviant in their classrooms, a pervert on their team. They weren't all kids though. Jack Murphy, Liam's dad, was there with a bat. My best friend—the same kid who laughed when I snapped Liam's picture—held a brick. Kenny's voice in my head stated the obvious. *Dude, he ain't your friend anymore.*

The rest of that night passed in a blur. I remember the police arrived, broke up the crowd. Dad and Pop nailed boards over the broken window. My mother cleaned up the glass. The brick that broke through the window skidded over the dining room table, gouging a deep scar through the surface. I stared at the gouge. Me. The table. Both scarred. I'd stood there with my thumb up my ass, unable to think, let alone help. Then there was a suitcase in my hand, and my mother was tugging me toward her car.

We'd fled. It was ten o'clock at night. We'd driven to the next county and holed up in a Holiday Inn for the night. Pop and Dad were there when I woke up the next morning, comforting me while I screamed myself awake. My parents sold the house with the help of lawyer number three, and we moved an hour or so west of my Jersey Shore hometown. The new house was bigger than our old one was, and it even had a pool. All my old stuff somehow managed to get shipped to us.

Except for the scarred dining room table.

I hated it, hated every minute we spent away from the shore. I enrolled in ninth grade, but by April, it began all over again when the kids at my new school discovered I was the same kid on the news. And then we had to move. We tried Maryland. Then Delaware. Finally, New York, under a new name. It was somewhere, sometime between New Jersey and Delaware, I think, when I'd tried to anesthetize myself to all my issues. I didn't like smoking, so marijuana wasn't much use, but drinking helped. For a while. When I reached a point where I was drunk by breakfast, Pop and Dad decided to knock some sense into me.

I'd stumbled down the stairs one morning, saw my bags packed by the front door, and totally lost it. They were sending me back. I knew it! I knew this would happen someday. I screamed, cursed, broke stuff, raged like a wounded animal while they tried to talk to me. It wasn't until Pop pointed over my shoulder and I saw my mother sobbing on the floor, knees tucked to her chest, that I was able to listen. "You did that," they'd told me. I'd pushed her, knocked her down. I didn't remember doing it, and that scared the fucking hell out of me, so I listened. They weren't sending me back as it turned out. Instead, they were taking me camping.

I'd stood there, blinking, trying to get my well-lubricated brain to process that. Camping?

We were away for a week. I don't know where the hell we went. I'd spent most of the week puking up my guts inside the camper they'd rented. "Talk," they'd said after my stomach had finally settled. And I did. I told them everything. Almost all of it—I left out the Kenny parts—to how I'd earned every last scar. "So what now?" I'd asked them.

"Now we save you," my father had answered.

"What if I'm not worth it?" I'd replied. I was a fourteen-year-old juvenile delinquent with a hangover, and they wanted to save me. I had a hard time understanding why. Hell, I still wasn't sure I understood why. I only knew something in me shifted during that trip, and instead of wanting to die, I wanted saving like I wanted air.

I sobered up. Got my head on straight. Took on as much extra work as I could manage to help the family. But I'd missed so much schoolwork during my *pickling*, as Pop used to call it, I'd had to repeat the ninth grade. It was somewhere, sometime among all these stops when Pop grew cold, brusque, and finally avoided me altogether.

Guess he hoped to be left in peace instead of traipsing all over the eastern seaboard. The first time, he was all for it, but now? Maybe— A dark thought filtered through my panic. Could he want me dead?

Probably does.

Before I could retort, piercing shrieks made me jolt and turn. In the busy parking lot, a little girl had broken free of her mother's hand and run, run until she'd tripped and sprawled on the pavement right behind an SUV about to back up.

I ran before thinking, pounded on the rear of the SUV. I reached the toddler before her mother did, a heavily pregnant woman doing her best to move fast. I picked up the girl, propped her on one knee to see how badly she was hurt. Her knees were scraped raw and filthy.

"Oh God! Thank you. She outruns me now." The toddler's mother panted, rubbing her belly. "Emily, Emily, you're okay, honey." She cooed at the wailing tot. "Oh, she's hurt. I have some first-aid stuff in my bag." Her mother rooted around in a diaper bag nearly as large as Julie's satchel. I scowled because things like purses now reminded me of Julie.

I scooped up the shrieking toddler and offered her mother my other arm to lead them to my picnic table so the SUV could leave the lot. "You okay?" I asked the mother.

The woman looked up at me with a wince. "Yeah, just a stitch. He didn't like me trying to run."

She eased down to the bench, huffing, and removed from her bag a lollipop, a bottle of water, a package of Band-Aids, and a tube of antibacterial ointment. My God, was there anything women did not carry in their bags?

"Come on, sweetheart. Let's fix up your knee."

Emily was having none of that. She turned and hid her face in my shoulder. That made me feel kind of warm inside.

"Emily!" the woman scolded, but I laughed.

"It's okay. I can hold her while you bandage."

The toddler squirmed in my arms while her mother squirted the water bottle at her wounds. I distracted her with my car keys while Mom dabbed her knees dry before covering them with the bandages smudged with antibacterial ointment.

"There you go. All better." The woman smiled, but little Emily shook her head.

"Oh. Right. She needs kisses too." Her mother sighed. With obvious discomfort, the woman bent down to kiss one knee, then the other. "Better now, honey?"

Again, Emily shook her head and pointed to me. I hesitated. Legally, I wasn't allowed near children, but she seemed to really like me.

Come on, man, get over it. Nobody will know, Kenny groaned.

Really? Somehow, *nobody* found out at in the last three towns we'd lived. But one look at Emily's big blue eyes, eyes that reminded me of Julie's, and I was toast. I lifted her higher and kissed two chubby knees with loud smacks, and she giggled.

"Okay, I promised her an Italian ice." Mom stood and reached for the girl.

"I'll get it," I offered. "What kind?"

"Small lemon."

I left Emily with her mother, stood in line to buy her treat. A few minutes later, the girl was happily back on my lap, digging in. "How old is she?" I finally asked just to make conversation.

"Eighteen months."

"She's…um, cute."

"Thanks. And thanks for catching her. If you hadn't been here, she could have been—" she squeezed her eyes shut and I squirmed while she mopped her eyes with one of Emily's napkins. Emily had inherited her mother's eyes, though Emily's were still watery.

"No problem. I'm glad I could help." I tickled Emily under her chin.

"You're good with toddlers. You know, she hates strangers but really seems to like you."

My face warmed, and I looked down at my feet, grinning. "Chick magnet. What can I say?"

My face got hotter when Emily's mother laughed. Kenny nearly went into convulsions in my head.

Emily fisted the spoon in her hand and shoveled in a mouthful. It was cold and sour, and she shuddered from head to toe. She did it again, and I laughed.

"When is this one due?" I asked.

Emily's mother sighed and patted the mound under her shirt. "Monday. Hope he plans on keeping that appointment."

"You're having a boy?"

"Yeah. We still can't settle on his name though. My husband likes Ian, but I like Kenneth."

Good thing the toddler dropped a spoonful of her lemon ice on my leg. It disguised my flinch.

"Go with Ian," I said. When I looked up, there was another set of icy blue eyes on me. They did not, however, belong to the pregnant woman or the toddler.

Julie Murphy was in the Italian Ices line, staring at me. My legs bounced with the compulsion to run.

Jeez, man, paranoid much?

"Yeah, maybe." Emily's mother said and braced her hands on the table to heave herself upright. "Thanks for rescuing us. Looks like bath time for a certain sticky little girl." She held out her arms, but I tightened my grip on the toddler.

"Please. Let me."

Yeah, I knew I was tempting fate. Sue me.

With Emily on one hip and her mother leaning on my free arm, I escorted them back to the minivan parked across the lot from the table. Emily now clutched the lollipop in two hands. I put Emily in her car seat, stepped back while her mother fastened the straps, and then I helped her mother into the driver's seat. With a wave and a honk of the horn, they were gone. I didn't know why that made me sad.

I glanced back at the shop, saw Julie had already been served. I hesitated. Should I leave or try to talk to her?

Talk to her, you ass.

Okay. Fine. "Hey." I shoved my hands into my pockets and strolled back to the table.

"Hey, Dan. You know them?" Julie jerked her head at the disappearing minivan.

"No, she needed help and—"

"Right. Somebody needs rescuing, and you're right there to do it. You can't help yourself." One corner of her mouth tilted up, but her eyes were sad.

"No, I guess I can't," I retorted with the same level of hostility and turned to leave.

"Wait."

She looked up at me like she was trying to calculate the distance from Earth to the moon, the line on her forehead in full sight. "You may as well sit," she finally said.

Like an idiot, I did. "What flavor is that?" I sat opposite her at the table.

Julie shrugged. "Something red. Cherry, strawberry, doesn't matter." She took a lick, and my stomach coiled.

"Why not?"

She looked blank for a second, then nodded when something occurred to her. "Sorry. I forgot you're not a girl—"

"You *forgot*?" I battled to ignore Kenny belly-laughing deep inside my brain.

"Well, when I was little, my sister and I only ate red Italian ices because it made our lips look so good, see?" She puckered her lips at me.

Yeah. They did look good. Bet they tasted pretty good too. God! I quickly thought of Jeff, the scars on my body, anything else horrible that would take my mind off Julie's luscious berry lips.

Julie turned to me, her face confused.

I stared back at her for a moment. "What?" I demanded when I couldn't take her scrutiny a second longer.

She grinned and shook her head. "Nothing. You just looked different when you were fussing over that baby."

"Different," I echoed. I didn't hold babies at school, so, yeah, I guess I would look different holding one.

Julie huffed out an impatient breath. "Yeah, different. You were like a big teddy bear instead of a big scary—"

"A big scary *what*?" I didn't like where this was going.

Julie's expression changed, softened. I watched her stand, deposit her trash in the can, and walk back to my side of the table. "Nothing. It doesn't matter. You just looked...I don't know...very sweet and gentle taking care of a baby."

"And you liked that?"

She took my hand, leaned closer, and kissed my cheek. "Yes," she murmured in my ear.

Oh. My. God.

The weekend couldn't end fast enough. Friday night, I couldn't focus. Saturday, I mowed the same patch of lawn twice. By Sunday, I was sure my mother would schedule extra Dr. P. sessions if I didn't get my feet back on the ground.

Julie Murphy kissed me.

Kenny was worse than I was. Every time I looked for him, I found him in the room he'd set up deep in a dark corner of my mind, lying on his bed, staring up at the ceiling.

What did it mean? Were we friends now? Were the icy glares and cold shoulders over?

By Sunday afternoon, my euphoria had given way to paranoia. She didn't like *me*. She liked the big goofy guy holding the adorable baby. I knew girls dug sensitivity in men. I peeked at my mother's *Cosmo*.

It didn't mean anything.

Familiar melancholy crept back into my chest, and Kenny found his voice.

Talk to her. Go find her right now and talk to her.

That was a very good idea.

I grabbed my keys and drove to her place, next door to Brandon's, parked, and then sat in my car for the next ten minutes, paralyzed with my fingers white on the steering wheel.

What the hell was I doing? I couldn't be friends with this girl. It was entirely too dangerous. If she found out, if anybody found out, we'd have to move so fast I probably wouldn't even get the chance to say good-bye.

A tap on my window made me jerk around, which made me hit the horn, which made me jump again.

Julie stood beside me at the passenger window, the line between her eyes in full view.

I hit the power door lock button, and she practically leaped inside. Her hair was scooped back in a plastic band. Her glasses were blue. Just smelling her made me incredibly happy.

"What the hell are you doing here?" She didn't look at me. Instead, her eyes swept up and down the street.

"Need to talk to you."

"You could have called. You didn't have to come all the way here."

"Um. Yeah. Sorry about that. What's wrong?"

She whipped her head around, pinned her eyes to mine. "Nothing. Nothing's wrong. So, what do you want to talk about?"

Crap. My knees bounced, hitting the keys dangling from the steering column. "Um. Yeah. I guess I wanted to, um, you know, talk about what happened Friday."

"What happened Friday?"

My chest constricted. Okay. It was nothing. I knew it. "Forget it. Doesn't matter. Sorry I bothered you." I leaned forward, shifted into drive, the signal she should get the hell out now.

She peered at me through narrowed eyes. "You have any money?"

My eyebrows shot up. Was she going to mug me now?

"I don't have my bag. I feel naked without it, but there's no sense going inside to grab it if you've got enough money for food."

Food. What?

Kenny smacked my head. *Food, genius! You know, the stuff you buy and then put in your mouth? Tastes good and all that? She's asking you out!*

Right. My face burned. I drove down the street. "Where do you want to go?"

She shrugged. "That depends on how much you can spend."

I envisioned the contents of my wallet, mentally counted the money that should still be inside it. "Snack or meal?"

Julie patted her stomach and smiled. "I could eat."

I wasn't sure I could eat, but a meal it would be. I hit the Long Island Expressway, headed east, and got off an exit near school where I knew there was a strip of chain restaurants. She was quiet the whole drive. I pulled into an Applebee's. "How's this?"

"Great." She jumped from the car and jogged inside without waiting for me.

I locked the car, hurried after her. The hostess seated us near a window, but Julie shook her head. "Could we sit back there maybe?" She pointed with her chin toward the back wall, behind the bar.

Whoa. Dude. She, like, wants to be alone with us.

I couldn't deny it. My heart clenched in my chest at Kenny's assessment of the situation, but I tried to be cool as I slid into the chair opposite Julie. "I don't know what to get?" she said like she needed my permission. And I realized that she did.

"Get what you want. I can cover it."

She gave me one of those tight-lipped smiles and nodded. When the server arrived to take the drink orders, Julie closed her menu.

"Hi. I'm Paige. What can I get you to drink?"

Julie ordered fajitas and a Coke. I ordered the same. My stomach was knotted, so no use pretending to examine the menu. My knees continued their twitching under the table, making the flatware dance.

"Dan, you can relax. It's not like this is a date or anything."

Oh.

I lowered my eyes before she could see the disappointment that filled my eyes. It wasn't a date. It didn't mean anything. Just like the kiss at the Italian Ice store probably didn't mean anything. I wanted to bolt. I wanted to run, put as much distance between Julie and me as I could. But I couldn't just leave her stranded here.

"You said you wanted to talk to me," Julie prompted after the Cokes were brought out. She leaned forward and suddenly grinned, jerking her head after the waitress. "I sure hope her last name isn't Turner."

I didn't get it but laughed like I did, a short huff of nervousness. I sipped, coughed.

Julie waited and finally waved her hand. I shook my head. "It's nothing."

"You drove all the way to my place for nothing?"

"Yeah, I guess I did."

We fell into another uncomfortable silence. Neither of us ordered an appetizer, so I just sipped until I'd drained my Coke because I had no idea what to say to her. A safe topic, I thought. That's what I needed. "So, did you do anything exciting today?"

Blue eyes widened, darted to mine for one brief, surprised moment before they took interest in the flatware she was passing from hand to hand. And then it hit me. She was nervous. The thought made me pretty damn happy.

"No, not really. Just usual Sunday stuff. Chores, homework, studying, reading."

I nodded, uninterested in anything else but the answer to the question that had burned in my brain since Friday, and I blurted it out before I could stop myself. "Why did you kiss me?"

The hand lifting the Coke to her mouth froze. She looked at me over the rim of the glass, frown line visible. "Is that what this is about?" She didn't wait for me to answer, just leaned back in her chair with a sigh. "I don't know. I guess I got caught up in the moment. Seeing you with that baby totally contradicted your rep."

"What rep?" My hands tightened on my glass. We were barely into the school year, and I had a reputation already?

She watched me like I was a meter that could tell her at a glance how close I was to some red-line limit. "You know. The big bad new guy brave enough to face Jeff Dean."

I gulped air.

"It's all over the school. You're, like, famous, I guess."

I exhaled slowly just as the food arrived. The sizzling skillets provided a convenient cover for my silence. Famous. That was just awesome. I watched her blow on a forkful of food, the pucker of her lips doing interesting things to my body. "Julie, you can't talk about this. Please. It's—"

"Oh. Right. No problem. I'm not much of a gossip anyway."

Good. This was going well. I scooped some chicken and peppers onto a tortilla and folded it up. I bit through half of it and chewed, my eyes closing while my stomach did a happy dance.

When I opened my eyes, I found her regarding me with a strange, almost comical look on her face.

"What?"

She laughed and looked away, embarrassed that I'd caught her staring. "I'm jealous. I want hair like yours."

A happy laugh escaped from me. I leaned back to look at her sideways. "What? Beige?"

She rolled her eyes. "It's light brown and could go blond if you sit in the sun long enough. But I meant the texture. Thick, full, and wavy. Instead, I got fine and straight. I always hated it."

My smile faded, and I shook my head. I'd wanted to run my hands through her hair, feel all that silky, spun gold since the day I saw her. "No, yours is perfect. I wouldn't change a thing." My voice sounded weird. Deep and raspy like I just woke up.

Julie's smile faded. She ate her fajita with a fork and knife in dainty little bites. I'd eaten three to her one.

"Tell me something true about you." She dropped her utensils and patted the table with both hands.

Oh, crap. "Um."

Dr. Philips's homework assignment flitted across my mind. With a deep breath, I figured now would be a good time to start it. "Okay. What do you mean 'true'?"

"Jeez, Dan, relax. I'm not interrogating you, so stop trying to swallow your Adam's apple, okay? I just want to hear something about you that isn't through the *Gossip Girl* channels, you know?"

Sure. Fine. I could do that. "Sorry. Go ahead. Ask me a question." I responded in what I hoped was a cool voice because inside, I was saying, "Jesus! What if she asks if I've ever killed somebody?"

You know, it's a good thing you're already under psychiatric care or I'd worry about you.

Kenny, go away.

"Okay, let's see." Julie nibbled a nail and pretended to think really hard. "What about books? Do you like to read?"

Inside, I was breathing a very loud sigh of relief. Outside, I said, "Yeah, I love books. Promise not to laugh?"

When she nodded, I continued, "I loved Harry Potter. I read a lot of fantasy. *Lord of the Rings*, *Eragon*. I love the classics too. Did you read *Where the Red Fern Grows*?"

She pressed her hands to her mouth. "Oh God! I cried and cried at the end of that book."

Me too, though I did not admit that out loud. Eighteen-year-old men did not cry or admit to having cried. Ever.

"And I love Harry Potter too. I named my dog after it."

"You have a dog?"

"Yeah, he's a black lab."

After an awkward silence, she changed the subject. "Do you work after school?"

I shook my head. "No, not a real job, but I help my dad with the family business."

"Which is—" she prompted me with a curl of her fingers.

"Retail. He's got an online store." Which used to be a real store with employees and customers and a parking lot.

"What do you sell?"

"Um, wedding and party stuff. Favors, custom imprinted, that kind of thing."

She nodded. "Cool."

Not really, but okay.

"So, what do you for fun?"

"Uh—" Fun. What did I do for fun? "I like the beach. I go almost every day."

"Even now? With school and the cold weather?"

"Yeah, I go after. I like to run on the sand. Cushions the knees. Plus, it's a tougher workout."

"That's it? The beach? What else do you do when you're not baby-sitting Brandon Dellerman?"

"Julie, I'm not baby-sitting anybody. We hang out. He's a cool kid."

She rolled her eyes. "Yeah. Right. Dan, he's such a douche. Aren't you afraid of what people will say about you for being his friend?"

"I don't give a crap what people say about me." It couldn't possibly be worse than the truth. "Brandon's got a lot of problems, Julie. I'm hoping maybe I can help."

Julie stirred the straw in her Coke. "Good luck with that."

"Brandon told me Jeff blames him for his mother's death, but I figure there's more to the story."

She stiffened. "And you think I know the rest of it, right?"

I shrugged. "If you do, will you help me?"

"Help you do what exactly?" She pushed back from the table, looked at me sideways.

"Help me end it." I waited for her to say something, but she just pushed the food around on her plate. "Julie, Brandon is relentlessly targeted by just about the entire student body. Doesn't that bug you? He's not a bad guy. You think he deserves to be ostracized like this?"

Julie looked at me like I'd just announced an alien invasion. "Doesn't matter. You can't control it, and you sure can't change it."

"And that's it? You can't control it, you can't change it, so that means you sit back and just accept it?" I couldn't keep the sneer from my voice. "Julie, I've been watching him since the first day of school. Do you know Brandon won't use the bathrooms at school, no matter how bad he needs to go?"

She remained silent.

"Bathrooms, he told me, are where sixty-five percent of high school crimes take place. He's been pushed. Robbed. Threatened. He's had his stuff destroyed. His head shoved into toilet bowls. He's even been followed home." I paused, waited for her to express some opinion on the matter that wasn't a simple shrug.

"Yeah, and?"

"And why doesn't this make you mad?"

"You're doing it again."

I blinked at her for a full minute. "What is it you think I'm doing?"

She stood up, dragged the napkin across her mouth. "Judging me. You can take me home now." She whirled, stalked out of the restaurant.

"Yes, *ma'am*." I threw some cash on the table and followed.

In bed that night, I tossed and turned for what felt like hours, replaying the evening. I didn't judge her.

Sure you do. You think she should speak up for Brandon like you are. You think she should have reported the fight like you did.

I sighed. Okay. I admit I do think she should have done something.

We were having a great time until you pissed her off, Kenny noted. *She's funny.*

I shrugged. I guess she was funny when she wasn't hating me. Something she'd said tonight suddenly clicked in my brain. The server's name. Paige. Turner. I rolled over and giggled into my pillow.

CHAPTER 8

What's Not to Like?

By Halloween, the summer weather had turned crisp. Paul and I hung out at his place, watching horror movies and handing out candy. We ate more than we gave away. I'd taken the SATs last week, so it was great to get some time back in my schedule. No more prep classes, no more practice exams on the computer. I thought I did well but tried not to get too pumped about that. Odds were no schools would accept me with my record. My father was spending most evenings hip-deep in the court-required paperwork necessary to start the expungement process for just this reason. If the request gets court approval, I would be legally permitted to answer no on any form that asks if I've ever been convicted of a crime…except for law school. Lawyers had to disclose everything, even if their records were expunged.

No matter how cold it got, I still needed my beach time. Early Saturday morning, I grabbed my iPod and drove the thirty-minute ride to Smith Point, not surprised to see few other cars in the lot. I stuffed buds in my ears, pulled up my hood, and started to run, feet smacking the sand to Metallica's "Frayed Ends of Sanity."

The irony was not lost on me.

As long as the music was jacked up, I couldn't hear Kenny haunting me to *get me Julie* like a Happy Meal from the drive-through, so running with music had become my new favorite pastime. In the time that had passed since our not-really-a-date date, Julie and I had said maybe two or three words to each other.

I ran, my breath coming in pants that pulled the salty air into my lungs, reminding me of Julie. Stone Sour played next. I slowed to a walk, singing quietly along. The sun hanging low over the water was the same color as Julie's hair. I tried looking at the sky instead of the sun. It was the color of her eyes.

Damn it. I stopped and flopped down to the sand, ripped the buds out of my ears. I'd hated her indifference, her icy streak. I couldn't make sense out of her refusal to care about Brandon's problem, but damn it, I liked her anyway.

"Okay. You win," I said out loud, waiting for Kenny's cheers.

There were none.

"Kenny?"

I whipped around. I checked the corner of my mind where he lurked, pushed open the door. His room was empty, but my gaze lingered on the posters of sports stars I no longer admired. "Kenny, come on, where are you? This isn't funny."

I was still panting and forced myself to pull in deep breaths, hold them, and slowly exhale. He was…gone. Worry—irrational, I knew—exploded in me. Hadn't I wished—no, *prayed*—for this day since Kenny first appeared? Whatever had tethered him to me had cut him loose. I should have been throwing a party. I was no longer insane.

I breathed in deeply, tried cursing him and saying the things that always pissed him off.

Nothing.

"Woo-hoo!" I did an end zone dance in the sand. This was great. This was incredible. Maybe I could cancel next week's session with Dr. P. I was free! Free to leave Julie alone now.

No.

For a second, I thought Kenny had whispered the word in my mind, but the denial was mine. I shook my head. *No.*

Being friends with Julie was a mistake. Leave her alone.

No.

Okay, this wasn't funny anymore. "Kenny! Enough joking around."

My head was silent except for the flurry of my own scattered thoughts.

Abruptly, I felt lost. Abandoned. Alone. He was always with me. I'd hear his whispers in my head when I was calm and relaxed, his shouts and taunts when I wasn't. But the first night I was attacked in juvie, he'd left my head and appeared in front of my eyes. When they'd slashed me again and again, I'd seen his face. My face. At the center of the burning and the screaming, I'd heard his voice. My voice.

I'd heard *him*. Kenny. He'd guided me, told me how to protect myself, how to fight back. How to survive. Even then, even as I lay bleeding on the concrete floor, I knew it was crazy, but I kept the secret. I didn't know why. I didn't know if I was protecting Kenny or myself. I only knew that I had to keep the secret.

I was cold. I stood, brushed off the sand, and headed back to my car, the iPod tucked in my pocket. Gulls cried over my head. The wind whipped. The sounds echoed in my hollow head.

I walked without seeing where I was going. I got to my car, climbed in, let my head fall back, and even though eighteen-year-old men didn't cry, I did. I wasn't ready. I just wasn't ready to be alone.

"Okay. Okay. You win. I'll make friends with her." I wiped my nose on my sleeve.

A hand patted my arm. I looked over and saw Kenny in the passenger seat. He was smirking.

Thirty minutes of silence later, my car was in front of her house. She was in the leaf-littered street, walking a shaggy black dog. I cut the engine, got out, and watched. She hadn't noticed me, a small comfort because I had no idea what to say that could explain my presence.

Kenny's voice made me jump. *There she is.*

"Yeah. Thanks." I rolled my eyes and fell back against the side of my car. What would I say? What the hell was I going to say?

"Hey."

For the second time in as many minutes, I jumped at the sound of a voice.

"Sorry." She grinned, pleased with herself, and then angled her head. "What are you doing here?"

"I…I'm not sure. I just—" I shrugged, looked at the ground, hoping to find inspiration in the pavement. No such luck.

You could ask her about the dog, jerk.

Genius. I could have kissed Kenny.

"Who's your friend?" I crouched to his level, held out a hand, let him sniff it.

"This is Hagrid."

I caught her gaze and grinned. She was wearing purple eyeglasses today. "Hagrid? Really?" I laughed. "When you said you named your dog after them, I thought you meant Harry. But Hagrid is, um, really cute. He kinda looks like Hagrid." I couldn't resist teasing her.

Her eyes narrowed. "Hagrid was an important character in those stories. What's not to like?"

"Nothing." I put up my hands, grinning. "It's just…cute."

"You said that already." Her lips curled into that mocking smirk, and it pissed me off. I busied myself scratching the dog's head. "He likes you."

"What's not to like?" I retorted and was rewarded with a little laugh. "So tell me, why Hagrid? I mean, why not go with Harry or Dumbledore or Snape?"

Hagrid tugged on his leash, so Julie began walking. I fell in step beside her. I saw Kenny out of the corner of my eye, walking behind Julie.

"Remember the first book? Harry's this poor little orphan, abused by the people supposed to raise him. He finds out he's a wizard, but what does he really know about any of that world? Nothing until Hagrid shows him the way."

I nudged her with my shoulder. "You telling me you're an orphan?"

She didn't laugh. Nor did she look at me. "Not exactly. My parents split up when I was a baby so my dad could marry someone else. My mom remarried like six years ago, made herself a new family. I used to see my dad every other weekend, but ever since…well, something happened when I was thirteen and now he doesn't visit anymore."

"You haven't seen him since you were thirteen?"

She shrugged. "He shows up when Mom needs money."

Jesus. My mouth hung open, but she wasn't done yet.

"I had a hard time adjusting. I got into a lot of trouble…intentionally. For attention."

I was intrigued. "What kind of trouble?"

Another laugh. "I smoked. I drank. A lot. I pierced…things." She indicated her nose, her eyebrow. "I took pills. I stole. I—" She glanced at me and remembered she didn't like me. "Forget it. Let's just say it didn't take me long to figure out that the only thing getting into trouble got me was the trouble." She smiled, and I swear it was like the sun came out. "So my mom and Carl adopted this little guy. As soon as I saw the black fur, I thought, *Hagrid.* But it fits his personality too. He shows me the way." She laughed again, and the sound tickled me. "He hated my emo phase. The black hair color must have smelled funny. He kept chewing it, so I cut it off, let it grow out." She raked a hand through it, fluffing it. "He must like it this way because he doesn't try to chew it anymore."

I stared at her and shook my head with a laugh. "I can't picture you doing the all-black emo thing." And then a disturbing thought flitted across my mind. "Did you cut too?"

Her eyes hardened. "Yeah." She showed me her hand. I saw a row of silvery scars. "I stopped when my razor blades started looking like the answer to all my problems, you know?"

Yeah. Yeah, I did know and couldn't stop the shiver when I thought about my own dark days. I wasn't into the whole emo scene, but I had messed around with blades. Kenny always stopped me. Said I had enough scars.

She stopped while Hagrid did his business, scooped up the mess into a plastic bag, and tied a knot with the ends. She glanced up at me, wrinkled her nose.

"You're a mess."

"Yeah, I just went for a run."

"With your car?"

I nodded. "I like to run on the beach."

"Right. You said that. So which one did you go to today?"

"I hit Smith Point."

"Hagrid loves the beach. Mind if we come with you next time?"

Say no, dude. Say you don't mind one bit.

"Sure, if you want." I shrugged.

"So, how come you're here?" she asked again.

There it was. I drew in a deep breath. Honesty would be good now, so I had to give her that much. As much as I could. "I really have no idea. I was on the beach, running, listening to music. And couldn't get you out of my mind. You remind me of the beach."

She gasped, a tiny sound that said she was pleased. "You hate me."

"Funny. I thought you hated me." She didn't reply, so I continued, "I just couldn't stand that you wouldn't help somebody who needed it."

She nodded with a frown that made the line between her eyes leap. "It'll always be in our way."

I frowned. Helping Brandon? I didn't understand.

But Julie did not elaborate. "So, you're not pissed off anymore?"

I laughed once. "No, I guess not."

Julie looked up at me. "What are you saying then? Are we, like, friends?"

"I hope so." I grinned wide and was rewarded with a bright full-wattage smile.

"Guess I'll, um, see you in class Monday?"

I nodded. Kenny was grinning ear to ear. My work here was done.

CHAPTER 9

Kickin' Butts and Takin' Names

I drew my jacket edges together, shivering in the cold November air, and jogged straight to class, not even bothering to stop at my locker first. I was ridiculously eager to see Julie, and as soon as I let myself think that, I forced myself to slow down. "Friends. That's all," I repeated.

I saw Brandon. "Hey, Brandon!" He burrowed into his jacket and kept walking.

What the hell was that about?

Relax, dude.

At least Kenny was speaking to me. I didn't know why that was comforting.

Told you, bro. I'm a gift.

Yeah. Whatever.

I grabbed my seat, opened a notebook, and reviewed my work. I was the only member of my team in speech class so far. Then the airhead brigade arrived, the scent of mousse, body spray, and flavored lip gloss trailing behind them. They spotted me. I quickly averted my eyes. No eye contact. That was the first rule of staying incognito. I occupied my time jotting down the highlights of an article I'd found in one of Dr. P's waiting room back issues that supported our law.

The air changed. A subtle shift that made my skin tingle. I lifted my eyes, watched Jeff and Julie walk into the room together. His lips twisted into a smirk, so I watched Julie instead. She settled into her seat. Her eyes met mine, held. Where my skin tingled before, it almost sizzled when she grinned. I hardly heard Paul and Lisa sit down and say good morning.

"Just friends," I repeated.

"Okay, everyone, let's get started." Mr. Williams walked to our team, dropped a pile of handouts on Lisa's desk. I took one, read the list of topics. *School terms should be twelve months instead of ten.* Hm. *Smoking should be banned in all public places.* Okay. *Hunting for sport should be banned.* Good luck. Mr. Williams was now taping signs to the walls in each corner of the classroom. The first said, "Strongly Agree." It was joined by "Agree," "Disagree," and "Strongly Disagree." "You have one minute to decide your position on the first topic. I want you each to consider not just how you feel about the topic but why. Then get up and stand in the appropriate corner. Ready?" He pulled a stop watch from his pocket and clicked it. "Decide."

Over the cacophony of chairs scraping the floor, shoes squeaking, and voices laughing, the entire class met up under the "Strongly Disagree" sign in the front corner by the window.

"Hm. I shouldn't be surprised." Mr. Williams smirked. "Guess nobody wants to go to school all year." He crossed his arms, grinned like the devil. "Now convince me why it's a bad idea." His eyes scanned the crowd gathered beneath the sign and settled on me.

Of course.

"Mr. Ellison! Enlighten me."

My face heated when I felt everyone's eyes on me while I scrambled for something to say. "Uh, um, summer jobs, summer internships. Both are important for seniors considering college, and a twelve-month school term would eliminate opportunities."

"Excellent."

Kiss ass.

I smirked at Kenny and turned to watch one of the airheads blush and stammer her way through a response. "Um, well, like, summer is for the beach and you know—"

"No, Ms. Magee, I don't know. What about the beach?"

"Um, well, society relies on the money people pay to use the beach, and if teens are still in school throughout the summer, the economy could, like, suffer?"

Williams angled his head. "Better. Next. How about Ms. Murphy?"

"Yeah, okay. How about the increase in taxes in an already-strained economy for the funds needed to pay the staff for two more months of service?"

"Excellent. Mr. Oliva."

"Yeah, I got nothin'."

The class erupted in laughter.

"Not good enough, Mr. Oliva. Find a reason."

"Okay, what about tourism? If summer vacations end, so does the tourism industry."

"Eh. Weak, but I'll take it. Mr. Dean, your turn."

"Yeah. What about electricity and utility bills?"

"I don't know, Mr. Dean. What about them?" Mr. Williams responded, and the entire class laughed.

"Well, all classrooms would need air-conditioning, and some are pretty old."

"Good point. Next!" Mr. Williams moved on until each student made an argument.

"Okay, next topic. You have one minute to decide your position. Ready? Decide!"

For the topic on whether smoking be banned in all public places, I hurried over to the "Strongly Agree" corner. This time, the class was more evenly divided among the four choices.

Williams clicked his stopwatch. "Time! Ah, now we've got ourselves a debate. Okay, in my two 'Strongly' corners—I want to know if I've got nonsmokers in the 'Strongly Disagree' corner and smokers in the 'Strongly Agree' one." He crossed one hand over the other as he pointed. "This makes for a more compelling argument."

A quick glance around the company in my corner told me we were all pretty much nonsmokers. Everyone was shaking their heads, pointing at each other. Except for Julie. She looked a bit sheepish. When I cocked an eyebrow at her, she shrugged. "Former, still-recovering smoker."

"Okay." Mr. Williams clicked his stopwatch. "Strongly Agree, you're up."

We all stared at Julie, waiting for her to step up.

"Um. Yeah. I used to smoke in tenth grade. Until I got caught and was grounded. I was pretty much forced to quit. And I'm glad I did. The problem is that smoking is not just a personal choice. It affects everyone standing close to the smoker. So people who choose to smoke are forcing me to join them because

I can't exactly hold my breath while I'm at the beach or walking into a building. And for those of us who quit, sometimes that's just way too tempting."

Mr. Williams applauded. "Well said, Julie! Okay, let's hear from the 'Strongly Disagree' side."

One of the airheads spoke. "I don't smoke, but I don't think it's fair that people who do are treated like lepers or something, forced to stand behind some wall with others of their kind. It's a form of discrimination."

"That's lame, Ashley," some guy from the "Agree" corner said. "They're not segregated because they're smoking. They're segregated because the smoke was proven hazardous to those around them."

"Yeah, so for the few minutes it takes for someone to finish a cigarette, people can move if they don't want to inhale too," Jeff added from the "Strongly Disagree" corner.

"How far?" I spoke on a sudden inspiration. "The chemicals in the smoke you guys exhale lingers long after you do. They're still in the hotel rooms after you check out and in the rental cars after you return them. How far do I have to go to avoid your smoke when it's so, so permanent?"

I grinned when I felt a hand clap my back.

"So maybe you should just not breathe," Jeff said, fist-bumping a guy who found the comment hilarious. "No big loss if you, um, die."

A morbid thought crossed my mind. If I died today, only two people in the whole world would mourn me. I couldn't even count my own grandfather. An elbow jerked me out of that misery.

Julie gave me a funny look. "Ignore him. He's just trying to piss you off." I managed a tight smile and a nod.

"Okay, okay, let's keep the personal arguments out of the debate. Mr. Cutler, I believe you had a point to make?"

The kid named Cutler said, "Yeah, I was gonna say that's why hotels and car renters ask if you want smoking or nonsmoking, so people who are bothered by the odor have a choice. What's wrong with just, you know, continuing that instead of outlawing smoking altogether?"

The rest of the guy's argument faded into the background when I sensed Julie's eyes on me. I turned, caught her gaze. "What?"

She shrugged. "You're good at this."

"Arguing?"

"No. Thinking on your feet. I am so nervous."

"You did great." I grinned. Her eyes widened, and her mouth went slack for a minute.

Easy, Romeo.

I grinned wider. I'd been told I had a killer smile.

Kenny's derisive snort echoed in my mind. *Yeah, by Mom. Are you really counting that?*

I ignored Kenny. I was having fun. Class ended all too soon. I decided to find Brandon, find out if he was mad at me or something.

I headed to his locker but didn't see him. It was nearly time for homeroom, and those were assigned alphabetically, so I started in that direction when I caught sight of Brandon down at the far end of the corridor.

I walked closer and was about to call out his name when I saw him glance around and shove a folded piece of paper through the slats in one locker.

It wasn't his locker.

What the hell was he up to?

"Hey, Brandon!" I called, and he leaped about two feet high.

"Jesus, Dan." He clutched his chest. "You scared the piss out of me."

"Sorry," I smiled. "Isn't your homeroom back that way? What are you doing down here?"

"I'm not doing anything!"

My grin faded. "Yeah, okay. Don't bite my head off."

"I gotta go. I'm gonna be late."

With a squeak of shoes on linoleum, he was gone.

Weird, man.

Definitely.

Just as I turned into my own homeroom, I heard a locker open behind me. It was Jeff. He bent to retrieve the folded paper I'd just seen Brandon shove inside his locker. As he read it, his face tightened into an expression of pure malice.

A shiver skated down my back.

"Kenny." I was in the privacy of my car, but the little deviant was hiding. "Come on, Kenny, I need your help."

Keep your panties on, Danielle. He was suddenly sitting beside me.

About time.

You're lucky I answer you at all. You treat me like crap.

I couldn't stop the laugh that escaped my mouth. Me? You're the one who never lets me forget what I did to Liam. Here, it's about to start all over again, and instead of helping me stop it, you'd rather make popcorn and watch.

Doesn't matter what I want. Only what you want.

He made a valid point. I didn't often see his wants as relevant. In this case, however, Kenny's wants were entirely relevant.

I know what you want, Kenny. You help me stop this, and I'll give it to you.

He rolled his eyes and smirked. *Yeah. Right.*

I'm serious, Kenny. Brandon's planning something. I have to stop him.

And how exactly are we supposed to do that?

No idea. That's why I need your help. You kept me alive when I was trapped in that hellhole. Help me do the same for Brandon. Please.

In exchange for?

Julie.

Kenny's eyes gleamed. I supposed that meant mine gleamed too. *Take Brandon home.*

With a jerk of his chin, he alerted me to Brandon walking between some parked cars.

I hit the horn, startling him. "Want a ride?"

His eyes narrowed, and he shook his head. "Nah, I can take the bus."

"Come on, man. I'm heading over to Julie's anyway."

"I don't need a friggin' baby-sitter."

I inclined my head. "Brandon, I thought you were my only friend in this place. You telling me I'm wrong?"

A ghost of a smile flitted over his lips. "Thought Julie was your friend?"

I shrugged. "Julie's a girl, man."

He stared at me, disbelief plain, and finally climbed into the passenger seat.

The days passed. Kenny was still acting, well, weird. Brandon was growing more sullen by the day. And Julie and I were…still friends. We'd been working on the big speech project after school with Paul and Lisa whenever we had the time. I liked them. Paul had an after-school job. Lisa had her club activities. It was cool, almost like having real friends.

Because Julie and I were the only ones with nothing going on after school, we often found ourselves alone—now that I'd stopped making up excuses to avoid her. Today was Wednesday. There was a study date scheduled for this afternoon. I tried not to be jacked about it when I pulled into the student parking lot that morning and cut the engine.

Heads up, man.

I went into defensive mode the second I detected Kenny's tone. I spotted Jeff chillin' with a few friends. One was beefy with a buzz cut. The other was a tall, popular kid the girls were all crazy for. Hm. The darting eyes. Stiff postures. They were plotting strategy. One of the pals smacked Jeff's arm, jerked his chin to the west.

Brandon. Should have guessed.

I whipped open my cell, dialed the school, and got the cavalry coming, never taking my eyes off Brandon as I talked. He wasn't hurrying. He was strolling. What the hell was he trying to do? Get himself killed?

Time to kick ass. Kenny was at my side, his eyes—my eyes—cold.

"Intimidate first. Kick ass *only* if it's necessary," I said out loud.

Three against one. I'd faced worse odds before. I could do it if I had to. I really hoped I wouldn't have to. With a wince, I remembered the last time I'd fought off multiple attackers. So much blood.

"Hey, guys." I was going for calm and cool as I approached the group, positioning myself between them and Brandon. By the way they'd jumped, I must have been anything but.

"Back off, Ellison." Jeff took a step toward me.

"Can't do that, Dean."

He grinned, took another step. "Uh, not sure you noticed, but I brought friends."

"Yes, I see that." And just to totally mess with their minds, I held out my hand to one. "Hi. Dan Ellison." And then the other. "Hey, I'm Dan. Good to meet you. You should know I've already called the police and school security." I cupped a hand to my ear when I heard a siren in the distance. "Ah. That must be them." I grinned. They backed up.

"Come on, man, let's get outta here," the first kid said to his pal.

"Good idea. I'd hate to mess up that pretty face. Might mess up your bid for prom king." I let the smile drip off my face. "But I'd do it."

Pretty Boy jerked his head, and Buzz nodded. "See you later, man."

"You guys suck." A vein throbbed in Jeff's neck. He shot a nervous look over his shoulder when the siren came a bit closer. "This isn't over. You can't protect the little dick forever." He stalked off. The siren kept going to wherever it was heading.

Brandon looked at me. "You never called the cops."

I nodded. "True. But they didn't know that."

"I didn't need your help." He wouldn't meet my eyes. What the hell was he thinking?

Give him the point, dude, Kenny suggested.

"You're probably right." I shrugged. "I saw three against one and had to even the odds a bit. But I really just gave them an out. I figured they didn't really want to fight."

"Dean does."

"Yeah, well, he's deranged." I was suddenly impatient with the game and blurted out what was really on my mind. "Okay, enough. Just what the hell were you trying to do?"

Brandon's eyes went round before they lowered. "Nothin'. I was just minding my own business."

"Yeah, yeah, yeah. Save it for the principal. I'm not buying it. I watched you. You were baiting the hook. I swear, if you were female, I'd have said you were working it, man. Now tell me why."

Brandon's face reddened. "None of your goddamn business. I didn't ask you to butt in."

"No, but I *am* in, and if I'm gonna get my ass kicked saving yours, I damn well wanna know why." I glared at him, and he caved under the weight.

"I was gonna do it, Dan. I was finally gonna stand up for myself and get Dean off my back."

I stared at him for a minute. I knew Brandon was hurting, but this was just crazy. "And the fact that he brought backup didn't change your mind?"

All the color fled from his face. "I…I couldn't back down now. It…well, it would have been worse."

He had a point. Still. It didn't sit right with me, this bravado of his, but the bell rang. I leaned down, grabbed the backpack he'd dropped to the grass. "Here. Next time, just call me, okay?"

He grabbed the pack like it was filled with treasure and ran into the school. I watched with my hands on my hips, thinking.

He lied to you, Kenny said.

Yeah, I noticed that.

He looked like you did in juvie. That "I'm not gonna take it anymore" look.

I nodded. I'd noticed that too.

I was late to first-period speech class. I had to stop at the principal's office and tell Mr. Morris what happened. Sure, it was snitching, but I was determined to make Jeff's life as difficult as I could. I didn't know Pretty Boy and Buzz's names—they'd never introduced themselves. Bad manners. Appalling really. Anyhow, there were only about twenty-five minutes of class remaining by the time I got there.

"Mr. Ellison, nice of you to join us today."

"Sorry, Mr. Williams. I have a pass."

He took it, glanced at it. "I hope whatever business you had in the principal's office is concluded."

I nodded. "Yes, sir." See? I had manners. I took my seat, my face burning, aware that every eye in the classroom was trained on me.

"What the hell happened?" Julie whispered.

"Dean," I muttered.

Just then, the PA system crackled to life, and the principal called Jeff Dean to his office. Every head in the classroom swiveled his way as he collected his stuff and left, glaring at me the whole way.

I heard her suck in air and then she scribbled furiously on her notebook, angling it so I could read it. *Lunch—fifth period?*

I looked at her, eyebrows raised. We never had lunch together. Well, we did—technically. Same lunch period. But we'd never sat together. Maybe Colleen and Beth had other plans? I nodded.

Just friends, I reminded myself when my heart threatened to break a rib. I forced myself to concentrate on Mr. Williams's lesson. The teams were poring over flashcards. I glanced at the one sitting on top of Lisa's notebook. It held a list of taglines from commercials.

1. Because you've got a lot riding on your tires.

2. A diamond is forever.

3. Don't leave home without it.

I recognized all three of the slogans. "What are we supposed to be doing with these?" I asked Julie.

"Identify the emotion each one makes us feel."

"What does that have to do with speeches?"

"No idea."

I grabbed a sheet of loose leaf and a pen and jotted down my ideas: "worry," "pride," and "trust." I slid my sheet to Lisa, who was busy writing her answers.

"Okay, folks, there isn't enough time to review your responses before the bell rings. Here's what I want you to do. Consider how popular commercials appeal to our emotions to sell products and apply those techniques to winning your arguments. I want each of you to take one of the slogans and write an essay about the emotion it makes you feel and why it would or wouldn't convince you to buy that product. Due by end of the week."

The bell hid our collective groan.

"See you at lunch." Julie offered me a brief, tight smile and left.

Do the American Express slogan, Kenny suggested with an evil grin.

"Why?" But he'd closed the door to his room, shutting me out.

CHAPTER 10

Peace, Love, and Hair Gel

I heaped a couple of burgers, a baked potato, an apple, and a bottle of water on my tray, lugged it to my usual spot, and wondered if the butterflies constructing a house in my gut would allow me to actually eat. I saw Colleen and Beth sitting at their favorite table, and my anxiety deflated. Julie would probably end up sitting with them anyway. No sense getting all worked up over nothing. I grabbed the first burger, bit in, and nearly choked when a tray slammed onto the table next to me.

"You're an ass, you know that?"

I considered that and shrugged. I'd been called worse.

Oh, tell me you're not gonna take this crap?

I would take his crap. For now. "Well, gosh, Brandon, I had no idea. Please enlighten me."

"Morris gave Jeff in-school suspension."

Again? It worked so well the last time.

"A whole week!" Brandon flung himself to the seat beside me, shoved the tray away with a sneer. "And he's benching him. No football."

I blinked, waiting for the part where this was bad enough to warrant calling me an ass. Kenny sat across from me, glaring.

Brandon huffed out a frustrated breath. "Come on, man, think about it. If he can't play football, he's going to be pissed, and I mean like volcanic eruption *pissed.* And then he's gonna erupt all over *me* for ratting him out. So, thanks a lot, man. Appreciate your help." He stood up, but I slapped a hand to his shoulder, pushed him back down.

"Hold it."

"You shouldn't have butted in. I had it. I had it, and you screwed it all up. I didn't need help. I *wanted* him to come after me."

I peered closely at him. His eyes looked okay to me. There were no marks on him that I could see. So he wasn't using. Then why the hell was he making no sense? "Okay, first, whether you know it or not, you were about to do the dumbest thing of your life. I don't like being called an ass because I stopped you from that. Second, ISS was the right call, if you ask me. And third, *I'm* the one who snitched, not you, so Dean's more likely to come after me, and fourth, he knows I'll be watching out for you if he does try to take you down. Even though you called me an ass." I released my grip on his shoulder. "Now you can leave."

He continued to sit, but he wouldn't look at me. After a minute, he moved his tray close and bit into a turkey sandwich. Swallowed. "Sorry," he mumbled.

Damn straight.

"No problem." I was about to say more when I smelled her.

Julie. Kenny sighed happily and grinned at a point over my shoulder.

"Um. Hi?"

I twisted my head around. She stood behind me, tray in hand, her shoulders clenched and her eyebrows raised over the rims of her glasses. That enormous sack she called a purse dangled off the arm holding her tray, yet somehow, she managed to keep it level.

Brandon leaped up. "I'm outta here."

"No. Stay. Julie and I have a project we're working on, but you can eat with us." I wanted Brandon to stay where I could see him.

Brandon's eyes darted from me to Julie and back to me. He nodded and slid over so Julie could sit beside me. She put her bag on the floor and grabbed one of her club sandwich wedges. She followed my gaze and managed half a smile. "I was able to get the club sandwich, and I'm not even a member."

Beside her, Brandon moaned.

"That was really lame," I said.

Julie smiled tightly and shrugged, twisting the cap off a Snapple, fumbling it. "Yeah, I know."

I couldn't stop my grin. "Why are you so nervous?"

My perceptiveness surprised her, and her mouth dropped. "I *am* nervous. I guess you heard about Jeff's suspension?"

"Yeah, Brandon just told me. Good."

She angled her head, thought it over. "Yeah. Guess so." She frowned, glanced around, and leaned closer. "You, uh, need to be careful. I heard him threaten you. He said he's going to get even with you for reporting him to Mr. Morris."

Beside her, Brandon gasped, but I shook my head. "I'm not worried, Julie."

Her eyes widened. "You should be. Jeff's got…a lot of problems."

Brandon went rigid beside her.

"Yeah. About that. Why don't you two clue me in." I waved a hand between them.

"It's your fault," Julie shot at Brandon, and he flinched.

"I was trying to help."

"Help? His mother *died*."

"I know!" Brandon said too loudly, and heads turned. "I know that, okay? But I did it to help."

"Did what?"

Julie stared at Brandon. Actually, Julie *dared* Brandon with a lift of her eyebrows.

He shoved his tray away. "Fine. I ratted him out to his parents."

Kenny whistled. *No wonder Jeff is pissed off.*

Julie glared. "It totally messed Jeff up."

"If he's so messed up, why do you hang out with him?" Brandon demanded while he stared at his ice tea bottle.

Julie shrugged. "I don't have much of a choice. He's going out with Colleen."

Brandon rolled his eyes. "Right, and you go everywhere Colleen goes."

"Hey, I don't—"

"Stop." I held up a hand before Julie got herself any further riled. "I'm still confused. You said you were trying to help?"

Brandon pressed his lips into a tight line. Julie cocked her head to the side, another dare. There were a few eavesdroppers hanging on to our conversation. I shot a look at one girl with spiky hair until she turned back to her own lunch.

"He...look, it's a long story, and you'll probably just take his side anyway, like everybody else, so let's just skip it, okay?" He grabbed his water bottle and got up. "Thanks for—" he started, shifted, looked down at the table. "Just...thanks."

"No problem," I said again, staring after him as he shuffled away, shoulders hunched and head down.

"Hey, you okay?" Julie nudged me with her shoulder after a few minutes of silence.

"Oh yeah. Fine. Just thinking."

"About Jeff? I'm sorry. I shouldn't have said anything."

"No, about Brandon. That kid worries me." I'd finished the first burger and was now chewing on the second, thinking. "He lives next to you. Does he have any family problems you know of?"

Julie shook her head. "No, not at all. They seem to get along pretty great." She picked the crust off her sandwich, popped it into her mouth. "You're actually the first person I've seen talk to him. Everybody did pretty much take Jeff's side. Except you. Maybe you're right. Maybe I should help him."

My face was suddenly burning, and I lowered my eyes, bit back the lame *Aw, shucks* that danced on my tongue. "Julie, I feel bad for him. I know what it's like, and I don't want to see anybody get hurt." I chugged half of my water.

"*You* know what it's like?"

The disbelief in her tone pissed me off. I capped the bottle, deliberately put it down before I responded, "Yeah, I do. You really think I built all this muscle just for the hell of it?" I watched her eyes flicker down my body and her lips part. There was a dark part of me—hell, it was probably Kenny—that was perversely excited by her obvious interest. But I didn't sweat all those hours running and lifting weights just for a girl's reaction. It was my only means of defense. I'd been no bigger than Brandon when I was locked up. And they'd come for me that first night. I was thirteen years old and luckily just hitting a growth spurt.

Let's just say I made the most of it.

She frowned again. "Jeff'll hurt you."

I laughed. "I'm not worried. Why are you? You don't even like me."

"Are we back to that again?" She sighed dramatically.

I didn't want to get into it all over again, so I changed the subject. "I don't hurt so easily anymore."

She squeezed her eyes shut for a minute. "You forgot the first day of school already? You were pretty easily hurt then. And that was one punch. The thing about Jeff? He doesn't fight fair."

"Neither do I." I leaned closer. "I took that punch because I knew Mr. Morris would see it." I winked.

You are such a liar.

She doesn't know that.

You sure about that, bro? Look at her face.

She knew.

"You glared at me. You totally hated me."

Okay. I guess we *were* getting into it again. I nodded. "I did. I was pissed off when I found out you saw the whole thing. You could have helped Brandon but didn't. You forced me to take a big risk I shouldn't—" I mashed my lips together. I'd said too much. Damn it. *You see?* I poked Kenny. *This is why it's too dangerous to be friends. It's easy to slip up.*

She drew in a deep breath. "What? The risk to your popularity? Or your pretty face? Oh, wait. I know. The risk to getting on the football team."

Popularity? Football? Please. I tried to laugh, but I was far too disgusted. "I don't give a rat's ass about football, Julie." How much could I say so she got it? What could I tell her without taking an even bigger risk? "There's a reason a guy starts a new school in a new town in his senior year. You could have stopped that fight, but you didn't. So I had to, and the whole time, I'm rehearsing the stuff I was gonna have to tell my parents when we were packing up to move. Again." I grabbed the water bottle in one hand and my tray in the other and stood.

"Dan, wait. I know about you, and it's cool really—"

What? Oh God, no.

The food congealed in my gut, and the world slipped away. My hand convulsed around the water bottle, and the plastic cracked under the strain. Run. Right now. Run.

"Dan? Daniel, stop it. Look at me." She pulled the water bottle away from me, forced me to look at her. "Everyone's been talking about your scars. We know you got into a bunch of fights and had to leave your last school because somebody got…got really hurt. And now whenever you see fighting, you have to stop it, but you're afraid you'll have to leave again. I get that. But you can't mess with Jeff. He'll do worse than your scars."

Relief washed over me, relief so great it was like plunging into the ocean on a hundred-degree day. Is *that* what everybody was saying? The whole school thought I was Tyler Durden. I could work with that. As long as they didn't know the real story, I still had a shot at getting through the next few months.

At the day's last bell, I hurried to my car, anxious to get away from everyone. I was pissed at Brandon for being stupid, pissed at Julie for forcing me to risk even more than I already had, pissed at Kenny for pushing me to make friends, pissed at myself for letting my guard down, and pissed at God for watching me splash in the deep end of the pool and not tossing me a ring.

Thinking about Brandon had me replaying the earlier scene when he baited Jeff. What the hell was he thinking? No sane person would seek out his bully's attention unless—

I froze mid-step.

Oh God, *no*. My brain started connecting the dots. Damn it, why hadn't I seen it? The way Brandon protected his backpack earlier? He packed a knife or gun inside it—I was sure of it. The problem with weapons was that you could be disarmed and the weapons used against you. That was exactly why I'd developed my own body into a thing of strength and power.

I got into the car, slammed the door, and threw my head against the headrest. How did I miss this? Brandon was plotting.

Kenny rubbed his hands in glee. *Epic! Next time, don't stop him. It will be better than* Fight Club.

I clamped my hands to the steering wheel instead of Kenny's neck. "I am not going to let him get hurt, no matter how *epic* you think it might be. He's not thinking straight. He doesn't know he can't possibly win." I choked when I realized what I'd just said.

Kenny's laughter ended. He stared at me from the seat beside me, eyes full of knowledge. *Maybe winning isn't his goal.*

With hands that shook, I raked hair off my face and tried to form a plan from the dozens of thoughts buzzing around my panicked mind. I had to stop him, had to stop Brandon from killing himself to get away from Jeff's torment or, worse, killing Jeff. I knew what it was like to live with blood on my hands.

Kenny's eyes—my eyes, whatever—gleamed dangerously in the sun beaming through the car's windows. *And how are you gonna do that? You're much better at causing suicides than preventing them, don't you think?*

"Shut up!" I roared. "Just shut the hell up!" I pounded the steering wheel. A tap on my window hammered a spike of terror through my chest.

"Dan? What's the matter?" Julie pressed her hand to the window, the line between her eyes fully defined.

My inner demon found great humor in Julie's question. Where could I start? While Kenny cackled, I shook my head slowly, mechanically. I flung my head back and shut my eyes. All I had to do was keep the secret. But then I met Brandon, and suddenly, keeping him safe was this impossible task. Sisyphus got off easy. Rolling a freakin' boulder uphill for eternity was better than this. The boulder couldn't resent my efforts.

I heard the passenger door open, and Julie slid in to the seat Kenny had occupied a minute earlier, filling the car with that scent I craved. She covered my hand with hers, squeezed.

"Dan." She didn't move her hand. "What's going on?"

I swallowed hard and finally opened my eyes. She watched me, her forehead creased, eyes grim. "Any ideas on how to stop a suicide?"

She snatched her hand from mine like I was caustic. Her eyes turned glacial. She took her giant purse from the floor and left the car, slamming the door behind her. I shoved through my door a second later. "Julie!" I caught up to her in a few strides, took her arm, spun her around.

"Don't touch me."

You upset her, Kenny shouted.

I'm aware of that.

Fix it. Fix it now!

I'm trying, Satan. Back the hell off.

Out loud, I demanded, "What the hell's your problem?"

"My problem? My problem? You can sit there with a straight face, make lame jokes about suicide to me, and ask me what *my* problem is?" She wrenched free from my grasp and strode off.

I didn't know why she thought I was making jokes about suicide, so I tried again. "Do I look like I'm joking? Julie, I think Brandon's gonna kill himself, and I don't know how to stop him."

She halted, hesitated a moment, and faced me. "You're serious? You're not making a sick joke out of my brother and me?"

My eyes popped. "Making a joke?" If there was a connection among teasing, suicide, and Julie, I wasn't making it. "You never mentioned having a brother." A cold knot settled in my stomach, slowly tightened across my gut.

"Had. Past tense." Her eyes bore holes through me as if I should have known this. "He killed himself when he was, like, twelve."

I pressed a hand to my open mouth to block the stream of curses I nearly cut loose. "Was his name Liam?" I blurted. I took her by the shoulders and gripped tightly. "Answer me!"

"No." She wouldn't look at me.

"Julie, please!"

She shot me another arctic look that almost freeze-dried me where I stood. "You're hurting me."

Abruptly sick, I let her go. "I swear to you I didn't know about your brother."

She stared a minute longer. "Fine," she said with a long sigh. "Let's say I believe you for a minute. Why are you so worried about Brandon?"

I was struck mute. I couldn't very well tell her that the little voice in my head noticed something funny about the way Brandon acted. "I…God! I didn't notice it, not until later." I spun around, pointed to the grassy median. "There. Right there. He was walking back and forth, slowly at first. Like he was pacing. But then I realized he was baiting the hook. He was doing all he could do to get Jeff's attention. Julie." I put my hands on her shoulders, looked her dead in the eye, and spoke the unbelievable truth. "He was *asking for it*." I raked the hair off my face, growing more certain Kenny's suspicions were correct with every word. "He had his backpack with him. When Jeff and his sidekicks approached, Brandon took it off his back, brought it to his chest. I didn't connect it, not then. The careful way he was cradling that bag. The wild look in his eyes. He had a *weapon*, Julie. I'm sure of it." I ignored her gasp and pushed the words out faster. "Worse, he didn't care that Jeff had backup and that even with a weapon, odds are he wouldn't have won the fight. And then at lunch before, he was pissed off at me for stopping him, and I didn't understand. But now I do. He…I think he was hoping Jeff would give him a reason, Julie."

Julie took my hand, led me back to my car, and got in. Only when the doors were closed did she speak. "Dan, this is—"

"Huge," I finished. "I know. What I *don't* know is how to help him."

She watched me for a long time, her eyes thawing. "You really mean it, don't you?"

I blinked at her for thirty whole seconds, bewildered. I was pretty sure it was English I'd been speaking. Helpless frustration made me twitch. "Damn it, Julie. If you can't help me, just say so. Stop torturing me." With my palms up, surrendering, I waited for her to trust me.

Julie picked up the giant bag from the floor of my car, rummaged through it. After a minute, she pulled out a large plastic bag that contained the remains of a Lego helicopter. A bunch of blocks floated loose around the bottom. I blew out a loud sigh. "Legos? Come on, Julie. I have to find Brandon."

She held the bag, staring at it with eyes glazed, mesmerized by the past. "This was my brother's. He…never got to finish it."

"So you carry it around in your purse?"

She laughed, a short, sad sound. "I bet you think that's crazy, but I like keeping it close. I keep everything that's important to me in this bag. Just in case—" She left the sentence unfinished.

"Will you tell me about him?"

A tendon leaped to prominence in her neck. The bag of Legos disappeared back in the cave of Julie's purse. "I don't talk about him. Ever."

I beat back my disappointment and nodded. "Okay. I understand. Look, I gotta go now. I need to find Brandon."

She opened the passenger door and called out over her shoulder. "Don't leave him alone. That's the one thing he'll want most. If he is thinking about suicide, he won't want to hang out." And she was gone.

I watched her walk away, her comical purse bouncing off her hip with every step. The burning need to know what else she kept in that sack battled with my other burning need—to help Brandon.

I waited in the parking lot, but Brandon didn't show. He must have boarded a bus before I got out there. By four o'clock, I was parked in front of his place, bouncing my knee against the dashboard and wiping my damp palms on my jeans.

You sure you want to do this? Kenny popped into the passenger seat. I jerked, accidentally hit the horn, and jumped again.

Damn it, Kenny.

I didn't have time to go a few more rounds with him. The front door opened, and Brandon came out to my car, no doubt attracted by my horn-beeping blunder.

"Hey, man," I said after I lowered the passenger side window.

"Hey. What are you doing here?"

"Um. Well, I wondered if you were up to anything? Wanna hang out?"

He did a double take. "You want to hang out? With me?" His eyes gleamed.

I nodded. "Sure. Why not?"

"Like, right now?"

I laughed. "Yeah, Brandon. Now. What's your problem?"

"Um. Well, I figured you'd have a dozen other things you'd rather do than hang out with me."

"I'm not working. I don't have to be home for hours yet. And maybe you haven't noticed, but you're pretty much my only friend."

His lips curled into a knowing smirk. "Yeah? What about Julie?" He jerked his head to the house over his shoulder.

I scratched my head and considered that. "I don't know if Julie and I are friends. Exactly."

He huffed out a short laugh and patted the doorframe. "Well, come on. It's getting cold out here."

I locked up my car, followed him inside the house. He led me up a flight of stairs lined with tons of framed pictures. "Are these all you or your brother?"

"Only child."

"Yeah? Me too."

He led me into his room. I whistled. "Wow, man. Nice."

His room was enormous, easily twice the size of mine. He had a cool flat-screen TV sitting on a stand on one wall. Opposite it was a twin bed shoved against the wall and lined with pillows so it could be used as a sofa. Under a huge window that faced the street, he had a large desk with another flat-screen. This one was for his computer. I couldn't help but notice the display. It was opened to a social networking site. I read several of the posts.

They were threats. All of them.

"Brandon, what the hell is this?"

He let out a long sigh. "Jeff and his pals. You're there too."

I managed to swallow my curses. "Figures."

"He's posting that you…and I—" Brandon inhaled deeply and exhaled slowly. "Well, you can read."

I could, and I did. It was a lot of *Brokeback Mountain* kind of stuff. I was relieved; it could have been a lot worse.

Dude, I know this is a stretch for you, but maybe you could imagine things from his point of view instead of yours?

Kenny's reminder served its purpose, and I winced. I looked at Brandon, but he wouldn't meet my eyes. His face was red.

"Brandon, this doesn't bother me."

That got his attention. "It doesn't?" His eyes were huge.

I managed a tight smile. "I've been called a lot worse."

Yeah, I guess "fag" pales next to "pervert."

My stomach clenched as it always did when I heard that word. Thanks, Kenny. Appreciate that.

Deliberately, I tuned Kenny out and remembered why I was here. "Does it bother you?"

He scoffed, laughed. "Me? Nah."

I noted the darting eyes, the muscle twitching in his jaw, the nervous laugh. "It's okay if it does. It's, um, normal, I guess. I mean, it's hard to understand how people can be so mean."

"There are so many," he whispered.

"Anybody besides Dean giving you a hard time?"

"Um, everybody?"

I almost laughed and then realized he wasn't kidding. There was so much I wanted to tell him. Like I knew how he felt, I'd been in his shoes, and not to do something in the heat of the moment he'd regret later. These weren't just platitudes. They were the wisdom of my own experiences, but I couldn't find any way to share them without also sharing my real identity.

Jeez, man. You're not a superhero. Your real identity isn't that big a deal.

Brandon suddenly brought his hands together in a single loud clap. "Hey! You up for some Xbox?"

He was wound tight and could use the distraction, so I agreed. We played hockey and then switched to war games. He kicked my ass, which Kenny found endlessly amusing. It wasn't until a voice called up the stairs that I realized we'd been in the house alone all afternoon.

"Brandon! I'm home." Footsteps padded up the stairs, and the door opened. "Oh. Hi."

Brandon's mother looked from me to him and back to me. Her face split into a wide grin. "You…you have a friend over."

Her astonishment was painful to witness, and from the look on Brandon's face, just as painful to experience.

"Um, Mom, this is Dan Ellison."

"Hi, Dan. Nice to meet you. Are you a senior?"

I nodded. "Yes, ma'am."

Her smile dimmed. I knew what she was thinking. I wished I could promise I'd remain friends with Brandon after graduation but feared it was a promise I wouldn't be able to keep.

"Well, it was nice to meet you, Dan."

"You too, Mrs. Dellerman."

For one suspended moment, I saw myself following Brandon's mother downstairs, telling her everything, and begging her to get Brandon out of danger. And I saw her asking me how I could be so sure. The moment passed, and I hated myself all over again.

What else is new?

"Sorry about that. She—"

"She's great, Brandon. It's cool."

He nodded, shrugged, and I stood up.

"I need to get home, Brandon. Hey, do you like to work out or run or anything?"

Another shrug. "I don't know."

"I'm gonna run on the beach Saturday if you want to come."

He blinked at me. "Dude, it's, like...*November*."

I shrugged. "Dress in layers."

He shook his head. "No, I don't think that will help my problem." He indicated the computer across the room.

"Don't focus on that crap, Brandon. Do stuff you like to do, get your mind off it."

"I don't know. There's not a lot I can do alone besides video games, and even that's—"

He didn't finish the sentence, but I got it anyway. Jeff and his pals were probably hassling Brandon on Xbox too. "Yeah, I remember. That's why I work out." Well, one reason anyway.

He thought for a minute and then smiled briefly. "Okay. I'll try it."

"Great." I smiled, proud of myself. It was a little step, but it would lead to bigger ones. "I gotta go. I promised my parents I'd get my hair cut today. Place closes at seven thirty."

Brandon angled his head and examined my hair. "What's wrong with it?"

"They think it's messy." It waved past my collar. I could pull it into a stubby ponytail if I liked that look.

Girl.

I sighed. "Wanna take a ride with me? Won't be long."

He bounced up and grabbed a beat-up canvas wallet from the computer desk. "Let's go. I'll get mine cut too."

Brandon's dirty blond hair was stringy and hanging in his eyes. It needed a cut more than mine did. With a shout to his mother, Brandon was out the door with me on his heels. We'd just reached my car when Julie stepped outside, Hagrid in tow.

"Hey." She looked from me to Brandon, eyebrows raised. "Where are you two off to?"

"Haircuts. Wanna come?"

"Sure. Just give me a few minutes to take care of Hagrid."

She climbed into the backseat five minutes later, and I drove to a barbershop in town. They took Brandon first.

"What'll it be, kid?"

Brandon's eyes darted to mine. I looked to Julie for help. "What do you think?"

She stepped back, angled her head, and eyed him critically. "Short. Gel the front."

She glanced at me, and I gave her a big smile to say thanks.

Brandon shrugged, and the barber starting cutting. Julie took the opportunity to analyze my hair. "You shouldn't go too short. Girls like something to run their fingers through."

Kenny and I both gasped. When it was my turn, I instructed the barber as Julie had suggested and ended up with a short, messy, bedhead style. Her eyes gleamed, and she nodded. "That looks really great."

A throat clearing had us both turning to Brandon with sheepish grins. "Um. Sorry, Brandon," Julie said. "Yours looks great too."

He shrugged, and I drove us home.

"So, what do you think?" I asked the too-quiet Brandon when I pulled in front of his house.

"I feel, um, kinda naked."

"Brandon, it looks good. You can actually see your face now. You know, I've lived next door to you for years and never knew what color your eyes were until now."

To my horror, Brandon turned eyes I could now tell were green to me and sneered. "I know what you two are doing, and you don't have to bother. It won't help anyway."

I blinked, speechless, and turned to Julie for a clue. She only shrugged. "Brandon, I don't know what you're talking about."

"I'm not a…a…freak show science project, okay? I don't need some extreme makeover."

I bit back the furious retort dangling off my lips and remembered to stay patient. "Brandon, if you feel that I forced you into cutting your hair, I'm sorry. That isn't why I asked if you wanted to come."

With narrowed eyes, he stared at me. "Then why did you?"

"Because I had fun hanging out with you and thought it would be cool to have company while I went under the shears."

"And she just happened to show up when we were leaving?"

"Uh, yeah," Julie said it with attitude. "Nobody forced you to cut it. I don't know why you're so freaked out now. It looks good."

"Everyone's gonna laugh."

"Yeah. Yeah, they probably will. But I'm not laughing and neither is Dan."

I am.

I shoved Kenny into his corner and slammed the door. "Brandon, tell me this. Do *you* like it?"

He looked from me to Julie, then back to me, and I shook my head. "No, don't *ask* us. *Tell* us. Do you like the way your hair looks now?" I flipped the visor down, opened the vanity mirror above his seat. He tilted his head from side to side, carefully examined his reflection.

"Yeah, I guess."

Julie mockingly punched his arm. "That's all that matters."

Brandon just sighed and got out of the car.

"Hey." I stopped him. "Want a ride tomorrow?"

With a shrug, he kept walking. "I guess."

"Six forty-five. I'll bring the hair gel."

"Guess I should head inside too," Julie murmured from the backseat.

I swiveled around to face her. "What do you think?"

"Your hair looks good."

I waved a hand. "No, about Brandon."

"His hair looks good too."

"Julie."

"Okay, okay." She climbed over my center console and into the passenger seat. "I think you did a good thing today. He's uncomfortable, but he likes it. He kept checking out his reflection all the way home."

"Thank you. For being nicer to him, I mean."

She looked down at her hands. "Yeah, well. Maybe you're right. I could do more."

No! No doing more. Kenny insisted from the passenger seat, where he'd suddenly materialized.

I tried to disguise my flinch as a cough. I didn't know if Julie bought it.

"Is that why you came with us?"

"Yeah." She pushed her glasses up. "Too obvious?"

I glanced at the light in Brandon's window. "I don't know. Maybe. Doesn't mean it wasn't great."

Julie looked up at me. "You...you thought it was great?"

My heart pounded when Julie's eyes, barely visible in the dashboard lights, lowered and fixed on my mouth. Which suddenly filled with cotton balls.

Holy crap, dude. Kenny breathed beside me. *Tell her she's great. Tell her!*

I swallowed and shook my head. "No, I think *you're* great, Julie."

Her eyes bounced back up to mine. She stared at me, eyes soft, and slowly lifted her hands to my neck, tugging me toward her. I went. Deep in the back of my mind, it occurred to me that this was wrong, that I should resist. She stroked her hands through my hair, leaning closer, close enough to take me away. When I closed my eyes, it felt like I was on the beach. The warmth of her hands on me was the sun. Her words in my ear were the breeze. I filled my lungs with her scent and snaked my right arm up to hold her, grip her, and then I waited for the panic lodged in my throat to weaken and fade.

It was the most perfect moment of my life.

She shifted. I pulled back, my head pressed against the seat back, afraid I'd offended her, but she touched my face. I watched, hypnotized, as she stared at my mouth, angled her head between the front seats, and closed in. I didn't stop her. I should have. She didn't know what I *was*. She wouldn't want to kiss me if she did. But I couldn't make myself question that perfect moment. Even Kenny was quiet.

Her lips covered mine, and I swear to God my heart jumped so hard I expected to see it lying on the upholstery between us, still beating. I didn't want her to stop, so I ignored the pain, hid it with the silk of her hair through my fingers, the scent of her skin in my nose, the taste of her lips against mine, the sound of her little moans, but *still*, I felt the friggin' pain. I thought, *More!* If I could only have more, the pain would end. My hands shifted, roamed, and tightened, clutching Julie closer. Her mouth opened, an invitation I wouldn't have refused even if I could have, and I took, took as much as she offered for as long as she let me. And finally, I could feel nothing, hear nothing, think nothing—nothing but Julie.

We broke apart, panting and staring at each other in amazement. Okay, *this* was the most perfect moment of my life. Until the guilt rushed back and I had to push her away.

"Um. Wow," she said.

No kidding, Kenny said.

"I should go," I said.

Are you crazy?

"Oh. Right. Okay. See you tomorrow."

And she was gone.

Why did you do that? She kissed us, man. She likes us. Now she'll probably never talk to us again.

She'd be better off if she didn't.

CHAPTER 11

Bigger Things to Worry About

I flopped onto my bed and threw an arm over my eyes. My parents had been waiting for me when I got home. They liked the haircut but weren't happy to hear about me kissing Julie, so I escaped to the solitude of my room after they'd tag-teamed me with reminders about how important it was not to slip up, not to get too close, not to have a damn life.

Shouldn't have told them.

So much for solitude. I moved my arm and cracked an eye open. Kenny sat at the foot of the bed, smirking.

"Kenny, I am so not in the mood." I rolled onto my side to turn away from him. It didn't help. Kenny swung his feet onto the bed, stretched out beside me.

So. Julie. That was sweet, dude. Seriously.

My lips quirked. It *was* pretty cool. Wrong though. But cool.

What was so wrong about it? She kissed us, man. We liked it. Don't even bother trying to deny it. She liked it. Everybody's happy.

"It was *wrong*. We're not…I'm not who she thinks. If she knew, she'd never—"

Exactly! Changing your name was probably the smartest thing you ever did! She'll never know.

His words hung in the air, seductive. I knew it was wrong, so wrong, but damn it, I wanted it. Wanted her. If I could just keep my mouth shut, I could have her. It was that easy. And that hard.

Bro, we have to talk to her. Get to know her better. Go on a date or something.

I snorted. A date! Yeah. Sure. I had this image of me meeting Julie at some club, imagining how that conversation would go. "Hi, I'm Dan. I like running on the beach, working out, taking walks in the rain, and camping. Oh, by the way, I'm an adjudicated juvenile criminal, and by law, I can't be alone with anyone under the age of eighteen. Can I have your number? You are eighteen, aren't you?" I'd drape an arm around her, flash her the killer smile.

Yep, I'm a real *playa.*

My laughter dried up, and I swung my legs over the bed, hanging my head. There was more, much more to my script.

Shut up, man.

Kenny and I hated thinking about that part.

She never has to know.

"She'll find out. Everyone will find out, Kenny. They always do. It's just a matter of time, and we'll have to move again."

She likes us, bro. She kissed us.

"What's with all the we's and our's? She kissed *me*, not you."

Without me, asshole, you'd still be curled up on the floor of that bathroom in juvie, so how about backing the hell off for once, okay?

I blinked. He was right. Damn it, I *hated* admitting that. Hated even more that he *knew* I hated it. I changed the subject. "You'll see, Kenny. Tomorrow, she'll be all weirded out over the whole thing. Wait and see."

You're wrong, man. Julie's different. Special.

I let my eyes close and thought again about Julie, about kissing Julie, smelling that scent, looking at that smile. Kenny was right. Julie was pretty special. I hoped he was right about being different too. Unlikely as it was—I didn't have that kind of luck—a man could still dream.

I bit my lower lip and realized I'd been rubbing my finger across it for the past several minutes. Damn it, it still tingled. Tomorrow, when she once again pretended that I didn't exist, it would be torture forgetting that kiss.

I'd been tortured a time or twelve. I wasn't looking forward to an encore.

Stop being a dick. She likes us. She won't pretend we don't exist.

"Kenny, give it a rest already. I'm just being realistic."

A knock on my door prevented Kenny from finishing his argument. Mom poked her head inside my room. Kenny didn't bother hiding. Nobody saw him but me.

"Hey, you never ate your stew, so I thought you might like a bowl." She handed me a steaming bowl, a hunk of bread perched on the rim. "What are you being realistic about?"

Crap. I took the bowl and tried to hide my wince. I'd been keeping Kenny's presence a secret for the past five years. I was determined to live a life the closest thing to normal as I could manage. Seeing and hearing myself at thirteen was not normal, and I knew it.

I dunked the bread into the stew gravy, popped it into my mouth to buy some time. Mmm. God, that was good. I chewed and considered the best way to respond to my mother's question and finally decided to appeal to her feminine side. "Just preparing myself for Julie to be uncomfortable around me tomorrow."

She sat beside me on the bed. I tried not to laugh when Kenny scrambled out of the way. "Are you worried about falling for her or leaving her?"

I swallowed another bite. "Both, I guess."

She patted my knee. "Sweetie, give her some credit. She chased after you because she obviously cares about you. And you should give yourself some credit too. You're not the big bad monster you think you are. Your sincerity and honor must have made an impression."

Almost against my will, I smiled. "Why do you say that?"

Her gray eyes softened, blurred, even though she smiled. "I know your heart."

It gave such a pang at her words, I was certain my heart failed. Sometimes, I wasn't sure I had a heart. Maybe I never did. Before…before I did what I did, I didn't remember feeling love for anybody but myself. *I* was all I cared about. And now? Well, I couldn't say I loved myself much these days.

"Honey, why does that surprise you?"

I stared at Mom. Wasn't it obvious? Did I really need to say it out loud? "Mom, come on. If Julie sees any honor in me, it only means I'm a damn good actor."

I expected her to deny it, so I shoveled more food into my mouth and waited for the inevitable Mom lies. You know, things like how great you are, how much you have to offer the world, how proud she is of you. In other words, Mom propaganda.

But she surprised me by staying silent.

I lifted my eyes and found her staring clear through me. "That's what this is really about, isn't it? That Julie can't see the real you. She kissed you but can't know who you really are."

I slid my bowl to the table beside me bed, abruptly ill. I raked my hair back, forgetting it was short, and sighed.

I really hated when she did this—this reading me like I'm a friggin' dashboard indicator light. She made it seem so easy, so obvious when I knew it was anything but. "Okay," I finally admitted. "That's part of it. She likes the *me* she thinks I am enough to kiss me. But that's not the worst part." I glanced at Kenny, still sitting with his knees tucked to his chest on the corner of my bed. His head was leaning on the wall, his expression flat and bored. "I liked it, Mom. Oh, not just the kiss." I waved away her knowing smile. "It hurts that she believes the lie, but I don't think I can stand her knowing the truth. I *like* the lie. I *like* the whole friggin' special effect."

I shut up when I saw her brows climb. She didn't get it, and I was suddenly furious. Was she unable to *see* or unable to accept what she saw?

With a sound of frustration, I jumped to my feet and shouted at her. "Don't you get it, Mom? I'm liking all the wrong things for all the wrong reasons! It means I *am* bad."

The sound echoed in my small bedroom, the crack of skin meeting skin. It was the sound, not the pain that had me staring at my mother, jaw hanging. She'd...she'd...God, she'd *slapped* me. I couldn't remember her doing that before. And then I saw the disappointment on her face. My stomach clenched.

I couldn't remember her ever looking like *that* before either. Not when

I was arrested, not when I was sentenced. Not even when she visited me in detention.

"If you believe that," she said in a low, trembling voice, her eyes shimmering with tears, "if you really believe that, you've got bigger things to worry about than Julie being weirded out." She turned and left my room, the door closing with a soft click.

I was alone with the knowledge—the certainty—that, yes, I really did believe it.

CHAPTER 12

Resistance Is Futile

Thursday morning, I grabbed a quick shower, combed my hair, and grabbed one of the hair products I'd picked up over time to rake some gel into it. "Bedhead," Julie'd said. I shrugged at my reflection and saw Kenny.

Lookin' good. He ran his hands over his—my?—okay, *our* hair and grinned.

"Gotta go." I wasn't in the mood to start off the day beating my head against Kenny's.

"Hey, bud, where's the fire?" my dad said when I nearly tackled him at the kitchen door.

"I'm picking up Brandon."

"Brandon. Who's that again?"

"Kid at school."

"The one you protected?"

I nodded and caught the frown he tried to hide. "What?"

Dad shook his head. "Dan, I thought we settled this last night. I worry how you'll handle this if you have to say good-bye."

I sighed. "I won't. It won't happen. I promise."

Dad put down the pair of coffee cups he held in each hand and gripped my shoulders. "Danny, I don't want to see you hurt again."

I frowned. "Dad, I know what I'm doing."

His hands tightened on my shoulders and he gave me a little shake. "What aren't you telling me?"

I raised my hands, spread them. "Dad, Brandon's in trouble. I think." I blew out air. "Well, I'm sure. I just…you know…I'm not sure how to help."

Dad looked at the watch strapped to his wrist. "You've got about five minutes before you're late. Condense it for me."

"Okay." I nodded, pulled in a deep breath. "He's got no friends. Only child with a ton of high-tech toys he uses to read all the lies and crap other kids are saying about him. Yesterday, I watched him bait the guy who's been hassling him. He wasn't happy I stepped in."

My dad's eyebrows shot up. "Why not?"

"I think he was planning to get even."

He was shaking his head before I finished speaking. "Danny, no. This is too much. You can't get involved."

"Dad! I *am* involved. I can't ignore this, not when I know what I know." I pulled out of his reach, grabbed my books.

"Dan."

Frowning, I turned back.

"Why don't you take this up to your mother?" He held out one of the cups of coffee.

"I'm late." I grabbed my keys and bolted, passing my grandfather on the way. He didn't say a word to me. He hadn't in a very long time.

At Brandon's house fifteen minutes later, he was outside waiting for me. "Hey."

"Hey," I greeted him. "Here. Keep it." I handed him a tub of hair gel. "I've got like a dozen of these products." He didn't need to know that I had so much because different hairstyles helped me conceal my identity.

He grunted, stowed the stuff in his backpack. "So, you up for more video games?"

I moaned. "So you can kick my ass again? Pass. I have to practice with the speech team today. Hang and wait if you need a ride."

"Nah, I can take the bus home."

"You sure? I don't want Dean to have another shot at you." I pulled into a spot and cut the engine.

"I'm not worried. He won't have time to come after me for a while."

Right. ISS.

"Still. His friends might try something."

He jumped from the car and slammed the door. "I told you I don't need a friggin' baby-sitter," he yelled over his shoulder.

Good job, dick.

Shut up, Kenny.

Brandon never waited for me that afternoon. The next day, he avoided me. Saturday, when I called him, he gave me some lame excuse about having to rake leaves to get out of running on the beach with me. The days passed slowly, and Brandon grew more tense and weird, like he had some kind of internal clock counting down the minutes until some momentous event. When he wasn't actually avoiding me, he was too quiet, like he was there in body only.

I had to face facts. I wasn't helping.

Not one bit.

Julie did not look up when I walked in to first-period speech class on Monday morning. She was too busy with her close, personal, whispered conversation with Jeff. Jeff, unfortunately, did notice me and shot me his usual glare. Guess he thought it scared me.

As if.

Julie's head whipped around and then back again.

I stared at the back of her head for a long moment and finally jerked back to reality when Paul elbowed me. I never even saw him sit down.

"Come on, man. Stay focused. We need you."

I tried, but it was hard to sit close enough to smell Julie and not touch her, not even talk to her. When the bell finally rang, I hung back, deliberately gave her the chance to apologize. She was the first one out of the classroom.

You have to catch up to her, find out what's wrong.

I already knew what was wrong. She regretted it.

Oh, come on! You probably just suck at kissing.

Really not helping, Kenny.

I kept my head down the rest of the day, and by dismissal, I was over her, certain I'd finally convinced myself she was better off not knowing me. I got in my car, started driving.

I ended up on Circle Court, parked in front of her house. Fifteen minutes later, the bus squealed to a stop, and there she was.

The line between her eyebrows made another appearance. She looked up and down the street and finally approached.

"You can't be here now."

Why the hell not? Kenny demanded.

Good question. "Why the hell not?"

"Because it's not a good time."

My eyebrows shot up. "Oh, sorry. Why don't you tell me what time *is* good and pencil me in?"

She smiled a big, cheesy, fake grin. "Sure. How about when hell freezes over?" With a flounce of hair, she strode into the house and left me standing out in the cold.

What the hell just happened?

I huffed out an unhappy laugh. "I'll let you know when I figure it out."

CHAPTER 13

The Spare Girl

It was Wednesday, the day before Thanksgiving and a four-day weekend. I had to drag my ass out of bed that morning. I lay there, mentally counting all the people avoiding me. There was Brandon, the only friend I'd made in like five years. My mother, who'd cook big meals each night but mysteriously fall ill when it came time to eat them. And Julie, a girl who had no idea what I was but kissed me anyway and then couldn't stand the sight of me. And rounding out the list, the grandfather who hadn't spoken a civil word to me in freakin' *years*.

My life couldn't possibly suck worse than it already did.

Stop whining. What more could possibly happen?

Kenny had a point, so I pried my butt out of bed, showered, and dressed. All too soon, I was parking in front of the school, my breaths coming in pants against the cold lump of dread that sat like day-old oatmeal and stuck to the sides of my gut. A knock on my window stopped the hyperventilation. And the flow of blood. And possibly the operation of several vital organs.

Julie stood outside my window.

I sucked in air, winced at the burn, and powered down my window.

"What?" I demanded without facing her in what I hoped was a preemptive strike, a sort of cold offense, my flat tone pretty damn believable. Zac Efron had nothing on me.

"Not a morning person, are you?"

I frowned. "Just following your lead."

"Yeah? How's this for a lead? Let's cut class."

My head whipped up.

Julie's hair was down. I loved it best when she wore it like this, a gold halo. Today's glasses were pink with purple flowers that matched the pink jacket she wore. The bag was hanging off one shoulder, making her hunch a bit, and I realized I was grinning. I couldn't help it. Julie smiled, and it was like the sun came out.

Unlock the doors, jerk.

My hand reached for the control before I remembered I wasn't listening to Kenny. My eyes tracked Julie as she hurried around the car, climbed in the seat beside me. She tucked the bag into the well beneath the glove compartment, and I couldn't resist a poke. "You ever leave that beast at home, where it can, oh, I don't know, gestate or mutate or something?"

She speared me with a fierce look. "This," she said and stabbed a finger at the bag, "goes everywhere I go. I never leave home without it." And then she blushed. "Except for that one time when you took me for dinner."

There was something in her tone, something almost feral that made me believe the bag was a kid and Julie its mother. I made a mental note not to tease her about it again.

Good idea. Kenny flipped pages in a pocket-sized pad in my mind.

Great. I was hallucinating secretaries now.

"So," Julie was saying, and I focused my attention on her. "Where should we go?"

I cocked an eyebrow at her. "You're serious about cutting class?"

She shrugged. "Why not? Yesterday was, uh, intense. I figure we could use some down time. Together." She put extra emphasis on that word, and my stomach flipped.

"Together. That's, um, funny. You haven't been able to look at me since we kissed."

Kenny groaned in my mind. *Jeez, man. She's trying to apologize.*

Okay, I conceded. That did sound pathetic, even to me.

Julie, however, didn't think so. "Can you forgive me for that?"

I started the car and didn't answer even though Kenny was chanting *yes* in my head. "Where do you want to go?" I asked once I'd hit the main road.

She fastened her seat belt. "How about the beach?"

My eyes widened. "I'm always up for the beach, but are you sure? It's freezing." It hadn't snowed yet, but it was cold. I had a blanket in the back of my car. My mother worried I'd get stuck in a snowbank or something. There was probably a packed picnic basket back there too. A spear of pain pierced my heart when I thought of Mom. I would apologize when I got home later, I vowed.

Julie and I were silent as I drove to Smith Point. Long Island had a lot of beaches, one of the things I loved most about living here. I'd spent a satisfying—if lonely—summer exploring them, starting with Jones Beach. I'd been to Sunken Meadow (didn't like the rocks), Montauk, which was good for fishing and surfing but not much else, Robert Moses, and the Hamptons. I liked Smith Point because it wasn't very far from my Holtsville home. I liked to walk around the memorial erected to honor victims of the plane that crashed off the coast years before I'd moved here. It was peaceful.

The access road was deserted, except for the occasional Parks vehicle. I pulled into a spot near the Pavilion, closed for the season, and cut the engine. A few brave gulls battled the cold, circling the beach. I jerked my head toward them. "Must be fish near the surface. See how they hunt?"

Julie watched for a minute. "Wanna walk?"

I glanced at her feet—beige suede boots. "No, it's too cold. You're not dressed for it. Those Icks things you're wearing will be soaked in under a minute."

She laughed. "They're called Uggs."

"Same thing." My eyes followed the boots up the curve of her body. She wore dark jeans exactly the same shade of blue as her eyes. She'd unzipped the pink jacket. Underneath, I could make out a purple shirt whose buttons strained over the swell of her chest. My face grew hotter, and I quickly averted my eyes, fixed them back on the circling gulls. I waited for Kenny to make some smartass remark, but he was strangely quiet. I did a quick scan for him, found him in his corner, lounging with his hands clasped under his head, his legs stacked one over the other.

Weird.

"You hungry?" She grabbed the bag and foraged for a minute. I had this bizarre image of her in a helmet with a carbide lamp. She emerged, a wide smile on her face, bearing two breakfast bars.

I took one, unwrapped it. Strawberries and cream. Mm. Good. I hadn't realized I was hungry until she suggested it. "Seriously, if I ask for a scalpel, a flashlight, and a skeleton key, are you gonna dive back into that purse and find all three?"

She shrugged. "Flashlight, yes. No scalpel. No skeleton key."

"You know what's in there?"

"Every item."

"Is it bottomless or enchanted or something?"

Her smile widened. "Oh, like Hermione's bag in the last Potter book? I wish. It would be nice to carry something smaller."

"Then why do you carry it?" Curiosity burned in me.

Her smile dimmed, and her eyes misted. "Remember when I told you about my brother?"

I nodded. It wasn't something I was likely to forget. "You have his Lego project in there."

"Yeah, I have a lot of his stuff in here. To protect it." She focused her attention on the bag's zipper. "When I was thirteen, my brother...um...died. Well, half-brother really."

I swallowed hard, wishing I could ease the pain I heard in her voice.

"It was hard. After the funeral, I wanted to be with my dad more than anything, but my mom said Dad and Erica were having a hard time just taking care of themselves right now. It would be easier if they didn't have to take care of me too. My sister had already taken off with her boyfriend, and my dad...just seemed to forget about me. Days passed. Finally, I couldn't take it anymore. I cried and cried until Mom took me to his house. I had to see him. I had to—I don't know—feel that connection, I guess."

Julie stared through the windshield, the cereal bar in her hand forgotten. "I ran up the front steps and into the house. At first, I didn't think anybody was there. And then I heard this sound. It was coming from upstairs, so I followed it, even though I didn't know what it was. You ever hear the howl a cat makes when it's in pain? That's kind of what I heard. I ran up the stairs into…into my brother's room and found my dad having…like this fit or something."

Julie pushed the hair off her face and sank lower into the leather seat. "He was crying and charging through my brother's room, smashing stuff, swiping things off shelves into a big pile in the center of the room. He'd brought all the garbage cans in from the yard and was just shoveling stuff into them. I knew he was grieving. I knew how much pain he was in. I swear I knew. I thought he'd regret it. When he calmed down and saw all of my brother's stuff destroyed—gone—he was going to hate himself. I didn't know what to do, so I did the only thing that came to mind. I wrapped myself around him in a huge hug, you know, because I didn't know what to say, but—"

She broke off, raised a hand to her cheek, and rubbed. A shiver of dread ran over me when the significance of that gesture hit me. I shook my head. "No."

"He hit me. He hit me so hard I landed across the room. I was so stunned, so hurt I couldn't even cry. I just…shut down while he raged about how it should have been me, not my brother. It should have been *me* because I was the spare girl and he had only one son."

Tears rolled down her face, and I thought about Liam. Is this how I made his father, his sister feel? Did Liam's sister carry around his treasures in a huge bag so they wouldn't be lost?

Doubt it. Dad said he didn't have siblings, Kenny reminded me, but it did little to soften the ball of guilt that sat petrified in my gut like crappy cafeteria food. I'd *done* this. Maybe I hadn't done it to Julie, but I'd done this, made somebody else feel as horrible as she felt. And the old familiar urge to drown myself in the pounding surf caressed me.

"My mom and Carl, my stepdad, stopped him from doing any more damage. They took me out of the house. I never went back. Everything I have in this bag is all I could rescue from the trash."

I took her hand, squeezed it. "I'm sorry, Julie. I'm so sorry."

She tugged her hand free. "That's not the worst part of the story."

Oh God. I waited for her to continue.

"Do you know what happened to my brother?"

I shrugged. "Only what you told me."

"I was there that weekend. I was the one who found him, hanging from the rod in his closet."

My body went numb. Liam had hanged himself. And during my first month in juvie, a kid also hanged himself. It's not a clean, fast death like it is in the movies. If the noose isn't tied right, your neck doesn't break, and you slowly strangle. Your face mottles and swells. Your tongue and your eyes protrude. I had nightmares for weeks, seeing Liam's face on this kid's body, knowing it was my fault, that I was responsible. The guilt chasing me, biting my ankles, finally caught up to me, and I had nowhere to go. I had to turn and face it.

Don't ask her, man. Please don't ask. Please, Kenny begged.

I pressed my hands to my ears in a futile attempt to silence him. I wasn't even sure what difference knowing would make. I only knew I had to know.

"Julie, please." I whispered. "What was his name?"

She paled. "I…I can't, Dan. I'm sorry. I can't say his name. Please don't make me. It hurts too much."

And she was in my arms, sobbing into my shoulder. I smoothed her hair, pressed a kiss into it. "It's okay, Julie. Shhh. It's okay."

But—big surprise—I lied. It *wasn't* okay. It was light-years away from okay. Was I the one? Did I kill Julie's brother? Destroy her family, carve the groove deep into her forehead? The questions were eating a hole through my heart.

Bro, relax. If you'd been the one, do you think she'd be crying on your shoulder?

She was quiet for a long moment. I glanced at her, wondering if she was disgusted. Shocked. Plotting my imminent demise. Something. But she just stared back at me, eyes dark and brooding.

Finally, she took a deep breath and lowered her eyes. "My dad lived in…in um, Maryland, when we lost my brother."

I shut my eyes and let my head fall back against the seat. It wasn't me.

It. Wasn't. Me.

I wanted to shout it up and down the beach. I'd grown up in New Jersey, not Maryland. Relief so profound filled me, and for a moment, I thought I had actually swapped places with one of those gulls. It was the lightest I'd felt in years.

Still, the similarities were, like, eerie or something. I drove a kid to suicide and then fall for a girl whose brother died in exactly the same way.

You know, some people don't believe there's any such thing as coincidence.

I sighed. Kenny, can't you just leave well enough alone for once?

I frowned as I mentally counted all the ways he always shut the sun out of my life. Something else she'd said finally registered. "So you're already eighteen then?"

"Yeah. Last April."

April, huh? "Mine's in April too. The thirtieth. When's yours?

She grinned. "I'm older than you by ten days."

I laughed. "So you were held back?"

Julie's eyes faded. "Had all that trouble to cause."

Right. Her goth phase. Still, two for two. I didn't usually have this kind of luck. Panicky thoughts started circling and attacking. Would I return home to find my parents abducted by aliens? Our house under six feet of water?

Something would happen to balance out this spike in my good fortune.

It always did.

You know what, man? You're right. We should just enjoy it for once.

I tried to do that, but my thoughts turned to the girl who'd just bared her darkest pain, the one sitting beside me. I extended my hand, waited while she stared at it for a few seconds before she finally took it. I squeezed, a gesture meant to be reassuring but falling way short. "I know you hate this, but I *am* sorry," I repeated.

She waved a hand. "Don't beat yourself up."

I burst out laughing.

"Hey," Julie said and lifted her head off my shoulder a few minutes after—hell, maybe it was hours. "I'm really hungry now."

So was I, now that she mentioned it. "I don't suppose the bag contains two extra value meals, does it?"

She shook her head. "Nope. Sorry. Guess you'll have to take me to lunch."

I started the car, visualized my wallet. It held thirty bucks. I could swing lunch at a fast-food place. I left the beach, drove toward home. The silence grew heavy.

"So how did you actually get your scars?"

I gasped. "Jesus, Julie." Where the hell did that come from?

"Sorry. I just thought…never mind."

"What? Tell me?"

"Well, I thought you might, you know, trust me."

Kenny bleeped. *Red alert! Red alert!*

Yeah, no kidding. I felt the panic rising up. "I can't."

"I wouldn't tell anyone."

I wanted to believe that. I really did.

I saw a Wendy's up ahead and pulled in, let the engine run to buy time. "It's not a matter of trust. It's one of safety," I finally said. I turned off the ignition, got out of the car, and walked around to open her door. She wouldn't look at me.

Inside, I ordered a few burgers for myself and a salad for Julie. We silently waited for the food. I hoped she understood that I couldn't say any more than I already had. But, of course, she couldn't. Nobody could understand it without first knowing the whole story—and the whole story was off-limits.

I stole a glance at Kenny. He hated talking about it. He wouldn't meet my eyes, and he just sat, listening, his arms folded over his body. I recognized that posture. Defensive. Wary. As far as Kenny was concerned, what happened in juvie should damn well stay in juvie.

That's right. So don't open your mouth.

Relax. I won't. I can't.

Sit back and enjoy the attention. The girl likes us. You did something wrong…So what?

Kenny again sat opposite Julie, just looking at her. It had always been his role to point out my shortcomings, errors, faults, and lack of character.

You're doing fine without me. He did not take his eyes off her.

Yeah. Right. You just don't want to lose Julie.

"You have scars on your face." Julie's hand moved up, but she quickly lowered it.

I did. A few.

"And you can't tell me—"

I shook my head. "No. Well, one's from Jeff, but no, I can't tell you about them."

She frowned at her salad, and I caved in. "Okay. I can tell you this much. I did something wrong. I was punished for it."

"Punished? Like in jail?"

I searched her face for the disgust, but all I saw was concern. I shrugged.

"That's it?"

I blew out a loud breath. "Julie, please stop. I told you. I want to, but I can't. I have to protect my parents."

She chewed her food quietly, avoiding my gaze.

I changed the subject. "So, your dad. You must miss him a lot."

Her hand came up to rub her cheek, and I kicked myself. Well, Kenny did it for me.

"Not that much anymore." She shook her head and then squared her shoulders. "Let's get out of here."

I followed her to the door, dumped our trash, and unlocked the car.

I wanted to rub that cheek for her, comfort her. I wanted to touch her so badly it was becoming a compulsion.

Beside the car door, I turned her around to face me. With my knees wobbling, I held out my hand and waited. She watched me, her face the picture of surprise. But slowly, she placed her hand in mine. I had to pull in a great big gulp of air then. Her skin, soft and smooth, was warm and made my hand tingle. I rubbed the knuckles with my thumb, my eyes glued to the sight of her small hand engulfed in my huge one. I stole a cautious glance at her face, saw her expression had gone from wide-eyed surprise to forehead-creasing confusion.

I wanted more, so much more. Deliberately, I moved closer, put my other hand against her cheek, the same cheek she rubbed whenever she thought of her father. I moved closer still, pressed my lips against the deep groove in her forehead, and heard her sigh. Her hand tightened around mine, and I couldn't help myself. I knew it was wrong, knew it was a lie, knew I'd burn in hell, but I wanted this. I tilted her face up and kissed her.

As kisses went, there was nothing tender about it. She was all fire and fury. I outweighed her by a good hundred pounds, and yet, she held me captive with this kiss. Wrong, wrong, God, this was so wrong. That was all I could think while the fire scorched me. I'd thought she was cold after she watched Jeff bully Brandon. Even that was wrong. Julie was a volcano—still and imperial on the outside, but inside…steaming, churning, and surging.

For me.

For *me*?

I tangled my hand in her hair. Melted gold, pouring between my fingers. I had to pry my lips from hers so I could bury my nose in that scent like some deranged actor from a Febreze commercial, but I was past coherent thought now. Her hands on my face clung to me tightly, rubbed, moved into my hair, tugging me back. Dimly, it registered that I could stand only because we were braced against the car. My body reacted to her at every level—heart thundered, lungs bellowed, legs jellied, eyes shut, skin tingled, blood rushed—and still, it wasn't enough, not nearly enough. My hands traced the lines of her body from toned arms across the smoothness of her back and down the curve of her butt, drawing her closer, molding her to me, wondering if she'd devour me and hoping, praying she would.

When my ears started ringing, I figured loss of consciousness was only moments away. But Julie's hands moved to my chest, shoved, and suddenly, she was two feet away from me. Her eyes blazed. Her mouth was slack, and she pressed a hand to her heart. We were both panting like we'd just sprinted a few hundred yards. And then her cell phone buzzed. She dove into the bag, found the phone, and read a text. Her body stiffened, and she snapped the phone closed with tight lips.

"We should go. It's…um…getting late."

I blinked. It was barely two o'clock, but okay.

"Julie, please don't—"

"Dan, I said we have to go."

Fine. With my jaw clenched, I drove home and said nothing.

Neither did Julie.

CHAPTER 14
Talking to Yourself Can Be a Good Thing

When I got home, I was still replaying Julie's words, trying to figure out where exactly everything turned to crap.

That text message. It upset her.

Yeah, no kidding. I let out a loud sigh, dropped my books on the dining room table—I wouldn't be looking at them until Monday—and headed for the refrigerator. A sweet smell derailed me. Mom baked cookies.

Chocolate chip cookies. Yes!

Maybe she wasn't so mad at me after all.

The house was quiet—nobody was home. I grabbed a glass, filled it with milk, stacked half-a-dozen cookies in my hand, and sat down with the mail at one of the gleaming counters. The stack of college brochures in the pile made me wince, but I glanced through them anyway. Quinnipiac. Columbia. NYU. Boston College. USC. Wow.

Beside me, Kenny whistled. *Nice.*

"Yeah," I answered him out loud. "What a great campus." I flipped the pages in one of the brochures.

I was talking about the chicks.

I laughed and nodded. "Oh. Right. Should have known."

So. Kenny got really serious. *Do you…you know…think we have a chance at schools like this?*

I ate another cookie, could taste the butter, chocolate, sugar. God, I'd missed these when I was in juvie. Mom used to make them only for special occasions. When I got out, she started making them for no reason at all. I tossed another in my mouth but didn't chew it. I just let it melt on my tongue. I closed the brochure, stood, and threw the stack in the trash.

Damn it! Kenny slammed the door to his cave.

Yeah, I hear ya.

"Now why would you throw those away? You planning to flip burgers for a living?"

I whirled, spilling some of the milk from my glass, and saw my grandfather leaning against the door frame. "Pop," I managed with a stiff nod.

What the—

He didn't smile. He didn't make eye contract. He strode to the kitchen trash can. He was as tall as I was but moved with a silent purpose that shouldn't have been possible for a guy in his mid-seventies. He rescued the college brochures from the can, tossed the pile at me. I fumbled the catch, tracking him as he moved around the kitchen. He poured a glass of milk for himself, sat on the stool across from the one I'd just left.

"Sit."

When a man who hasn't talked to me in ages tells me to sit, I sit. And wait. Swallow another cookie. Drink some milk.

With my grandfather.

"I hear you at night sometimes. Talking to yourself."

I choked. He reached around, pounded my back.

"Talkin' to yourself can be a good thing, you know."

I doubted that. With my face burning, I glued my eyes to the crumbs on my plate and felt every molecule of oxygen leave my body.

"Look at me, son."

My stomach clenched and twisted, but I looked.

"Yes or no, did you mean for that boy to die?"

The words hung in the air between us, echoing in my ears. *How*, Kenny whispered. *How could he ask that?*

"Answer me."

"No." It was no more than a whisper.

"What?"

"No." Stronger now.

"No what?"

I erupted. "*No*. Goddamnit, I didn't mean to kill him. What the hell difference does it make, Pop? He's still dead. Jesus. Why would you even ask me that question? Do you hate me that much?"

His lips pressed into a tight line, and he glared at me for what felt like decades.

"When I was the age you are now, I was pointing a gun at the Chinese for control over a little mound of dirt. You study the Korean War yet?"

I opened my mouth but couldn't squeeze a sound out of it. I nodded once.

"Then you've heard of Suicide Hill." He ran a finger across his lip. "I was there after we'd taken control of it the first time. Hundreds of guys got killed that summer because the Chinese just kept coming and coming and wouldn't let up. One of my company, this hillbilly named Darrell, was a real piece of work. Arrogant smartass, funny as hell, and had a real way with the ladies. After all that fighting, we were exhausted, hungry, and terrified. The Chinese were rallying, and we knew it." He spun the glass slowly, letting it scrape against the granite. The squeak drew goose bumps from me. "Darrell was out of water. I'd just swallowed the last of mine. He got testy with me, like I was supposed to save it for him. Guess I should have. I just never thought to ask him if he needed any. He got real mad at me, and before I could stop him, he climbed out of our foxhole and stood up straight. He was shot through the head under his helmet." Pop pointed to the base of his skull. "He died in my arms."

The cookies and milk—so comforting a few minutes ago—roiled in my stomach. Pop ate another cookie, swallowed the last of his milk, and cocked his head at me.

"You think nobody understands. Nobody gets it. You're wrong. I understand. I get it."

"Yeah? Really? You understand?" I repeated, the words tasting as bitter as they sounded. "You get it? Then where the hell were you all this time?" I didn't wait for his answer. I shoved away from the counter, tossed my plate and glass into the sink with too much force, and the glass shattered. I muttered a curse, reached in to start cleaning up the broken shards when two strong hands grabbed my shoulders and spun me around.

"You wanna know where I've been? I've been waiting for you take your head out of your ass, son. Instead, you just crawl deeper up your own butt. You walk around moping every day, letting your soul decay a bit more than the day before, and I'm supposed to just pat you on the head? Where's the boy I used to know?" He shook me hard enough to rattle my teeth. "Since the day you were born, you were hell on wheels, Ken. Nobody told you what was what. You followed your own gut and now you let this—"

"This *what*?" I knocked his hands off me. "This *mistake*? This *ordeal*? This error in judgment? I'm sick to death of people trying to underplay it, Pop. I killed a kid! I didn't just forget to share some water with a GI. I *killed* somebody. You don't know the meaning of guilt like that."

He stood at eye level with me, the storm swirling in his brown eyes, the muscle clenching in his jaw. "You didn't kill anybody, Ken. You said so yourself. I killed sixteen. Sixteen times, I pointed a weapon at someone's skull and pulled the trigger. Counting Darrell, it's seventeen. Don't you tell me I don't know guilt."

"That was war, Pop. Nobody arrested you for those deaths. Nobody put you in jail. Nobody carved you up like a freakin' jack-o'-lantern, and nobody put *your* name on a list with rapists and perverts." Spittle hit his face when I popped a P. My chest burned from the acid my words stirred up. We stared at each other, waging our own war. Disgust against disappointment, guilt versus grief, revulsion fighting rejection.

Slowly, he nodded. "So that's it then. You plan to just roll over, go through the motions, while life passes you by." He turned away, looked out the kitchen window. "What about this girlfriend of yours? She likes you enough even though you insist on calling yourself a murderer and a pervert."

"She's not my girlfriend." The acid in my gut ignited a path to my throat, and I gulped it back down. "Besides, she doesn't know the whole story."

He took a step back and looked at me like it was the first time we'd met. "So you're lying to her too." His lips twisted in disgust.

"What choice do I have? Telling her the truth risks Liam's dad coming after us again, not to mention the media."

"The Kenny I know would never take this bullshit from anybody. He'd fight. He was the kid who begged me, 'Pop, let's go to the city and find all the people buried under the buildings.'"

I remembered that. September 11. The images on TV broke my heart. I was too little to understand what was really going on. But I understood that some things were beyond my control, beyond my ability to fix. This wasn't. I *was* fighting. There was a brand society carved into my forehead like the scars in my skin, a scarlet word that told the entire word what I did. What I *was*. How come he couldn't see that? How come he couldn't understand I didn't *want* to be Daniel Ellison? I *had* to be!

"You think I'm not fighting?" I forced the words through gritted teeth. "I fight every goddamn day to keep Mom, Dad, and you safe from the narrow minds out there who think I peep on little girls and grope old ladies. I've been fighting for years."

Pop stalked out of the room.

I dragged the trash bin to the sink, angrily chucked pieces of the broken glass inside, and cursed out loud when one cut me.

Apparently, I hadn't bled enough for one lifetime.

"Bud, what's up?"

I jerked, found my father standing in the kitchen door, staring at the blood streaming from my hand. "Hey, Dad. Didn't know you were home."

"Wasn't until five minutes ago. What's with all the shouting?"

"Pop finally decided to talk to me. It, uh, didn't go so well."

Dad took off his coat, tossed it on the kitchen table, and opened the cabinet where Mom kept the first-aid kit. He ran my hand under the faucet for a minute and squinted. "Doesn't need stitches. Let me just tape it up."

Sure. Why not? What's one more scar?

"So you guys talked, huh? What about?" He took out some gauze and a roll of tape.

"Let's see. Killing people. I'm a lying scumbag. Oh, and I've got my head up my ass."

My dad's eyes snapped to mine. "Not funny, Dan."

"Wasn't trying to be funny."

Dad tore open the gauze package and sighed. "Okay. Start with the killing people."

"Pop figures the sixteen guys he killed in Korea means he understands what I'm going through."

Compassion flickered in Dad's eyes. "Did he tell you about Darrell?"

I shrugged. "Only that he was a smartass and got pissed off that Pop didn't save him any water. He got shot, died."

Dad huffed out half a laugh and shook his head. "Figures." He folded the gauze around my finger. "Did he mention he spent years after that war with his lips glued to a bottle of booze until your grandmother tossed his sorry butt out?"

"No. Guess it slipped his mind." Light penetrated the fog, and I could see things a bit more clearly. "Did he drink to forget Darrell or the others?"

My dad tore a strip of tape from the roll and wrapped it around the gauze. "He spent a long time believing he killed Darrell. Finally, a priest told him that God only cares about intent. Pop put down the bottle and never touched alcohol again."

Well, Jesus. "Why didn't he finish the damn story? And why the hell didn't he tell me the story back when I was getting drunk every day?" I flung up my arms in a wide arc.

"He tried, bud. You weren't ready to hear it then."

"Jesus." I swallowed a lump. I had no memory of this.

There's a surprise.

Shut up, Kenny.

I shook my head, tried to shake loose what little I could remember. There was a whole lot of stuff I hadn't wanted to hear back then. I didn't listen, so now he wouldn't talk to me.

Poetic. I grabbed my head with both hands and sighed. "Dad, Pop asked me if I meant to hurt—"

"Stop. You're my son. I know you didn't. I *know*."

I tried to talk. Instead, I grabbed him in a bear hug.

"Okay, okay." He patted my back and pulled away, a smirk curling his lips. "Move on to the lying scumbag part."

I couldn't suppress the eye roll. "That's about Julie. Pop thinks it's wrong that I haven't told her the whole story."

"And what do *you* think?"

I shrugged. "It doesn't matter what I think. I have to keep the secret or we'd just have to move again."

"Dan, I told you when we went through with the whole name change thing...I'll stand behind you whenever you feel the need to tell the truth."

"I know, Dad. I'm just not—" I was going to say I wasn't sure, but that wasn't true. "Hell. I'm freakin' terrified to tell her. She'll run screaming into the sunset, never to be seen again."

Dad slapped my head. "Exaggerate much?"

I glared, and he laughed.

"Oh, come off it, Dan. A girl likes you for the first time. It's natural to want to impress her, to keep that going for as long as you can. But at some point, it's going to get serious. When that happens, guess what also happens."

I thought for a minute and shrugged.

"She'll either figure things out on her own or something will slip out. It's inevitable."

"So you're saying I should tell her?"

Dad shrugged. "When you're ready, yes. The longer you hide it from her, the bigger it'll get. And if she's as special as you seem to think, she won't go running for the hills."

"Sunset."

"Whatever." He put the first-aid kit away. "I'll finish cleaning this up. Go get your homework done or something."

Thank God. I was talked out for the day. I didn't mention that I had no homework. I wanted nothing more but the privacy of my room, but Kenny had another idea.

You need to apologize to Mom.

I blew out a loud sigh and turned back. "Dad, you seen Mom?"

"Check upstairs in our room," he said. "Oh, take this." He fished in the pocket of the jacket still lying on the table, tossed me a box.

"Chocolate?"

Dad winked. "Greases the wheels, buddy. Trust me."

I rolled my eyes and headed upstairs to my parents' bedroom. I found my mother curled in the comfy chair we used to share when she read me bedtime stories, staring into a cup of coffee. I swallowed and squatted down beside her, but she continued staring into the cup. Her hair was tied up in a messy ponytail, and her eyes were dull.

I did that.

Man, stop the pity party and take care of business.

"Mom, I'm sorry," I whispered and held out the box of chocolate.

She looked up and smiled, and I was forgiven. Just like that.

"Thank you, honey." She took the box. "Oh. Godiva. You've been talking to your dad, I see."

My face heated.

"And now you should tell me why you weren't in school today."

My eyes popped. "Um—"

"Let me guess. Julie?"

I nearly convulsed.

"Relax," she laughed. "I'm not giving you 'the talk.'"

God, take me now. Please.

"Okay. Changing the subject. From the noise downstairs, I'm guessing you and Pop finally talked."

I was still dumbstruck, so I merely nodded.

"And that it didn't go so well."

Another nod.

"Okay. Here's my take—and this is just an opinion. I don't know if it's fact." Mom slipped the ribbon off the box of chocolate. "I think Pop knows he lost Nan because of his own thick skull. He's trying to make sure you don't follow in his footsteps."

I blinked. "Mom, Julie and I aren't together like that."

"Why not? I thought you really liked her?"

I winced. "I do. It's not that simple. She has...problems of her own. Her brother killed himself, and it destroyed her dad's family. She lives with her mom."

"Suicide? Oh God. You said her name was Murphy. Do you think it's the same Murphy?" The coffee cup rattled on the saucer.

Been there. Done that.

"Mom! Calm down. It's not me. She said it happened in Maryland."

My mother's eyes slipped close for a second. "Thank God." She sipped from her cup again and smiled. "Sorry. Panicked. So, are you thinking of telling her the truth?"

I stared at my feet. "I...God, I hate all the lying, but I'm afraid."

Mom patted my hand. "Okay. Some advice? Give it some more time. See how things go. Teenage girls, well, we're an erratic bunch."

I laughed.

"What?" she said. "My teens weren't that long ago, you know."

I laughed harder, and she pretended to swat me.

"Come on. Let's get dinner."

She stood up, and instead of walking to the door, she grabbed me in a frighteningly strong hug. I hugged back and heard her sniff.

"I'm sorry, sweetheart. I'm so sorry. We raised you right. I know we did. This never should have happened to you, and I'm sorry I let it—"

Dread swelled. "No, Mom!"

She pulled away, rolled her damp eyes. "Okay, okay. No more tears. I just can't believe how big you are now. I sent the county a little boy, and they gave me back a man."

I didn't know what to say. "I'm sorry."

"No more sorry either. Just be happy." She rubbed my face, the same side she'd slapped. She popped another chocolate in her mouth, grabbed the box, and hurried downstairs with me on her heels, laughing.

We ate…together. Just pizza, nothing fancy. Pop didn't say much, but he stayed instead of eating in his room. I went to bed happy for the first time in a very long time.

Thanksgiving was a quiet event. Mom and I cooked the turkey. It had been a tradition since I was released from juvie. I liked cooking. Not just because I liked food. It took a lot of food to maintain my six-foot-three, 220-pound body. Cooking gave me back some control. We had fun. Mom did the turkey and stuffing. I was in charge of all the trim. It was just us for dinner—Mom, Dad, Pop, and me. We had no other family. When dinner was over, Mom curled up with a book while the football game was on. Pop was…civil, I guess. It was better than nothing. Even Kenny was uncharacteristically quiet.

It was about as perfect a day as I could hope for.

The next day, I called Brandon.

"Hey, man. Got plans?"

A long silence. "Um. Not really."

"Wanna hang out?"

Another silence. "I guess."

Oh, he's psyched.

"If you have something better to do—"

"No. No, it's fine. Come over whenever."

"Okay. See you in like twenty minutes."

Just after noon, I parked in front of Brandon's house. I got out of the car, and Hagrid barked out a hello from the house next door. Julie appeared in the window, stared at me for a second, and then disappeared.

Hagrid went quiet. I stood for a long moment, my hands clenched.

Don't just stand there. Knock on the door. Ask her what's wrong.

Isn't it obvious, Kenny? She's ashamed.

I shook my head and strode up Brandon's front walk.

"What's up?

I shrugged. "Got bored. Thought I'd let you try to beat me at *Call of Duty.*"

Brandon snorted and quoted Yoda. "'There is no try.'"

I rolled my eyes. "Are we playin' or not?"

We wasted a few hours shooting at things and blowing things up.

"Jesus, man, you suck at this."

Kenny laughed his butt off at that.

I sighed. "Sorry. My head's not in the game."

Brandon ended the game. "Let me guess. Your head is next door. At Julie's."

With a wince, I shrugged. "I don't know. Maybe. I can't figure her out."

"Can't help you there," he snorted. "I've lived next to her for years and never really talked to her until I met you." The grin faded from Brandon's face. "You didn't come here to hang out, did you?"

My head snapped up. "Yeah, I did. Really, I did."

"Bullshit, man. You're just using me."

He's got a point.

My jaw dropped. "No! That's not true."

Brandon grabbed the controller out of my hands. "Just…just get out of here, man."

"Brandon, come on, man. I swear I came over because I thought we were friends."

He laughed once. "You know, he said you'd say that." He reached behind him and shifted the flat-panel display around so I could see it.

Brandon's favorite social network was open. I clenched my teeth as I read Jeff's latest post:

> *You're such a loser. You don't even notice Ellison is just using you to get into Julie Murphy's pants.*

I will kill him, Kenny raged in my head.

Chill. Let me think. I sucked in a deep breath, tried to regain control over my temper. "Let me get this straight. This guy—he used to be your best friend—hasn't talked to you since his mother died, tries to beat you up every chance he gets, but posts one comment about the guy who not only tries to save your ass but actually likes hanging out with you, and you believe him…just like that?"

I stood, the fury making me shake, waited for Brandon to deny it.

He didn't.

This is when I'm supposed to say 'I hate to say I told you so,' right?

Shut up, Kenny! I pressed my hands to my temples.

"Sorry you feel that way," I muttered.

Brandon said nothing. I turned, left his room.

Outside in the cold November air, I huddled into my hoodie, fished for my car keys. It was freakin' cold, but I needed a run.

Now.

I got behind the wheel, started my car. While it warmed up, I took one last glance to my right.

Brandon stood at his window, arms crossed, face stony. While I glared up at him, he uncrossed his arms and waved one hand with an exaggerated flourish toward Julie's house.

Julie also stood at her window, arms crossed, face stony.

I clenched my teeth.

Let's get out of here. Now.

I shifted into gear and drove to the beach, leaving them both with their faces pressed to the cold, cloudy glass.

CHAPTER 15
Black Friday

I couldn't call Dr. Phillips—she was away for the holiday—so I ran on the cold sand until my lungs were ready to explode. I didn't have my iPod, but the whipping wind and crashing surf did much to drown out Kenny's ceaseless ranting. I came to a stop, chest heaving, choking on my own spit.

Alone again.

I turned and stared at the waves that pounded the shoreline for a long moment, erasing the footprints in the sand. There was a broken shell at my feet. I heaved it as far as I could, watched it splash down, and thought, This would be so easy.

So, so easy.

The waves could have me. Pound me. Erase me.

Guess again, Einstein.

Kenny stood beside me, pointing down at the retreating surf.

There was the broken shell I'd just tossed into the ocean, coughed up like the brussels sprouts I could never make myself swallow.

You'd just get spit out. So come on, let's go home. You know it's Black Friday, right?

So what?

Good sales. We need to get Julie a Christmas present.

My lips twitched.

I knew he wouldn't let me do it.

I headed back to my car, surprised to find another one parked next to it. I hadn't seen another soul since I got there.

I aimed the key fob at my car to unlock it. Stowed in the back of my car, I found a towel and a dry shirt. I quickly stripped off the hoodie and the sweat-soaked T-shirt underneath and while I was at it, ripped the bandage off my hand. I coughed and wished I'd brought some water bottles with me.

"Dan."

I spun, instinctively coiling into a fighting stance and cursing Kenny for not giving me any warning.

He sat on the rear bumper pretending to be casual. *You afraid of girls now?*

"Julie." I stared at her, then Kenny, then her. Yeah, she was real. "What the hell—"

"Sorry. I didn't mean to...um...scare you." Her eyes honed right to the scars on my chest, and I cringed, quickly shrugged into the new shirt, and covered it with the sweat-damp hoodie.

"Oh, Dan, I—"

"Don't."

My single-word plea sounded like a harsh curse. Maybe it was. I didn't know.

I slammed the rear door down on top of my Kenny apparition and got into the driver's seat. Julie slid into the passenger seat. Unfortunately, Kenny was unharmed and now in my backseat. When he held up a middle finger, I turned to stare out the windshield and ignored them both.

We sat there for a long moment, me coughing and staring over the steering wheel, Julie rubbing her hands together and blowing on them. She wore a thick ski jacket, a hat, and gloves, but she was—

She's cold, dude.

I cursed and started the car, jacked up the heat, and went back to staring out the window.

"What do you want?" I demanded between coughs.

"To apologize." She dove into the bag and pulled out a bottle of water, broke the seal, and handed it to me.

I guzzled half of it, wincing against the cold burn.

She still hadn't said anything.

"Thanks," I muttered, tipping the water bottle at her.

She shrugged in response.

"How did you know I was here?" I asked when I couldn't stand the silence for another minute.

"I followed you."

"Why?"

"To apologize."

"Yeah, you said that already," I prodded.

"Dan, could you, like, look at me? Please?"

I cursed again and turned my head.

"There are some things about me you don't know—"

I cut her off with a loud laugh. Her secrets couldn't possibly be worse than mine.

It's not a contest, dick.

I sneaked a glance at her face and sobered up quickly. "Sorry."

"Remember when I told you about my brother and…and my dad?"

I went still when her hand rose to rub her cheek. But I didn't say anything.

"He's…well…he's a mess. That's why I don't see him."

I turned to face her, swigged more water.

"He shows up sometimes. Without calling first. Then there's all this…this…tension and anxiety and crap. And you…I don't want—"

Feeling like a total jerk, I held up a hand. "Stop. It's okay. I get it."

She whipped her eyes to mine. "You do?"

Jeez, she looks worried.

Kenny was right, so I backed off. "Julie, I didn't mean to make this harder for you. I just thought you and me—" My face burned, so I left the thought unsaid.

She smiled, and damn if that didn't wipe my mind. "You and me what?"

"I thought we were kinda more than friends, you know?" As the words left my mouth, it hit me like a kick to the head just how much I hoped they could be true.

Her smile widened only to suddenly dim. "We are, but—"

But? My temper spiked. "But what?" I demanded, out of patience.

"Dan, I—" Her face reddened. "Hell, I like you. A lot. I want us to be way more than friends, but we shouldn't be. We're seniors. We'll be going off to different schools, different careers. I mean, why start something we can't—" She trailed off with a loud sigh and pressed her head against the seat rest.

She's wrong, man. Tell her she's wrong. We won't forget her.

My mind was stuck on the *way more than friends* part and that got my heart pounding at an erratic pace. I stared at her for a long moment.

"Julie, all that stuff? It's the future. It's like a year away. And your dad? That's the past. Can't change any of that, no matter how much we want to, and believe me—" I stopped myself, swallowing hard. "All we have is this." I waved a hand between us. "Right now."

She didn't look convinced, so I reached out and took her gloved hand. She let me hold it and then changed the subject. She rubbed her thumb over my knuckles. I tried not to combust.

"You and Brandon fight? You looked pretty upset when you left."

With a frown, I shrugged. "I'm really not sure. We were playing video games. I was...well...I wasn't paying attention. He got mad. Said I was using him to get close to you."

"Are you?"

I was about to retort when I saw the teasing glint in her eyes. "Julie, I don't know what's going on with him. I mean, the mood swings—I never know which way he's gonna go." I blew out a loud breath.

"I warned you. He's got a lot of problems."

"No, you said *Jeff* has problems." I smiled and then shrugged. "Besides, I just...I thought I could help."

She leaned over and kissed me, a soft, barely there touch to the corner of my mouth. "It's pretty great that you tried. I just would have minded my own business."

Heh. She's smarter than you.

I mentally cursed Kenny and curled my arm around Julie, pulling her closer. "I think it's pretty great that you tried too. You know...lunch. And the haircut."

"I...well, I don't want Brandon to do what my brother did. If I can help, I will." Her shoulders lifted in a brief shrug and then she wrinkled her nose. "Um, Dan? No offense, but you're *gross*." She puffed out her cheeks, pretending to hold her breath.

I pulled away with a groan while Kenny nearly wet himself laughing. "I just ran like three miles."

"I know," she said and held up both hands. "I'm just sayin'."

"You wouldn't happen to have a stick of deodorant in there, would you?" I tugged at the bag. "Moist wipes?"

"No." She frowned. "But that's a really good idea." She took out a pad and pen and actually made a note.

Laughing, I opened her door. "It's cold, and like you said, I need a shower. I'll follow you home."

She got out of the car, slung the bag over her shoulder, and headed back to her car. Just before she slid behind the wheel, she grinned at me. In that moment, something happened to me.

Admit it, bro. We love her.

"Kenny." I swallowed. "What the hell am I gonna do?"

The next few weeks passed in a blur. Lisa, Paul, Julie, and I spent all our afternoons practicing for the big speech at the end of the semester.

Which was Friday, just two days from now.

Julie and I had no more cold-shoulder moments, and even though I knew they'd had nothing to do with me, I hated that she didn't trust me enough to let me help.

And that was usually when Kenny would butt in with some snarky reminder that I still didn't trust her much either. I tried explaining the difference between *didn't* and *couldn't*, but Kenny was a stubborn ass. That was usually when the door to his room would slam deep inside my brain and the rap music would rattle my teeth.

Kenny and I kept fighting about telling Julie the truth—the whole story, my real name, and why I'd changed it. So, I had a long talk with my dad about it one night after dinner.

"Something on your mind, bud?" Dad took a brick of ice cream out of the freezer, grabbed a few bowls. "You're quieter than usual."

I nodded. "Yeah."

"Let me guess. Julie." He dug out a pair of spoons, nudged the drawer shut with a hip.

"Dad…I think…well." I chickened out. "I like her. A lot."

Come on, dude. Just spill it, Kenny groaned in my mind.

Dad filled a bowl, slid it over the kitchen counter to me, then hit the cupboards for toppings. "So…did you tell her…everything?"

I shrugged and poured some fudge topping over my bowl. "I want to, Dad. But I'm—"

"Still scared?" He added a spoonful of sprinkles to his dish and one to mine.

Disgusted. Ashamed. Embarrassed. But *scared* worked too. I blew out a frustrated breath. "Yeah."

He carved out a spoonful of ice cream, stared at me over the top of it. "Well, it's not real if you're not a little bit scared." He shoved the spoon in his mouth and groaned. "Cookie dough. Good stuff."

Real. Oh, crap.

Kenny's gasp deep inside my brain halted the spoon halfway to my mouth. I let out a long, slow sigh. Real?

"Uh-oh. You look the way you did when you found out Pop was Santa Claus."

"Dad." I dropped the spoon in the bowl and waved my hand in the air, trying to find the right words. "I don't...I mean...how do I—"

Dad grinned around another spoonful of ice cream. "How do you know if it's real?"

I swallowed. Shrugged. "Yeah."

"Okay." He leaned over the counter. "You like her, right? Can you imagine living with her?"

My eyes popped. Me and Julie? Living together?

Whoa, Kenny whispered.

I thought of the bag and her eyeglasses collection. I thought of reading Harry Potter books and walking Hagrid. I imagined us working together at side-by-side desks, the way we did on our speech project, except we were older and had real jobs. No, wait—we'd have *careers*. We'd discuss each other's days. I would help her when her dad upset her, and she'd trust me.

Fingers snapped under my nose, and I jerked.

"Okay then. The goofy grin on your face tells me you *can* imagine living with Julie very well."

I nodded enthusiastically.

"Now imagine living without her."

My goofy grin disappeared.

"When you're sure...when you feel it deep down in your gut...when you'd rather suffer in hell sitting through back-to-back chick flicks or enduring endless hours of shopping, holding her bags just so you wouldn't have to live a day without her, that's how you know it's real."

I considered that for a minute. Could I live without her?

I can't. Neither can you.

"Give it some more time before you decide to tell her. See if she feels the same way, you know?" Dad polished off another spoonful.

That was what Mom said. I bit back a smile.

"So, what's happening with your friend Brandon?"

I shoveled in more ice cream. "He's mad at me. Thinks I'm using him just to get to Julie."

"Are you?"

"No!"

Bull.

I dropped my spoon. "Why does everyone keep asking me that?"

"Okay, see this from his point of view. School started how many months ago, and you've never invited Brandon over here."

I stared at the ice cream melting in my bowl and sighed. Crap.

"He lives next door to Julie, so—" Dad rolled his hands.

"Okay. I get it. I'll fix it."

"Good man." He clapped my back. "I'm going upstairs to bother your mom." He headed for the door. "Oh, one more thing. If this thing with you and Julie *does* get...you know, *real*...you be safe, okay?"

I shut my eyes. "Oh God. Dad." I let my head fall to the counter.

"Okay, okay. Just checking." He held up his hands. "Good talk."

Awkward, Kenny sang.

CHAPTER 16

Toughen Up, Buttercup

Friday morning arrived, gloomy and freakin' cold. Snow was in the forecast. It was our last day before a week-long Christmas break.

And it was "speech day."

I had practiced for so many hours. I'd dreamed about the damn speech. I had index cards of notes tucked in my back pocket. Wait—I patted my pocket just to make sure—yep.

You faced a judge sentencing you to juvenile detention, and this has you nervous?

My mouth went dry. I'd passed *nervous* and was now heading into *panic attack* territory. On the way to the lockers, I saw Paul and Lisa. They waved, asked me if I was ready for the speech. I shrugged, but I didn't stop to chat. I was a man on a mission. I strode with single-minded purpose directly to Julie's locker, where she stood in front of the open door.

I skidded to a halt, abruptly blank and sweaty and embarrassed and totally drained of confidence. "Um. Hey." I smiled wide. She wore jeans, boots, and a soft sweater nearly the same shade as her eyes, plain wire frames around them.

Julie jolted, whirled. Gave me a tight smile, the kind that showed no teeth, and then turned away. "Hey."

The smile fell from my face. Julie kept her head in the locker, flipping through books, hanging up her jacket. I finished my inventory, and she still hadn't said anything else. She still wouldn't look at me.

I gave her the benefit of the doubt. "Nervous?"

"I'm fine," she said over her shoulder and removed every last shred.

After all that talking. And the kissing. And we were back to this? Cold seeped into my pores. I wanted to take her in my arms, shove her against her locker, and force her to look at me. When my hands twitched, I whipped around and walked away, my shoes squeaking from the speed.

What the hell are you doing? Go back. Kenny poked me.

"No," I said out loud, not giving a crap that half the damn corridor heard me. I was done with this. Done, period, full stop. I was done with the whole does-she-or-doesn't-she-like-me issue. We had a speech to make, so I strode to the auditorium by myself.

"Dan!"

I spun and saw Brandon behind me. I waited, not patiently, for him to catch up.

"So. Speech day. You, uh, okay?" He grinned.

"Uh." I'd caught sight of Julie coming down the corridor. "Yeah. Speech day."

The smile waned a bit. "You still up for watching a movie tonight?"

"Yeah, sure."

The smile disappeared. "Hey, look, if you have better things to do, I get it."

"Brandon, it's fine. I wouldn't have invited you over if I had better things to do."

Shut up, idiot.

As the words fell out of my mouth, I wished I could suck them back in. Brandon's face reddened, and his eyes drifted down.

"Shit, Brandon. I'm sorry. That's not what I meant."

"Yeah, no problem. I…um…have something else going on tonight anyway."

And he was gone.

The sound of slow clapping filled my head. *Nice job, moron.*

I gritted my teeth on my way inside the auditorium. I would fix things as soon as the speech was over.

Dozens of kids filled the seats. Panic descended on me like sharks on chum. Classes had been suspended this morning for the big event.

Terrific.

I breathed and tried to remind myself that we'd practiced until we were hoarse. We were ready.

We *hoped.*

By the strength of sheer willpower alone, I stopped obsessing over Julie and Brandon and went over the speech plan one more time before we took the stage. We'd agreed that the girls would argue against the proposal while Paul and I would argue in favor. Paul and Lisa didn't care that much one way or the other, but Julie and I had strong opinions. No matter what I said, how much evidence I showed her, she remained stubbornly convinced that a "duty to respond" clause was a bad idea. I was just as strongly convinced it was good. According to the assignment, each of us would take turns presenting an argument. Paul would go first as a proponent of the law, with Julie next as an opponent. Then I would talk, and we'd end with Lisa.

The hard part was what came after the speech—the rebuttal. We're supposed to take notes during each other's talks and then ask a question that could be twisted around to prove your own point. I hadn't been very good at this in our practice sessions. So we'd tried to plan this part by preparing questions ahead of time. My questions and responses were printed on the cards I'd tucked into my pocket.

Holy crap.

My knees were already knocking. I was sweating and suddenly needed to pee.

So let's sign up for another speech class next term.

Not helping, Kenny.

But Kenny, traitor that he was, chuckled deep in my mind and left me to twist.

It was two minutes. Just two minutes. I could talk for two minutes without choking, right? I wasn't going to puke. Nobody was going to laugh. It was all going to be just fine.

Toughen up, buttercup.

I couldn't stop the irrational giggle that left my lips. Julie walked through the auditorium's side door, her eyes looking everywhere but at me, Paul and Lisa following behind. I stopped laughing after that.

We waited anxiously behind the drawn curtain, the first group up, probably the only good thing about the whole ordeal. Mr. Williams agreed to let us sit two to a table. When we addressed the audience, we would have to stand but, thankfully, not at the podium. We would also be wearing lapel mics, which, I was willing to bet, would broadcast the pounding of all four hearts across the auditorium.

Mr. Williams stood on the other side of the curtain, explaining the format to the assembly. I took another look at Julie, who immediately turned her head.

As soon as the speech is over, take care of this, bro.

Oh, I intended to.

I shrugged when Paul looked at Julie and then at me, his eyebrows raised. I knew as much as he did about her moods. We sat on the stage, and I tried not to swallow my tongue when the curtains parted with a soft swish. I didn't look at the faces I could make out under the bright lights. Some of them would be bored. Others would be thrilled at not having regular classes today. I would have paid good money to exchange places with any of them, even if I had to steal the good money first. Wish I'd thought of that sooner.

Mr. Williams introduced our topic. "Resolved. Existing Good Samaritan laws should be expanded to include a 'duty to respond' provision."

A few seconds after the bored applause faded, I elbowed Paul in the ribs, and he climbed to his feet, leaving his notes on the table in front of us. I suddenly remembered mine, fished the cards out of the rear pocket of my jeans, and fanned them out on the table.

"Paul Oliva, arguing in support of the resolution." Paul's voice shook. I heard him suck in air and start the speech, leading off with a list of crimes in which people were killed while witnesses did nothing, like the 1964 Kitty Genovese case, Princess Diana's death in 1997, and the rape and murder of a little girl in a casino bathroom while the killer's friend watched. He ended with the major ethical philosophies that supported our law.

But my eyes stayed glued to Julie. Each time Paul nailed one of his points,

Julie moved a note card to the pile on the table in front of her. My hands went damp.

"Time," Mr. Williams said, and I jerked in my seat.

Paul sat beside me, sighing heavily. I gave him a nod.

Julie stood and pushed her glasses up.

"I'm Julie Murphy, arguing against the resolution."

Julie's voice didn't tremble at all, which both impressed and upset me.

"In 2004, a woman pulled her coworker from the wreckage of a car, leaving the victim a paraplegic. Crash investigators later said the victim could have walked away from the accident if someone who knew what he was doing had rescued her instead."

Paul elbowed me. Right. We'd practiced this one. I knew what to say. I grabbed one of my cards from the table, moved it to the front of my deck, and waited for Julie to finish her argument.

"This law is trying to legislate morality. That violates our rights *and* fails Kant's categorical imperative test because there's no way you can predict the right response in all situations," she argued.

I wiped damp palms on my pants and added another card to my response deck.

"That 1964 example? What if the widowed mother of several children tried to stop it and got herself killed? That would have left her children orphaned, so doing nothing was the right thing for this mother to do," Julie finished with a sigh of relief.

"Time."

Crap. I was sweating in rivers now. Where the hell had Julie pulled all that from? I barely had time to make a note of her point when Mr. Williams called time. I was up next.

I stood, drew in a deep breath and began. "Daniel Ellison, arguing in favor of the resolution." My voice shook. No surprise there. I sucked in another breath to calm myself and locked eyes with Julie. Suddenly, there was nobody else in the room but her. I didn't need to convince Mr. Williams or the assembly or the faculty. I only needed to convince *her* that this law had merit.

"Mr. Ellison, ninety seconds left."

I jerked and cursed myself for wasting time.

"Um. Sorry," I mumbled, drawing another deep breath. "The Constitution protects our rights with a system of government that passes laws. For example, there is a law that says parents have to rescue children. There is a law that says married people have to rescue spouses. And there are laws that say doctors, police, and firefighters have to rescue people when off duty. It's pretty clear the law already does legislate morality. But *this* law isn't about *rescuing* people. It's about *responding*. Just open a cell phone, call 911, and you've complied." I looked down at one of my cards. Right, I nearly forgot about the categorical imperative. "And because today's technology addresses special needs, like people with physical handicaps, anyone can make that call. Therefore, the categorical imperative is satisfied as well as the different variations of the Golden Rule preached by all the Abrahamic religions." I never stopped looking at Julie.

"Time."

Thank you, God. I blew out a gust of air. I did it. Lisa was up last. I held my breath. So did Kenny.

"Lisa McKenna, arguing against the resolution." Lisa faced the audience and returned to the major ethical philosophies and said something about how forcing a duty to respond on everybody violates utilitarianism's *maximum happiness* principle. I was still watching Julie and hardly heard a word Lisa said.

"Time."

I jerked back to attention. Julie gave me a mean little smile I didn't understand. I smiled back, but she would not acknowledge me again.

"The team will now refute the arguments they've presented in a cross fire round," Mr. Morris notified the assembly.

All four of us stood. Paul grabbed his first card. "You mentioned the maximum happiness principle. But doesn't utilitarianism theory *support* this law on the basis that it serves the greater good?"

Oh, that was good. Paul phrased his question so Julie and Lisa pretty much had to say yes. They not only had to remember the theory but twist it around to argue their own point...and do it in less than a minute.

"Yes, but only as long as the greatest good for the greatest number of people is *always* served. In the Kitty Genovese example, that test fails if three children were orphaned to save one life," Lisa answered.

You guys are toast, Kenny jeered.

I had the next question and tried to follow Paul's lead. But I abandoned our script. "If you were in trouble—the victim of a crime or an accident—would you be mad if bystanders did nothing to help you?"

"Yeah," Julie shrugged.

"Would you wear a seat belt or wait until you were twenty-one to drink if the law didn't force you?"

"Probably not."

"So you agree the law already limits our rights?"

Julie's eyes went cold, and she wasted precious seconds glaring at me before she muttered a terse yes.

The assembly applauded.

"Okay, we're out of time. Summary review. Who is the team's last speaker?" Mr. Williams interrupted.

Julie was our designated summarizer. She was supposed to close with a bias against the law. She turned wide eyes to me, and I recognized the look. Stunned. Paralyzed. It was the same look as the day I'd met her. And suddenly, I realized it was the same look from this morning. Lisa was frantically nudging Julie, who remained immobile. Paul looked at me.

"Do something," he mouthed.

Um. Right. I could do the closing. But I couldn't argue her side! I stood up on knees that knocked and cleared my throat. With my eyes glued to Julie, I began our closing.

"In summary, we agree that responding to emergencies needs qualified experts. That's why we think a law should be passed that says we only have to call 911 when we see a crime or an accident. Calling 911 is always the best thing to do because it doesn't put anybody at risk, which makes utilitarianists and Kant happy and prevents bigger tragedies."

I did it. It was over.

I was suddenly aware of the sheer number of eyes pinned on me at that moment and took my seat before I fell over. Dear God, if you ever were to open a hole and swallow a whole human being, now would be a really good time. Amen.

Mr. Williams, still standing at the podium, turned his back on the audience and applauded. In seconds, the entire auditorium had joined him, but I knew they were just being polite. I watched Julie, but she sat with her head down. Judging by the tendons straining in her neck, she was upset, and it was taking everything she had to hide it.

I smiled tightly, and the four of us stood to leave the stage. There were four more groups scheduled to speak next, and we had to stay to watch. Once backstage, Paul held out a fist to bump.

"Hey, man. Wow. Seriously. That was way cool. You saved our asses. Where did you learn to talk like a *Law & Order* episode?"

From my attorney, my court-appointed shrink, and my caseworker. But because they were all part of the whole secret identity thing, I only said, "Here and there."

Julie walked ahead, her mouth pressed into a thin line. Oh, yeah. She was definitely mad.

Apologize, dude.

Back off!

Kenny glared.

Fine. "Julie, hey, I'm really sorry."

She whirled around so fast I skidded to a halt and fumbled my landing. My hands came up to catch her after we collided, but she flung them off. "Really? Doesn't feel like it. You know what it feels like, Dan? It feels like an excuse. You do something wrong and then want to make it a law so poor, innocent bystanders have to share your blame. It…God, it's like winning is all you care about."

For a long moment, I stared at her, blinking, scratching my head. Winning wasn't my only goal. I wanted Julie to see my point of view, to make her understand why standing and watching when someone needed help was wrong.

Sorry, dude. You just wanted to win.

No. No! I—

You did.

Helpless, I shook my head. Julie made a sound of disgust.

"For God's sake, Dan, don't you understand how this hurts me?"

Hurts her? Why would this hurt? It was a stupid class project, not a Supreme Court hearing. I stared at her, trying to connect the dots in her leap of logic and couldn't get there from here. I stood, gaping, and she flung her hands in the air, then took off. Lisa hurried behind her, stopping once to skewer me with a dirty look.

Paul looked at me and smirked. "Sucks to be you."

Deep in my mind, Kenny laughed like a loon.

CHAPTER 17

I Tell Myself I Shouldn't

I drove down Portion Road on autopilot. Businesses had their holiday lights up, and some were already twinkling in the early dusk. Kenny was right; I should probably get Julie a gift. Assuming I could get her to forgive me. Dr. Phillips suggested a direct attack. Okay, she called it a 'direct line of communication.' Whatever. The plan was to come right out and ask Julie how she felt about me.

As I turned down Julie's street, I saw the Dellermans' house was dark. I hadn't seen Brandon since before the speech. I wish I could text him or something. I guess I could leave a note in the mailbox, let him know I was still his friend—assuming he was still mine.

I parked, headed up Julie's walk, and before I could ring the bell, Julie flung open the door.

"You have to leave."

"Julie—"

"Dan, not now. Just go. I'll meet you, I promise. You can't be here right now." Her arms were crossed over her chest, but one hand came up, rubbed her cheek. She stared at me, her eyes wild, her hair blowing in the December wind.

No. My muscles clenched. No, damn it. I wasn't going to let her do this to me again. I took her by the shoulders, turned her to face me. "I have to talk to you, to apologize. I know I upset you."

"I said not now!" Julie slapped my hands off her and went back to the door. "You have to leave before—"

"Before what?" I followed her. "Julie, you either like me or you don't. Which is it?"

She wasn't hearing me. Her eyes, glassy and too wide, kept scanning up and down the street. A few kids slapped around a hockey puck, and for a minute, I wished I could play too. A car turned the down the block, and Julie's eyes popped. "Leave! Leave right now. Go to the restaurant, and I'll meet you. I promise. Just go now."

The car drove past the house and parked at the end of the street. Julie's shoulders dropped in relief.

"Julie, I'm not going anywhere until you tell me what the hell is going on." I ran my hands down her arms, rubbed gently.

"Dan, I will, I promise." She put a hand to my chest, pushed at me. "Just…not now. He's coming. He'll be here soon."

"Who? Your dad?"

She didn't answer.

"Damn it, Julie. Tell me. Tell me why you keep pulling me closer one day and pushing me away the next."

Before my eyes, her features rearranged, going from worried and afraid to totally pissed off in zero-point-five seconds. "To protect you, you dumbass. Now go." She swung on her heel and escaped back into the house before I could recover.

I hesitated for a minute and walked across the grass to Brandon's door, dug an old scrap of paper out of my wallet, scrawled a short note across it, and stuffed into the mailbox bolted beside the door. I pulled my hood up, huddled deeper into my jacket, and hightailed it back to my car, Julie's words replaying in my head. As I pulled away from the curb, a beat-up, old Hyundai slid into the spot, facing the wrong way. I couldn't see the driver.

Come on, bro. She wanted us out of here, so let's go.

I took the Long Island Expressway back to the Applebee's where we'd eaten dinner that one time. I sat outside in the parking lot for twenty minutes, then thirty minutes, before a car pulled beside mine.

"I can't stay," she said when I got out and met her at the driver's door.

"Julie, I—"

"I know. I'll meet you. Tomorrow, I promise."

I searched her face for signs she was lying, but she met my gaze without flinching. After a moment, I nodded. "Fine. Where?"

"How about your beach? Tomorrow morning?"

I nodded again. "Eleven."

She flashed me a halfhearted smile and drove back the way she'd come.

What the hell was that about?

"I wish I knew."

I didn't sleep much that night. When the sun came up, I was itchy for a run but didn't want to be all smelly and gross when I met Julie. I still had five hours to kill before I met her at the beach. So, I headed to our basement, where my dad and I had a small home gym set up, to take out my frustrations on the Bowflex. I ran through my usual circuit in about forty-five minutes and worked up a lather. It did nothing to take my mind off Julie. Or Brandon.

I grabbed a clean towel from the pile of folded laundry sitting on top of the dryer and jogged back upstairs for a shower. I washed off the sweat, toweled off, gelled my hair, and dressed in jeans, a T-shirt, and boots.

By 10:30, I was in my car about to head to the beach when my phone rang.

"It's me. Julie."

Dread settled in my gut.

"Um, hi."

"I sent you a text, but you never replied."

I grimaced and let another lie drip from my lips. "Yeah, my phone's, uh…not working right. I haven't been able to text in weeks."

"Oh. So, listen…about the beach."

"You're canceling, right?" I let my head fall back against the seat rest.

"Not exactly. I just wondered if you'd rather come here where it's warm instead of the beach where it's below zero."

Yes! Kenny clapped his hands, and my head pounded.

"Yeah, absolutely! I'm already in the car. Bye." I snapped the cell shut. "Woo!" I did a lame fist pump thing that nobody saw.

I did.

"You don't count," I retorted with a wide grin. Not even Kenny would foul up my great mood.

Fifteen minutes later, I was sitting in Julie's toasty warm living room. There was a fake Christmas tree in the wide window that faced the street, a pile of presents under it. Julie handed me a bottle of water and then curled up on the sofa opposite the tree. She wore jeans with flowers embroidered on one leg and a clingy top that sparkled when she moved. Her glasses were blue today. I liked the blue ones the best.

"So, last night was messed up," I finally said.

"Yeah, I'm sorry about that. My dad showed up." She shuddered. "He has a lot of problems, and there's always a ton of drama whenever he shows."

She kept using the word *shows*. "You didn't know he was coming?"

"No, not until right before he showed up. I wasn't all that happy about it, to be honest."

"I thought you really missed him."

Julie shrugged and picked at a flower on her jeans. "I did, but—"

"But what, Julie?"

"You don't understand what it's like to be around that much hate." She twisted her hands. "I care about you. I tell myself I shouldn't. *He* tells me I shouldn't. But I can't help it."

I scoffed. "Right. Nothing says I love you like a door slammed in your face."

She shot me a glare. "Look, will you stop with the sarcasm already?"

With a loud sigh, I forced myself to stay calm. "Just tell me this...you said you wanted us to be more than friends. So yes or no, Julie? Do you like me as a boyfriend? I shouldn't be asking you this, I know that, but I just don't give a shit about any of that stuff right now. I need to know if you feel the same way." Holy crap. Did I really do that? Just come right out and demand an answer to a question that direct?

All I needed to hear was one word, just one word to make the butterflies in my stomach go away. Instead, Julie's eyes lowered.

"Julie, please," I begged.

"No." Her voice was strained like it hurt to say the word.

It hurt to hear it even more.

"I love you. I'm in love with you, Dan."

Oh my God. She loves me. My heart started palpitating. The butterflies hadn't disappeared. They'd called friends. She loved me! Nobody who wasn't related to me had ever said that to me before.

Whoa, Kenny whispered.

I should have stopped her. I should have put the brakes on. "I love you too," I blurted out. "And I'm sorry."

"Um…okay." She smiled halfway. "For what?"

I waved a hand, impatient and frustrated. "For everything. For the speech. For pressuring you. I…I just don't understand why you keep flipping the switch on me."

As I spoke, Julie's hand slowly crept to her cheek, where she rubbed it.

"Oh. It's because of your dad."

Her eyes nearly popped from her face. "How…how did you know that?"

I shrugged. "Every time you think about your dad, you rub your cheek. I'm good at reading people." I managed half a laugh. "I sort of have to be." I put my hand over hers. "What I don't understand is why you made me leave. I wanted to meet your dad."

The hand I held twitched.

She shook her head. "No." The word was shrill. "You can't meet him. Ever."

What the hell, dude? Why not?

Excellent question, Kenny.

She sighed. "You don't understand."

"You said that already." I spread my hands apart. "Then explain it to me this time instead of pretending you don't know me or sending me away."

Julie sat silently, twisting her hands. She adjusted her glasses, a slim finger sliding them back up her nose. She nodded once. What did that mean? Was she thinking about how to answer me or about sending me away?

I leaned back in the sofa, frustrated, tired, and angry. I took a gulp from the bottle of water. I waited while Julie fidgeted beside me. She stood up, walked to the window by the Christmas tree, and looked outside. I could see the side of her face, the sun outside turning her hair into a halo. But her eyes were cold and distant.

"Nobody knows this," she finally said. "Not my parents or my stepparents. Not my sister. I've never told anybody." She drew in a deep breath and turned, leaning back against the windowsill. "I *knew* my brother was being bullied. I knew it for months."

I shut my eyes tight, sympathy building.

"He was a real brainiac, got skipped a grade, and that totally bugged me. Like he needed more attention. My dad loved having a son…a lot more than he loved having daughters."

I nodded, understanding but trying very hard to contain my impatience.

"He was very immature for his age—physically, I mean. He was still baby-ish while the other kids were growing taller and stronger. He told me kids laughed at him, pushed him around, teased him, took his stuff." Julie shut her eyes for a moment. "But I never helped. I could have. I could have told my dad. But I did *nothing*. I didn't lift a finger and now he's dead." Her voice broke, and tears slid down her cheek.

I sat on the sofa, paralyzed and ashamed. "Julie—"

"No! I'm not done. There's more." She brushed a tear away, annoyed at it. "I was grateful. I was actually happy there was something less than perfect about him, something that my dad couldn't gush and brag about." She covered her mouth and squeezed her eyes shut in a gesture of self-hatred so familiar I was up and across the room in a single motion, pulling her into my arms.

"No wonder you hated me."

She pulled out of my arms. "No, I never hated you. You hated me." With half a shrug, Julie smiled tightly. "You *should* hate me. I'm…I'm such a piece of shit."

"No." I tugged her back. "I don't think that at all." It made sense. All of it. She'd said she was staring but not watching Jeff attack Brandon…that she was frozen in a flashback. It all made sense now, and I'm—

An ass, Kenny finished for me.

This time, I did not argue.

"Julie, I'm so sorry. I hope you can forgive me for making you feel so bad."

Again, she shook her head. "No, you were right. I should have done something. I had the power to help," she said and held up a hand, palm up. "But I just wasted it." She turned her palm, as if to spill whatever it held. She squared her shoulders and returned to the sofa.

"Anyway, my dad doesn't know any of this. He already hates me for…uh, surviving, I guess. He'd probably kill me himself if he knew."

I thought of my grandfather, about the guilt he carried. "Julie, are you sure he hates you? He's grieving. Maybe he feels the same guilt you do."

Julie shook her head. "No, my dad doesn't do guilt. All he feels is hatred. That's why he and Erica are having so many problems—that's my stepmom."

"I don't understand."

She pressed her lips down. "He can't hold down a job. He pisses through all his money, chasing down dead-end leads trying to find my brother's bully. Wants justice. Nothing else matters. I don't matter. Erica doesn't matter. My sister doesn't matter. Nothing but revenge, twenty-four-seven."

"Is that why you sent me away last night?"

She nodded and glanced at me from beneath her lashes. "Dan, we shouldn't be together."

Awesome. "Yeah, I got that part. So are we?"

"If he knew about you, he'd hurt you."

"Why?"

She shook her head slowly, her eyes still not meeting mine. "He blames everyone. Nobody is allowed to be happy. He can't stand it when we are." Her eyes slid shut. "If he…if anything happened to you—" She swallowed. "I couldn't stand it."

Tears escaped from her closed eyes, and I thumbed them away. "You…like me that much?"

She didn't reply. Instead, she leaned closer. Slowly, her damp eyes pinned to mine, she kissed me, and the world went away. "Told you. I love you. You should go."

I swallowed hard, but I didn't move. "I love you too. And I'm not leaving."

She looked like she wanted to pick me and throw me out, but when she grabbed me, it was to kiss me again. When we finally separated, I was panting.

"Jesus, Julie." I gulped air to regulate certain um, systems, but it didn't do a damn bit of good.

"I know," she whispered, a hand pressed to her chest.

"We—" I began, paused to remember what I was going to say because the look in her eyes was potent enough to scatter my thoughts in all four directions. "We should stop before we get, um, too carried away."

She shook her head, and my heart stopped for an instant, then pounded a frenzied beat against my ribs. Was she saying what I think she was saying? Oh. My. God. I can't.

Are you nuts?

I twisted Kenny's arm behind his back and shoved him into his corner in my mind, slamming the door on my way out, but his words kept echoing in my head. Could I? Could I really do this and not get zapped by a lightning bolt? I stared at Julie, at the full pink lips she kept pressing together like she was afraid they might run away or something, at the flush I could see creeping up her face, begging for my fingers to track, at the dark blue eyes that usually gave me frostbite but now scorched my skin. God, I wanted this, wanted her. But—

But it was wrong.

"Julie, we can't—"

Her mouth was suddenly fused to mine, swallowing the rest of my sentence. Okay. We *can.* Her hands tangled in my hair, and her tongue danced over, under, and beside mine. And then her hands were everywhere—my face, my shoulders, my pecs, my hips, my thighs, and then *there.*

God in heaven, I tried to say, but all that came out was a groan. The sound was harsh; it distracted me from what had suddenly become my mission in life, and I tore my mouth from Julie's, trapping her hands in mine.

"Julie, are you sure?" Be sure. Please, please be sure. Be sure. Be sure. Be sure.

She nodded, her eyes pinned to my mouth.

"Here? Now?" I pressed. If not here, then where? Someone was always home at my place.

She tugged her hands free and stood. "Right here. Right now." She took my hand and led me upstairs to her room. "My mom and stepdad are out all day today."

I followed her, my thoughts churning. There was a condom in my wallet. It had been there probably since I was released from juvie. That had been my counselor's way of making sure I was safe. I took it out, held out my hand, and waited.

With my breath burning in my lungs.

Julie took my hand, tugged me into her room, and shut the door. I looked around, but only certain things penetrated my mind. Kenny was shouting *Yes!* Pink walls. Purple bedspread. Really clean. I may have tried talking and failed. She stretched out on the purple quilt, moved over to make room for me. I lay down next to her, my eyes glued to hers. She breathed through her mouth, and I could see her pulse pounding in her throat. And then her lips met mine, her hair falling over us like a gold curtain. I pried my mouth from hers so I could bury my face in her hair, breathing deep. Her hands slowly moved under my shirt, lifting it. I raised my arms, let her tug it off in one move. She gasped, and I froze.

The scars. Jesus, the scars.

I'd tried to bury the shame, but it lived in those scars, and I couldn't let it ooze out, couldn't let it touch her. They were the first place her eyes landed, and I grabbed for my shirt to hide them. But she snatched it back. Slowly, she lowered her head and touched her lips to the longest line. The warmth, oh God, it almost blistered my skin when she kissed along the scar that crossed from my sternum to hip. My shirt fell from her fingers when she shoved them into my hair and tugged hard. I gasped, loud and long, and she grinned, all fire and temptation and need and distraction. And I forgot the scars, forgot the guilt, forgot the complications, forgot the confusion. I forgot who I was, what I did, who I needed to be, and all the reasons I never could be.

I forgot it all.

CHAPTER 18

I Can't Tell You

Julie scooted off the bed, golden and perfect. I watched, entranced as she wriggled into her bra and panties, pink wisps of material that looked way too delicate for their intended purpose. She pulled on her jeans and then moved to her dresser. She was a whirl of motion, pulling more brightly colored, soft-looking things from a drawer and tossing them on the bed. I grinned when she slid open the top drawer. She had at least a dozen pairs of eyeglasses organized in there. She deliberated a minute, then slipped on the flowered pair, followed by the floral top that had landed on my foot.

"Hey, are you okay?" she asked me over her shoulder.

I was light-years beyond okay. I was all loose limbed and warm and fuzzy. I managed a drunken grin and sat up. "What's with all the glasses?"

Julie shrugged. "Contact lenses bother me. If I have to wear glasses, may as well have fun."

"Must be expensive." I took the pair she'd left on the table next to the bed, ran my fingers along their curves.

"No, not really. I order them online."

I handed her the pair in my hand, and she slipped them into an empty spot in the drawer. That was when hormones and guilt teamed up to kick me in the gut, nearly taking my breath away. I'd slept with Julie. Oh God. I had sex with Julie. I should be shot. I had no right, no right at all.

Dude, do not ruin this moment for me.

Kenny's voice was like an electric shock, and I jumped.

"Dan, what's wrong?"

I didn't answer. I found my pants, pulled them on, looked all around the floor for my shirt but didn't see it. I flipped up the ends of the bright purple bedspread. No shirt.

"Dan, look at me."

"My shirt. I need my shirt." My voice was a hoarse croak.

"No, you need to look at me."

I shook my head. "I need my shirt." I checked the pile of clothes she'd pulled from the dresser. Not this one. Not this one either. Not this, this, or this. I ran my hands down my chest, tried to hold the edges of my wounds together, contain the shame I could feel spreading, dripping.

"Dan, please."

She put her hands on me, on my chest, right where the ugliest scar began. In her hand was my T-shirt. I snatched it, tugged it over my head, and only then breathed normally. I was dizzy and sat on the edge of her bed, propped my head in my hands.

Her quiet murmur penetrated the fog. "If you tell me you're sorry, I swear I'll hit you."

Yeah, so will I.

I laughed, but it held no joy. It should have. This was the best day of my life. I should have been giddy with the feeling. Instead, all I felt was an oily knot of shame rising from gut to throat. I lied to her. I was still lying to her. And now we'd slept together. More lies.

"Dan, I swear to God, if you don't talk to me—"

"Don't call me that!" I screamed, and she stared at me in shock. "Just…just don't call me that."

The line in her forehead deepened. "You don't like your name?"

I laughed again, but I knew the only thing she saw in my eyes was regret. "I like my name. But I can't tell you my name."

Her eyes narrowed. "You're telling me your name isn't Daniel Ellison? Is that what you're telling me?"

Slowly, I nodded. "I'm a liar, Julie. I've been lying to you since the first day of school, and I don't think I can take it anymore."

"I don't understand."

"I know."

"Why can't you tell me your real name?"

I paused, trying to inhale courage along with air, but it didn't work.

Go on, jerk, finish what you started.

I scrubbed my hands over my face and tried to find a place to start. The beginning seemed lame. I found my socks, tugged them on. Then my boots. I felt better when I was dressed. Covered. Hidden.

"You wanted to know about my scars."

She nodded.

"Five years ago, I did something…horrible. I served time, Julie. Nine months. But it wasn't enough. People keep…finding out what I did. They…make threats.

They show up at my house, my school. I'm never safe. My parents are never safe. This is the first town it hasn't happened because *this* time, we changed our names. Protecting this name, hiding my secret…it's the most important thing I do every day."

She covered her mouth with both hands. "Oh, that's why you were so mad at me for not breaking up that fight."

I nodded, kneeling in front of her. "Making enemies isn't smart. Jeff can make a lot of trouble for us. And you—"

"Me? I wouldn't do that to you!"

I winced. "I told myself to stay away. It was better if we were never friends. But the speech project made that impossible. I can't help but like you. And the more I liked you, the worse I felt. I just can't take it anymore, Julie. And I understand if you don't want to see me anymore."

She shook her head. "I never said that."

I blinked. "Does that mean…you want to keep seeing me?"

God, man, do you need a map or something?

I struggled to ignore Kenny. I'd divulged enough secrets for one day. I had no plans to tell Julie I talk to myself…or that myself talks back.

She slid to the floor in front of me and flung her arms around my neck. "Yes."

I wrapped my arms around her, lowered her to the floor, and kissed the breath out of her.

The holiday break passed too quickly. Julie dragged me shopping for her family's presents, and I took her home to meet my parents. December on

Long Island was cold, but it hadn't snowed yet, so Julie and I hit the beach to run or took Hagrid for long walks down leaf-littered streets. Whenever Julie spotted a pile of leaves, she would shuffle through it, sending leaves swirling in her wake. When I asked her why, she said it was something she used to do with her brother. She begged me to try it, to embrace my inner child. I nearly collapsed from laughter when I visualized Kenny and me wrapped in a bro-hug. While Julie stared at me, confused, Kenny flipped me off. That just made me laugh harder.

On Christmas Eve, I rang Julie's doorbell with a huge wrapped box under my arm, and my knees quivering like the Jell-O mold Julie's mom made. I'd spent some restless nights arguing with Kenny about what gift to buy Julie. We'd finally agreed on something. I bought it earlier that day, wrapped it myself. Silver paper and a red bow. Her stepdad opened the door, smelling like peppermint Lifesavers and cigarettes. I sat on the sofa between Julie and her mom, the box dancing on my bouncing knees. Julie covered my hand with hers and squeezed. My knees stilled.

"Cookies," Julie's mother decided and hurried off to get some. Her stepfather followed. I looked at Julie, felt the heat creep up from my collar. She stared back, swallowing a grin and shrugged at their transparent attempt to give us some privacy.

"Um. So this is for you. Merry Christmas." I shoved the box into Julie's arms, and she huffed.

"Big."

"Yeah." I wiped sweaty palms down my thighs. "If you don't like it, I kept the receipt."

Julie tore off the red bow, shredded the silver paper, and lifted the lid. Under layers of tissue paper, she pulled out what I'd already dubbed "the Bag II" and gasped. "I don't know much about designer labels, but since you like large bags, I thought this one would work for you."

It wasn't a handbag, though I'd found it in that section of the local Kohl's department store. It was a *weekender*, the sales rep told me, and I repeated her script for Julie. It was canvas with the designer's logo repeated in a patchwork pattern, and it had an adjustable strap. "Look inside. It's got dozens of compartments and pockets so you can keep your brother's treasure safe." I'd already pulled out all the wadded-up paper the store stuffed into its bags. Inside one of the pockets, I'd tucked a Christmas card I hoped she'd find later.

She glanced up at me, all misty eyed and soft voiced. "Treasure. My brother's treasure. I like that. I like this. It's perfect." She pressed a light kiss to the corner of my mouth. "Thank you."

She jumped up, darted across the room to the Christmas tree near the window, and found a small box under it. It was wrapped with recycled paper and tied with twine. "This is yours. Merry Christmas." Feeling like I was four years old again, I worked through the twine and the paper and found a medallion nestled on a square of cotton. A religious medallion. I peered at it closely but couldn't tell who the saint was.

Julie lifted the silver chain from the box and let the medallion dangle between us. "I wasn't sure if you were really devout or anything, but I liked Saint Maria Goretti's story. Have you ever heard of her?"

I shook my head. My family and I weren't particularly faithful these days.

It felt like God was already out to get me. Going to an actual church would be just giving him the home-field advantage.

"According to the story, Maria was a young girl when a neighbor stabbed her after she said no to his advances. The neighbor was arrested, and Maria was rushed to a hospital. While sitting in his cell across town, the man who stabbed Maria claimed she visited him in jail and forgave him for what he'd done to her. But she couldn't have been at the jail because she died in the hospital. That's her miracle. The church calls her the patron saint for both sexual assault victims and forgiveness."

My eyes darted from the medallion to Julie. I smelled the peppermint Lifesavers and Christmas cookies and her tropical scent and thought, I'll never forget this.

"You just…look like you needed forgiving, you know?"

It was several minutes before I was able to talk. "Julie." I opened my arms, invited her in. She wrapped her arms around my back. "Thank you. It's…perfect," I whispered in her ear.

CHAPTER 19

When the Time Is Right

Every day during Christmas break, I tried to reach Brandon. My phone calls were sent to voice mail. My emails were ignored. When I knocked on his door, nobody answered.

I drummed my fingers on the computer desk in the family room and tried posting on his profile.

Come on, man. Are you crazy?

Kenny, I have to get in touch with him.

Okay, but not online. You post, "Brandon, I'm sorry. Please call me," and the Internet'll crash under all the LMAO comments.

I winced. Good point. I thought for a few moments and stood. I was fixing this today.

Now.

I grabbed a few DVDs and some snacks and drove to Brandon's. I'd camp out in his driveway until spring thaw if that was what it took.

It took about an hour. I'd parked in front of Brandon's house, waved to Julie at her window, and settled in. It was around one o'clock when a car pulled into the drive.

"Hi, Mrs. Dellerman." I waved when I got out of my car.

"Hi, Dan! Happy New Year."

"Um, yeah. Thanks. You too."

A door slammed behind me. I turned. Brandon carried shopping bags and glared at me on his way to the front door.

"What brings you here?"

"I brought some DVDs. Thought Brandon and I could watch a few movies."

Mrs. Dellerman smiled wide. "That sounds great, doesn't it, Brandon? You weren't doing anything. I'll make you boys some popcorn." She unlocked the door to the house, waved me inside. "Come on in. You can leave your jacket here." She indicated a chair.

Brandon said nothing. He shoved past me with the shopping bags, slammed them on a kitchen counter.

"Brandon! Careful. I've got this. Go hang out."

Brandon turned with a sigh and stomped up the stairs.

In my mind, Kenny whined, *This is gonna suck.*

I squared my shoulders and followed.

"What are you doing here, man?" Brandon asked without looking at me.

"You won't answer my calls or emails, so—"

"Sorry, *mom.*"

"Dude, I'm serious."

"So am I. You made it clear you had better things to do."

"No, Brandon. That's why I've been trying to reach you. I'm sorry about that. The words…well, they came out wrong. I didn't mean it."

He lifted a shoulder. "Whatever."

I opened my mouth, but Kenny shut me up. *Leave it alone.*

"Um. So, you feel like watching *Iron Man* or *Transformers*?" I dug in the bag, pulled out the DVDs.

He tried to glare, but his lips twitched into a halfhearted smile. "*Iron Man*. Definitely."

I handed him the disc, and he set it up.

"So, we cool?"

Another shrug. "I guess." He aimed the remote control at the flat-screen. "So, you still with Julie?"

I nodded. Grinned because I couldn't help it. "Yeah."

"She's not home?"

"Um. No, she's home. I talked to her this morning."

"Why aren't you next door?"

"Because I'm here."

Brandon's eyes whipped over to mine. "But if you have something better to do—"

"Uh-uh. Foul." I waved my hands. "Not falling for that again. I'll see Julie another time. Right now, I'm watching movies with a friend."

Brandon managed a slightly bigger smile.

Now we were cool.

The rest of the break passed way too fast. It finally snowed, a dump of like a foot of powder I shoveled for hours. I couldn't run on the beach in that, so I stayed close to home and jogged in the tracks cut by SUVs until the plows came through.

Julie had found a job at a chain restaurant, so my evenings were free. Brandon and I decided to hang out at a bowling alley one night when Julie was at work.

We haven't been bowling since Jake McGuire's tenth birthday. Remember? They put the bumpers out.

Right. They put the bumpers out for me because I'd never gone bowling before and sucked. I two-handed the ball, rolling it between my legs like a toddler. The guys all laughed and harassed me about it, but I didn't care. There was cake. And pizza. And friends.

"Dan, you're up."

I grabbed the sixteen-pound ball and hurled it down the alley the way Brandon did—with one hand curled around the ball like I was carrying a baby.

A baby you hurled down an oiled wood alley?

Okay. Bad metaphor. Sue me.

I watched the ball skid down the alley. I knocked down one pin.

Kenny laughed his ass off. I let him.

We'd already bowled two games. Brandon got a 168 and a 170. I bowled a 30. Twice. On the third game, he took pity on me and joined me on the approach.

"Jesus, dude, unclench. It's a game. It's supposed to be fun." Brandon took the ball from me, stood next to me, and demonstrated proper technique. "Hold the ball like this. Walk to the foul line as you're getting ready to let it go, then let it go gently."

"So, no bounce?"

Brandon laughed. "No bounce. You're not pitching a softball game."

"Okay."

I held the ball, approached the line, and let it go. It landed smoothly on the polished lane and stayed straight and level until the last second. Then it veered into the gutter.

"Try it again. This time, don't forget to follow through."

"Huh?" What the hell did that mean?

"Here. Like this." Brandon pretended to release a ball and then brought his hand up straight, aiming with his thumb.

I tried it his way, and this time, I got half the pins. "Yes!" We high-fived and then spun around at the sound of raucous laughter.

Jeff and some friends stood behind our lane.

Kenny cursed in my mind. Brandon's face went stony.

"Oh, come on, Brandon. Don't let us interrupt your hot date," Jeff shouted. One of his friends made rude kissing sounds.

"Come on. Let's get out of here," I said.

With his jaw tight, he shook his head. "We were here first." He turned to Jeff. "Why are *you* in a bowling alley?"

Oh, that sounded like a dis.

Jeff's grin froze, and he took a few steps closer. "To bowl, asshole."

Brandon scoffed. "Let me know how that goes for you. I'll be here for about six more frames if you need lessons."

Jeff's sneer disappeared, and he strode off. "Let's go." The entourage headed to a lane at the end of the alley.

I let out a low whistle. "Impressive handling."

Brandon's eyes stayed pinned to Jeff's back. "He was never as good as I am at bowling."

"You guys used to bowl a lot?"

"Yeah. Used to. You done?"

Hell yeah. I sat on the U-shaped bench, tugged off my tricolored rentals while Brandon packed up his way-cooler shoes and ball into his bag.

Outside in the blustery January night, I aimed the remote at my car and unlocked the doors. The pounding of feet on the wet pavement just as Kenny shouted a warning had us spinning around.

Jeff shoved Brandon before I could move. The bowling ball bag fell on its side with a heavy thud. I grabbed Jeff in a lock, let him dangle a bit.

"We don't want any trouble, Dean. Walk away while you can."

"Fuck you," he ground out.

Brandon ignored us both, unzipped the bag, and examined the ball. "Damn it, Jeff. Goddamn it."

I tightened my hold and glanced down at the ball in Brandon's hands. There was a deep crack in the finish entirely visible even in the streetlight that cast dark shadows over the parking lot. I didn't know much about bowling, but I figured the ball was trash now.

Heads up, man. He's really pissed.

Crap.

"Gonna cry now?" Jeff jeered, breaking free of my hold.

"You son of a bitch!" Brandon shouted in Jeff's face. I stepped between them before things got physical.

"Back off, Dean. Now."

Jeff swung his gaze from Brandon to me and back again. He grinned broadly, wiggled his fingers in a mockery of a wave, and jogged back into the alley. I bent down to help Brandon set his bag right, but he knocked my hands away, shoved the bag into the car, and slammed the tailgate. He stalked around the car and settled into the passenger seat, his face thunderous.

I got behind the wheel, started the car, and drove home, silent while Brandon seethed. When I pulled into his driveway, he opened the door without a word. Before I could unlock the tailgate, he tugged on the handle hard enough to rock the car. With a loud curse, he stalked to his front door without a backward glance at me.

He left the bowling ball behind.

CHAPTER 20
Hearts, Flowers, and Bad Ideas

January blurred into February. More snow covered Long Island. Things with Julie and me were good.

I think.

We had an understanding, I guess. We saw each other after school when she wasn't working, and after work, she let me pick her up on nights she was certain her father wasn't in town. In the car, we'd talk about books and school and life. But the future—life after high school—was somehow off-limits. I knew only that Julie planned to go to one of the state schools. I was hoping for USC. Ever since my dad submitted all the paperwork to get my record cleaned up, I was starting to think I had a good shot at admittance. Dad was all for it. Mom, on the other hand, not so much.

When are you gonna tell Julie, dude?

Soon, Kenny.

I had plans for a special Valentine's Day date, when I intended to not only tell Julie—*gulp*—everything but also talk about the future.

Our future.

Monday night, I brought her flowers. That was my mom's idea. I took her to this Italian restaurant close to my house, all decorated with red and pink balloons floating over heart-shaped candles on every table. She wore red glasses to suit the holiday and a black dress that totally killed my ability to speak for like an hour. When the server placed a covered basket of hot buttery bread on the table, my stomach let out a loud rumble, and we laughed.

"You look amazing," I finally blurted out.

"Thanks. You look good too."

I resisted the urge to roll my eyes. I wore a tie.

Dork.

Also Mom's idea.

Julie sipped her soda and nibbled at the antipasto. I cleared my throat. "Julie." My voice cracked. Jeez, it hadn't done that since I was twelve.

Kenny nearly lost consciousness from laughing.

I tried again. "Julie, there's something I want to talk to you about."

Our server arrived with our entrees. I wiped sweaty palms on my napkin.

"That looks good." She nodded at my plate. I cut off a portion of chicken parmigiana and forked it on top of her fra diavolo.

We ate in silence. The food was great. Not as good as Mom's but really good. I waited until she was done, my stomach pitching like a carnival ride.

Oh my God, I'm getting old here.

"Julie," I tried a third time. "What do you want to do…you know, after graduation and stuff."

She stiffened and then put down her fork with a little frown that made the line in her forehead wink at me. "I don't know. But after meeting you, I think I could be a counselor or something."

"Me?"

"Yeah, you." She paused to sip her soda. "Since I met you, I wonder how many people are like…disturbed, I guess. You know. Like Brandon. Or like my brother. Or my—"

She stopped abruptly when I sucked in a sharp breath. I was doing as much as I could to make sure Brandon wasn't *that* disturbed.

"I thought about you today."

My whole body got warm when I heard those words.

"This girl dropped her books all over the main hallway. Everyone was laughing. I figured you'd be on your knees picking everything up. So I helped her. And she was really grateful. I mean, all these people are laughing, and I was just one person helping. She didn't seem to mind them because of me."

"Wow."

"I know, right? It got me thinking…we should all be looking for ways to help instead of laughing. Counselor." She flushed and looked at her plate. "I'll probably suck at it." She picked up her fork, speared a piece of chicken.

I grinned, shook my head. "No way. You'll be great."

"What about you? What do you want to do?"

"I'm hoping to go to USC."

Her fork froze in mid-flight. "California?"

I nodded. "Come with me, Julie."

Her eyes went wide. "I…I can't."

"Sure you can. There are loans, grants, and scholarships. We can get an apartment together. I know you applied to state schools, but it's not too late."

She put down her fork, stared at me. "Dan, are you asking me to live with you?"

I nodded. "Yeah, I am. I love you, and I don't want us to end at graduation."

"Why California? Why didn't you apply to any state schools?"

Kenny leaned forward. This was it.

I stared at the heart-shaped candle for a moment. "I want distance, Julie. I want to put miles between my parents and me so I don't have to worry about them."

"Are you ever gonna tell me why?"

I was trying, damn it.

"USC has a law program. I want to help make sure kids like me get punishments that fit their crimes." I gulped my soda, hoping for courage. I thought of Dr. P. and what she'd said about the judge using me to send a message.

"Is that what happened to you?"

"Well, some people think maybe the judge could have cut me a break since I was thirteen and never in trouble before."

Julie hung on every word, the food in front of her forgotten. "He didn't?"

I swiped my napkin over my mouth, swilled more soda. "They were able to twist some other law to fit my crime. To prove it. And punish me for that."

"But you don't think you deserved it."

Her mouth went tight, and she wouldn't look at me. Damn it, I knew it. I knew this would happen.

"No, I did deserve it. Just maybe not so…extreme. I don't know. What I did was, well, it was bad, Julie. There's no way to shine that up."

She digested that for a moment. "What about me? Aren't you gonna worry about me after I know the truth?"

My mouth fell open. Every minute of every day, I worried only about Julie's reaction to what I did. But it never occurred to me that telling her would put her in the same situation as my family. Crap.

"Dan, relax before you break your glass." Julie's hand stroked mine, clutched tightly around my soda glass. I let go of the glass so I could hold her hand.

"You're right, Julie. I'm sorry. Let's just forget the whole thing." I shoved a hand in my pocket and removed a small box. "Here. This is for you."

Kenny cursed. *That went well.*

Julie took the box but didn't open it. "No, no. I don't want to forget it. I like that you asked me, Dan. I'm glad you like me enough to—"

"Julie, I *love* you."

"I love you too. And I promise you whatever you did, it won't change that."

Come on, bro. She just opened the door.

Kenny was right. I gulped hard. "What if I…killed somebody," I whispered, unable to look at her.

Her hands stilled on the box. "Did you?"

I nodded once, swiped a hand over my mouth, hoping that dinner wouldn't make an encore appearance.

"No, you're not a murderer. Even if that's what they say you did, I don't believe it. I know you."

No, you really don't.

Shut up, man.

"Come on, Dan, would you hate me if you found out I did something, you know, bad?"

"No," I said with certainty. "I couldn't."

"You did," she reminded me.

I waved that off. "I didn't know you then. I do now, and I couldn't hate you. No matter what."

She stared at me, unconvinced, her eyes almost ink blue in the dim light. Her mouth opened, but whatever she wanted to say stayed locked inside. Instead, she unwrapped the box, lifted the lid, and smiled. "This is beautiful. Thank you." She held up the pendant, fastened it around her neck before I could do it for her.

Heh. Gold heart on Valentine's Day. Aren't you original?

I bit my tongue.

"Dan, you okay?"

"Peachy. You want some dessert?"

Julie opened her mouth to answer me just as my cell buzzed.

"Dan, it's Brandon. I need help, man."

The tremble in his voice had me on my feet, tossing cash on the table before he finished his first sentence. Julie frowned, the line on her forehead vivid, but she stood and grabbed her coat without complaint.

"On my way."

Kenny slammed the door to his room, grumbling about timing.

At a local Friendly's restaurant, Julie and I found Brandon alone in a booth. I slid in next to him, Julie across, while a bunch of girls giggled at another table. "Hey, man, sorry we're so late," I said loud enough for the girls to hear.

The giggles stopped.

Under my breath, I added, "They set you up?"

"It was probably Jeff." Brandon shrugged. "Anyway. Um. Thanks."

"No problem." I grabbed a menu. "You guys want some ice cream?" I took note of Brandon's flushed face and murderous eyes. "Or not."

But he shook his head. "If we all get up and leave, they'll know."

"So what happened, Brandon?"

"I got a text message telling me to meet some girl here."

My eyebrow lifted. "Who?"

His eyes met mine and then quickly lowered. "Doesn't matter. I should have known it was a scam."

A server came by, and we each ordered a sundae. She left some water glasses on our table and drifted over to the girls' table.

"How long were you stuck here?"

"Like twenty or thirty minutes." He played with the napkin-wrapped flatware. "I didn't want to mess up your dinner."

"You didn't. We were paying the check when you called," Julie assured him.

The sundaes arrived, and we dug in. Except for Brandon. He just sort of played with it, chopping and dragging his spoon through the layers of ice cream and toppings without actually eating any.

I nudged him. "What's up, man?"

He glanced at me for a second and then back at the bottom of his bowl. "Ever wish you could kill somebody and, like, get away with it?"

I jerked and gripped the table just for something to hold on to. What the—

"Forget it. I didn't mean that. Just sayin'."

"I used to do that all the time," Julie admitted, and my mouth fell open. "I used to plot out elaborate schemes to nail my dad." She said it like she'd just commented on the weather. "Who do you want to kill?"

Brandon leaned forward. "Everybody. Except you guys. You're cool."

Julie rolled her eyes. "Thanks."

"Seriously. I have no problems with you."

"I'm glad to hear that," Julie retorted. "You do realize you can't actually kill them, right, Brandon? Or I'd have to go to *your mother*. To *help*, I mean."

She's a genius. Kenny smiled proudly while Brandon glared.

I had to agree.

Brandon squirmed. "No, I wouldn't. I may want to, but I know it's wrong. I'm just sayin'."

The server put the check on the edge of the table. Before I could move, Brandon grabbed it and shoved at me to let him out of the booth.

"I got this."

"Worry?" I asked Julie when he was out of earshot.

She stared after Brandon. "Definitely. What do we do?"

I shook my head. "I'm not sure."

Brandon acted weirder as time went by. He worked out with me once or twice after the sundaes, but in March, he started blowing me off. A few times, he turned and walked in the opposite direction when he saw me coming. By April, he was ignoring my calls. Julie and I celebrated both our birthdays with dinner out. We invited Brandon.

He never bothered to reply.

By May, he was cutting classes. I didn't know if I should talk to Mr. Morris, maybe go to one of the counselors or directly to Brandon's parents. What would I say? That the little voice in my head and I had this feeling he was in trouble? What if he wasn't and reporting him got him kicked out of school? And then he couldn't go to college, and his whole life would be ruined. He could end up homeless, mugging people for their spare change just to eat. All because of me. But what if I was right? What if I didn't say anything and he ended ups in prison—or, worse, dead?

You know, I'm starting to think those little white pills you're so afraid of could be a good thing

Shut up, Kenny.

Relax, man! He's not the only kid in school with problems. You have your own crap to worry about.

No, I needed to talk to him, to look him in the eye.

I tried waiting for him at his locker, but he never used it. I even tried camping out in front of his house again, but Mrs. Dellerman came outside and said he flat out did not want to see me. He wouldn't even tell her why. Jeff knew something was up and did as much as he could to make it worse. I was slowly going out of what was left of my mind.

There was one thing left to try.

This is a bad idea, Kenny muttered as I strode up the walk to Jeff Dean's front door.

Whatever. I rang the doorbell.

Jeff was happy to see me. "What the hell are you doing here?" He leaned against the door, his hand pressed to the back of the glass, a furious scowl hanging off his face.

"Need to talk to you."

"Yeah, right."

"No, man. Seriously. I came to talk to you."

"Yeah? Well, I got nothin' to say to you. Get the hell off my porch."

Shouldn't have wasted our time.

The door would have crushed my nose if I hadn't planted my foot in front of it. "Five minutes, Dean."

He crossed his arms over his barrel chest. "If this is about Brandon, I—"

"It's not. It's about you." That wasn't a lie.

Okay, not *entirely*.

He stood in the doorframe, glared, while a vein pulsed in his neck. "This should be good."

I decided to ignore that. He stepped outside, wearing nothing but sweats and a T-shirt, and joined me on the large porch that extended the entire width of his house. He cocked a hip, leaned against one of the porch uprights, and waved his hand, impatient for me to get to my point.

"You need to talk to Brandon."

He angled his head, smirked a little. Heh. Seems like Jeff was smarter than I thought.

"Really?" He rolled his eyes and shook his head. "You're pathetic. You really are gay for the little dick, aren't you?"

I folded my arms and let that one go by. "Dean, I came here because there's a bigger picture than you're able to see. Did you know Brandon—"

Whoa, whoa, whoa! Don't divulge all the kid's secrets, dude.

Crap. Kenny was right. I was about to tell Jeff how frightened Brandon was, so I started again. "Did you know Brandon believes you're out to kill him because you think he killed your mother?"

Jeff flinched, pushed off from the porch post, his eyes dark. "You're about to cross a line, Ellison."

I held up my hands, surrender-style. "Dean, I'm not here to make trouble. I'm here to stop it. You keep coming after Brandon, you'll end up in the system, and trust me, it's not a place any sane person wants to be."

With his hands on his hips, he sniffed. "Yeah? What do you care if I do?"

I met the challenge in his eyes directly. "I wouldn't wish it on anybody."

Jeff broke eye contact first. "So it's true? What everyone's saying about you?"

My stomach pitched, but I hid it. "Yeah, it is."

Jeff thought that over for a moment. "How long?"

"Um. Almost a year."

He swallowed hard, waved a hand at my midsection. "That's where you got all—"

"Yeah."

"And where you learned to fight so…so—"

"I think the word you're looking for is *viciously*—and yes."

He nodded, still thinking.

"You guys used to be friends once. You really hate him that much? Enough to risk juvie?"

Jeff lifted one wide shoulder. "Maybe I do." He kept his eyes fixed to me, waiting for my reaction.

The words sent a chill racing up my spine, but I managed not to shiver. "You don't really believe he hurt your mother, do you?"

I saw a flash of grief and then it was gone, replaced with fury. "My mother died of cancer."

I waited a beat and then shrugged. "So what's that got to do with Brandon?"

Jeff paced barefoot down the porch away from me, then whipped back. "Nothing. Absolutely nothing. So run back and tell your boyfriend your little talk didn't work."

"Brandon doesn't know I'm here."

"Yeah, right."

I raked the hair from my face and blew out a frustrated breath. "Okay. Look. The only reason I'm here is because I don't want to see either of you do something you can't take back."

Jeff's lips twisted into a grimace. "Can't take back? Really? That's funny, man. Real funny. Why don't you talk to the guy who told my mother I was a drug addict the day before she died."

"I know he ratted you out. But he swears he was trying to help you."

"Help me?" Jeff echoed, his voice dripping in sarcasm. "Brandon *told* her, man. He fucking *told* her. I went to visit her, and she told me she was disappointed in me—" Jeff broke off when his voice cracked. "That was the last thing she ever said to me."

Holy crap.

I ignored Kenny and shut my gaping mouth. Jeff's admission hung there for a moment, suspended in the air, waiting for one of us to give it the attention it deserved. He walked to the porch steps and sat. After a moment, I sat beside him.

"The pot was hers," he said with a swish of his hand. "It's supposed to help with the side effects of chemo or something." He shook his head. "It didn't. So *I* tried it. And you know what? It helped. For a little while at least."

I cleared my throat. "I'm sorry, man. For what it's worth, I know Brandon never meant to get you in trouble. He was just trying to be a good friend, but you shot him down and, worse, took the whole school with you."

Jeff stared at his bare feet.

I stood. "I don't know if this matters to you, but I'm worried Brandon may do something, you know, permanent."

Jeff's head snapped up. "What? Like suicide?"

I nodded. "Yeah, you think you feel guilty now, try living with that."

Why don't you just write down your social security number while you're at it?

Jeff looked away but said nothing, so I headed down the walk.

"Hey, Ellison."

I turned and waited.

"Julie's not your friend, man."

My vision reddened, and I took a threatening step. "What the hell are you talking about?"

He stared at me, a muscle in his jaw twitching. "You know what? Just forget it." He walked inside, closed the door.

That went well.

I wish. The truth was it hadn't gone well at all. Instead of helping, my talk with Jeff made things worse. He amped up his efforts to harass Brandon—the latest being a classic shove in the corridor that had sent Brandon sprawling like one of the bowling pins he'd taught me to knock down.

That was three days ago, and nobody had seen Brandon since. He wasn't in class. He wasn't online. He was off the grid.

Mom and Dad kept telling me to stop worrying. Julie, of course, kept trying to see the bright side, telling me Brandon wasn't sad and lonely, the way he was in the first semester.

And she was right. He wasn't.

He was *mad*. And his mad was a simmering, festering thing that swelled and got hotter along with the weather as the days piled up into weeks. I had a bad feeling Brandon wasn't going to take it anymore.

Turned out I was right.

CHAPTER 21

Duty to Respond

By June, I couldn't take it anymore. Everyone was psyched about graduation, the prom, and signing yearbooks. But there was a buzz under all that usual stuff, an undercurrent of tension so potent it had its own pulse. I couldn't find Brandon, and by dismissal time, I practically shot out of my seat, ready to hog-tie him to the luggage rack on my car.

Paul stopped me at the school's main exit as I was heading to my car.

"It's Dean, man. He's coming for Brandon." He waved a hand in the direction of the parking lot. "Now."

I strode toward the cars. It shouldn't have surprised me, and it didn't, not really. I'd really hoped Jeff would understand, would stop before he got himself so deep into trouble he couldn't escape it. Like me.

"Is Brandon here? You seen him?"

Paul shook his head. "No, not since Monday."

Where the *hell* was he?

Dude, heads up. Kenny jerked his head to the north end of the student lot, where Jeff and some of his friends were getting loud.

"Dan?" Julie called to me from the bus stop, worry making the line in her forehead deeper. I smiled for a second or two.

I liked that she worried about me.

"Julie, it's okay. Go home," I said when she reached me.

"Not leaving you."

Kenny flashed to my side. *Move away. Put distance between you and her. Jeff's a few feet behind you.*

I took a few steps back. "Have you seen Brandon?"

"Um. Yeah." She pointed toward a side door the teams used that led from the locker rooms to the athletic field. "He was there a minute ago."

Awesome.

I turned to keep an eye on Jeff. He nudged one of his pals and jerked his head. It was a look I'd seen many times while I served my time. Alpha dog just gave the pack the command to flank and prepare for attack.

"Paul? Walk away."

Paul whirled, followed my gaze, and shook his head. "You're outnumbered."

"Paul, I can handle this."

Paul's eyebrows shot up. "You can handle four on one?"

Paul's words took me back to the night Kenny was…um…well, *born*, I guess. Suddenly, I was back in the dingy bathroom in the New Jersey juvenile facility I'd called home for almost a year. I remembered it all. The bad florescent bulb flickering in the farthest light fixture. The cracked tiles behind the faucet. The sour odor of piss and sweat mixed with soap. The hint of mildew that defied the industrial-strength cleaners clinging to the air, forcing me to take shallow breaths as four of my six usual tormentors surrounded me. I gulped when I saw Kenny. Saw *me*…standing beside me. Me, but…not me. The other me lunged and then he was *in* me, screeching like a wild animal until blood filled the cracks in the tiles and splattered the floor, the ceiling. And the only odor in the air was the rusty smell of it. All four were scattered on the floor, writhing, crying, bleeding. Except me. Both of me.

I swallowed hard. Yeah, we knew how to handle four on one.

The guys tried to look intimidating as they approached and fanned out. You almost had to admire their nerve.

Move away from Paul, Kenny reminded me. *They'll use him against you.*

I took a few steps and angled my body to protect Paul, watching as three of the boys hung back, making way for their leader. I didn't recognize these dicks, probably teammates.

"Didn't listen to a word I said, did you?" I tried to sound intimidating.

"Where is he?" Jeff ignored my question.

"Who? Brandon? No idea. I haven't seen him in days."

"He's here. This was his idea."

My stomach fell. "Dean, you have to let this go. You don't know what—"

"Oh, waaah!" He pretended to knuckle away imaginary tears. "I don't know what Brandon's going through?" Jeff's fake pout changed to a wide grin. "I don't care."

I didn't have time for this. I needed to find Brandon, figure out what he was planning. "What do you mean this was his idea?"

"He sent me an email. Said he was done trying to talk and that we should just do what we had to do."

Fuck! Kenny shouted in my head.

This was it—zero hour. I spun around. "Brandon Dellerman! Did anybody see him?" The crowd of spectators all looked at each other, looked confused, or looked disappointed. But a few looked toward the same door Julie pointed out just a few minutes before. "Go home, everybody. No fight today."

I ran toward that door, Jeff on my heels.

I burst through the door, found myself in the gym corridor right outside the boys' locker room. "Brandon! Brandon, you in here?"

"What a little pussy. He didn't even show up," Jeff sneered.

Okay, that's it! I've had enough—

Not now, Kenny!

"Go home, Jeff."

"Fuck that."

I searched the locker room, up one row, down another. No sign of him. Why the hell would he intentionally goad Jeff into a fight and then not show up for it?

Bro. Kenny stopped me with a hand on my arm. I followed his gaze. Brandon crouched beside a bench over his backpack. I watched and waited, my pulse hammering a staccato rhythm in my ear before it skidded to a complete stop when I saw what Brandon took out of his pack.

It was a gun. Holy God in heaven, it was a .22-caliber handgun.

Jeff snorted.

"Brandon."

He snapped upright, the gun clutched in both hands. "I don't want to hurt you, Dan. This is between me and him." Brandon never looked at me.

Jeff's lips twisted in a smirk. "You're not gonna shoot me. You don't have the balls."

My God, did he have no brains in that hard head? "Shut up, Dean!"

Brandon stepped closer and released the safety, leveling the gun at Jeff's heart. With dead eyes and a cold voice, he said, "Get on your knees."

When Brandon racked the slide, Jeff's sneer evaporated. He shook his head slowly. "Please. Don't."

"I said…on your knees!"

Jeff sank to the floor, tears filling his frightened eyes. "I'm sorry. I'm sorry."

Kenny was back. *Door's open on the locker behind you. Kick it closed.*

What? Oh, right. I lifted my leg behind me, slammed the locker. Brandon jolted, and I leaped before I could think twice, snatched the gun out of his hands, ejected the clip and the round—Jesus, the round he had in the chamber. I stowed everything in my pocket and then grabbed him.

"Are you out of your friggin' mind?" I took his elbow, led him away from Jeff, ghost white and still kneeling on the floor.

"Leave me alone."

"That's the last thing I'm gonna do," I managed to squeeze out of my clenched teeth. "Come with me. Now." I manhandled him through the room, out the rear exit, but he wrenched out of my grasp.

"Back off! This isn't your fight!"

"Brandon, don't—"

He broke into a run, and I was right on his heels. He ran around the school. I chased him around and back toward the visitor lot. I spotted Julie and tossed my keys to her. "Car!" She nodded, and I kept running. Was he planning to run all the way back to his house? At the edge of the school's property, I lost him. Squealing brakes, honking horns, and a stream of obscenities told me he'd run into the main road that bordered the high school. I stopped running then.

I was trying to keep him alive, not kill him myself. I stood hunched over, hands braced on my knees, and tried to stop panting. I heard the car behind me, climbed in the passenger side. "Go home. He's got to show up sooner or later."

"What the hell happened?" Julie drove slowly, cautiously.

"Julie. Jesus." I scrubbed my hands over my face, still unwilling to believe it. "He had a gun."

She was strangely silent. I glanced over at her, wondering what the rigid expression on her face meant. "What are you gonna do?" she finally asked.

I pulled in a deep breath, caught Kenny's eye in the side mirror, and grimaced. "Squeal."

CHAPTER 22
Nothin' But a Waste of Oxygen

Julie pulled to the curb in front of Brandon's house. Cars were now in the driveway, so I knew his parents were home.

"Thanks for sticking with me," I said and managed a weak smile when Julie returned my keys.

"Uh-uh. Not leaving you now. Come on."

I watched, astonished, as she strode up the walk and knocked on the front door.

"Julie! Hi, there." Brandon's mother smiled in the doorway.

"Hey, Mrs. D."

Brandon's mother's smile instantly evaporated when she noted our grim looks. "What's wrong? Where's Brandon?"

"Mrs. Dellerman, we're not sure where Brandon is. Can we come in?"

Mrs. Dellerman frowned, tucked the hair cut to her jawline behind her ear and nodded. "Pete? Come out here."

Julie and I followed Mrs. Dellerman into the living room and sat down at opposite ends of a long sofa. Footsteps from the kitchen called our attention to Brandon's father, a heavy man with a receding hairline and glasses.

"What the hell's wrong? Where's Brandon?"

I didn't know where to begin. "Mr. and Mrs. Dellerman, I'm sorry, but Brandon ran off when I tried to stop him. You know how much Jeff's been hassling him, and I think—"

"Jeff's been hassling Brandon?" Mrs. Dellerman looked at her husband, bewildered. "Did you know about this?"

His raised eyebrows suggested no.

I leaned forward, began again. "Okay, look. Brandon is pretty much despised at school. Everyone makes fun of him, and Jeff is itching to fight him."

Mrs. Dellerman gasped. "Fight him? Oh, no, Jeff wouldn't do that."

"What about you two? You his friends?" Brandon's dad asked.

I nodded. "I've been trying to help him. But I think today, I made things ten times worse."

Spare them the woe-is-you crap and get to the point. Kenny smacked me in the head.

"I've had this feeling Brandon's been plotting revenge. Today, he tried to get it."

"No." Mr. Dellerman shook his head, stood up. "No. Absolutely not. Brandon would never do anything to hurt anybody, especially Jeff. They've been friends since kindergarten. Thank you for coming, but I think we can take care of our son without your help."

"Really? You didn't know he was being bullied, so why are you so sure he wouldn't fight back?" Julie asked, her tone belligerent.

"Get out. Get out now." Brandon's dad looked like he was about to go nuclear.

I had to make his parents understand. I shoved past them and ran up the stairs to Brandon's room, ignoring Mr. Dellerman's furious shout for his wife to call the police. I headed for the computer. It was on. I opened a browser and typed in the URL for the social network Brandon had up when I was over the day before. Luckily, he'd stored his passwords, so I didn't have to log in.

"What the hell are you doing?" His father roared behind me and grabbed my arm. I twisted free. "Making you see the truth. Look. Look at this." I pointed to Brandon's screen, where post after post illustrated the kind of teasing and cruelty he'd been dealing with. "Do you see how people treat him? What they say about him?"

Mrs. Dellerman cried while she read the screen. A muscle twitched in Mr. Dellerman's neck. "How long has this been going on?" he whispered.

I shrugged. "A long time. Are you ready to hear the rest of it now?"

Brandon's father stared at me for a long moment and finally nodded. Slowly, Mr. and Mrs. Dellerman sat on Brandon's bed. Julie stood near the door.

"On the first day of school, I caught Jeff about to beat the hell out of Brandon and broke it up. I figured he'd been having some problems for a while just by the way he acted, but he wouldn't admit it. Then I found him pacing in front of the student parking lot where Jeff parks his car. There was something about the way he kept looking over his shoulder and holding onto his backpack. I realized he was baiting Jeff and that he had something in that backpack."

"Something like what?"

"A weapon."

"No! No, no, no, I refuse to believe it," Mrs. Dellerman said.

I clicked Brandon's mouse and displayed his Internet history. "Here. Does this convince you? Look at the websites Brandon's been visiting." I scrolled through the list.

Mr. Dellerman cursed and pressed a hand to his mouth when he saw the one about Columbine.

"I've been afraid to let him out of my sight."

"No. No, you're wrong. I know my kid. He'd never hurt somebody."

I held up my hand. "Mr. Dellerman, I'm not even sure he wanted to hurt *Jeff*."

Brandon's parents stared at me for a moment and then his mother's eyes popped. "What? You think he'd hurt *himself*? Oh my God, you're crazy." Mrs. Dellerman's voice shook. "Brandon wouldn't hurt himself. No. No, I won't listen to any more."

Now would be a good time to show them what's in your pocket.

Right. "Do you keep a weapon in the house?"

Brandon's father's face paled, but he nodded. "Yes, I have a handgun, but it's locked up in a box."

"When was the last time you checked it?"

"Linda, go get the gun box."

Mrs. Dellerman walked stiffly out of the bedroom. Mr. Dellerman and I stared at each other while she was gone. Julie moved to stand beside me. In a few minutes, Mrs. Dellerman walked slowly back in, clutching a box in her hands. Her face was white.

"No. No!" Mr. Dellerman leaped up, snatched the box from her hands, shook it though he knew it was empty. "Oh God. Oh my God."

"Mr. Dellerman." I stood up, lifted my hands over my head. "Check my left jacket pocket."

He swallowed but reached inside my pocket. When his fingers curled around his gun, a harsh sob caught in his throat. He pulled it out, stared at it like it was gonna tell him what happened. I took out the clip and the round I'd ejected from the chamber and put both on Brandon's desk.

Mr. Dellerman sank down to Brandon's bed, covered his face with his hands. I figured they were ready to hear it all now.

"There was all this talk at school today. So I started looking for Brandon. I found him in the locker room. He was hiding there with this in his backpack. He emailed Jeff and told him to meet him. To end it. I saw him. He told Jeff to get down on his knees, and he aimed this right at Jeff's chest. I disarmed him, and he ran off. I chased him for as long as I dared. Then I came here to tell you."

I sat back down at Brandon's desk because my knees were knocking together. Julie's hand squeezed my shoulder. I was grateful.

"I don't know what he planned to do, Mr. Dellerman. But he chambered a round, so I'm pretty sure he intended to use that gun. A whole bunch of people could have been hurt today."

"You son of a bitch."

Everyone's heads whipped to the doorway where Brandon stood, his face flushed, his hands clenched.

"Brandon! Oh God, Brandon." Mrs. Dellerman ran to him, but he swatted her away.

"I thought you were my friend," he seethed. "But you're just like the rest of them. You think I'm just a joke. Nothing but a waste of oxygen, right?" His entire body trembled with the power of his rage. "Why did you stop me? I had this all planned for so long, and you ruined it. Why? What did I ever do to you? To any of you?"

"I *am* your friend, Brandon. That's why I stopped you."

"Bullshit!" he shouted, his face twisting with the hate. "You're just like them. You don't know what it's like—"

"I know exactly what it's like, Brandon." I crossed the room in two strides to shout right in his face.

Dude. Shut up. Now.

There's no other way, Kenny.

I knew what I was risking, but Brandon needed to hear the whole story. My story.

I pulled up my shirt, showed him the scars, ignored the gasps. "You think I did this to myself? I know *exactly* what it's like to be threatened, Brandon. To feel so helpless you're sure you'll die. To do something so bad you can't make it right no matter how sorry you are, and you can't undo it or forget it no matter how hard you pray, no matter how much you drink. I *know*, Brandon."

I stood there, chest heaving, waiting for someone to say something.

"What did you do?"

The question was whispered, hardly even audible. I didn't even know who'd asked it. I couldn't look at any of them, so I stared at my hands, willing a plausible explanation to reveal itself. But there was no such thing. There was only the truth. Despite my best efforts to keep it hidden, the truth needed to be told here. Now. I walked back across the room, sat at Brandon's computer, hunched over my knees, and spoke to the floor.

"I—" I choked. Took a deep breath, tried again. "I clicked Send." I jerked my thumb at the computer monitor. "I posted some mean, vicious stuff about a kid in my class when I was in eighth grade. I uploaded a picture of him changing after gym class. He was wearing cartoon underwear. I thought it was funny. So did all the people who posted comments about what a loser he was. And always would be. Dozens of kids. Then it was hundreds. It wasn't so funny when I found out the next day that he—" I swallowed the lump in my throat. "He killed himself." Tears rolled down my face now; I couldn't stop them. "They said I was guilty of distributing kiddie porn, sent me away for almost a year."

Mrs. Dellerman gasped. "A year?"

I didn't acknowledge her. I was lost too deep in the past. I rocked on Brandon's desk chair, staring at my fingers. "You can't imagine how bad it is until it happens to you. You try to apologize, tell them you didn't know, you didn't mean it, that you're not a bad kid, but they don't listen and lock you up anyway. They put you in with the real bad kids, rapists, gangbangers, murderers. And you think this isn't real. This can't be happening—it's a dream, just a bad dream, only you don't wake up. You're just a kid, just a stupid kid who clicked Send, but it *is* real, and it's your life now. You're afraid. You're so friggin' scared, but there's nobody to go to, nobody but the kids you're afraid of. They come for you. They come for you at night, and they hurt you."

I trailed a finger down the first of the scars that crossed my torso like a fault line, the one that started at my chest and ended at my hip.

"The first time, you scream and you fight them. The guard comes, and you think you're safe, but he ignores the blood and yells at you to keep quiet. So the next time, they do worse. And you take it. Night after night after night. Until you finally grow some muscle and learn to fight back. And you get so good at fighting back, they run from you. And you wanna die because as bad as it is, as scared as you are, as much as you hate what you're becoming, it's nothing, *nothing* compared to the voice that lives in your head and reminds you *over* and *over* and *over* that you murdered somebody until you believe it. Until you believe you deserve to be locked up, cut up, shut up. And that's not even the worst of it. Because the judge wanted to send a message, he puts *your* name on the sex offenders' list with rapists and child molesters, and the whole world thinks you're a pervert and it just. Doesn't. End. Even when they let you out, it doesn't end."

A sob made me jolt, and I came back to myself, swiping knuckles under my running nose. The sob was mine. God, I was bawling like little Emily. I stood up, nodded to Mr. and Mrs. Dellerman. Brandon's mother sat on his bed, quietly crying. His father had taken off his glasses and sat with his head in his hand. I didn't dare look at Julie. I had to leave. I had to get out of here. Retreat.

Now.

"I have to go. I'm…I'm sorry you think I let you down, Brandon, but you really have no idea."

I was in my car before I realized I'd moved. I jammed the key in the ignition, started the engine. The stereo blared OneRepublic's "Secrets," and I punched the dashboard. I hit the steering wheel. When I finally got the radio off, I beat my head against the wheel.

Cut it out, man. That hurts. Kenny appeared in the passenger seat.

Oh God, Kenny. I could have used your help up there.

You didn't need my help.

I shot him a look. Yeah, like that's ever stopped you before.

Pull it together, dude. You need to get home in one piece and start packing.

He was right. I'd said way too much. It would be all over school in the morning. I wasn't worried about Brandon. I had more to fear from Julie. I managed a halfhearted grin. "Let's hope your dream girl can keep her mouth shut."

I think she will. She wouldn't have chased after you if she didn't care.

I whipped my head around. "Crap."

She was right beside my door. *Murder me, Kenny*, I begged silently.

That would be suicide, man.

I powered down the window. "Julie, I gotta get home. I'll talk to you tomorrow."

"Dan, wait." Julie put her hand on the doorframe. "I…I'm so sorry."

My eyebrows shot into my hairline. "For what?"

"For everything you went through. For the way I treated you."

I turned away, stared at the windshield at nothing in particular. "Julie, I—Trust me. You weren't wrong." Hadn't she said she thought I was a bigger bully than Jeff?

I was. I *am*.

"I don't know what you mean."

I drew in a breath. "I have to go. I already said too much." I shifted into gear. "I really have to go. I'll see you tomorrow."

"No! Not yet, Dan."

I shifted back into park, shut my eyes, and let my head fall back against the seat rest. "I'm talked out, Julie."

"Ellison, let her talk."

I whipped my head around. Jeff stood on the sidewalk near my passenger door. I shoved out of the car. "What the hell are you doing here? You have a death wish or something?"

Jeff held up his hands, palms front. His face was tight and pale when he shook his head. "No, I—" he said and then crossed his arms over his chest. "I need this to stop. I came to talk to him. I didn't know."

"You didn't know?" I rolled my eyes. "You tormented him for years and you didn't know?"

"Okay. I get it!" he shouted, his hands up again. "It's my fault. I get that. But you need to let her talk." He swung his eyes to Julie. "You need to tell him now. Before somebody really does get killed."

Dude, what is he talking about?

No idea, Kenny.

I turned to Julie, expecting to see the same bewildered expression I wore. But it wasn't there. Instead, she shook her head and stared at Jeff with pleading eyes.

"Tell him, Julie, or I will."

Her eyes closed, her lips moved. "Please. Don't."

"You're gonna get him killed, Julie." Jeff took a step toward her. "Is that what you want?"

Her hands flew to her open mouth and covered a sob. "No."

"Julie," I whispered. "What's he talking about?"

There was a long silence.

"Dan, please." She grabbed my hands. "I love you."

"Then tell me what he's talking about."

Silence. My eyes darted from one to the other, both of them anxious, but Julie...Julie looked guilty.

"Your name is Ken Mele. She told me...on the first day of school."

My heart skidded to a stop. My name—my *real* name—bounced around in my head for a moment while I tried to convince myself I didn't hear Jeff right.

You did, Kenny said.

I felt sick. "You...you knew?" The truth, hideous and sour, spit in my face, and I wrestled my hands out of Julie's, my heart cracking like a piece of glass.

Run. Run now.

But I couldn't. I was frozen in place by the thought that Julie had lied. Right on its heels was another, much more frightening thought, and I clutched my head, willing it to stay quiet. How?

But I already knew that answer. There was really only one way she could know. My eyes slipped shut, and my head dropped.

Liam Murphy was Julie's brother. Liam. Julie. Related. Liam, Liam, Julie, Liam. Suddenly, it all made perfect fucking sense. Liam, short and skinny, glasses sliding down his nose, unruly tangle of dirty blond hair, standing in his cartoon underwear while my pals and I skewered him with taunts. Liam, the son of Julie's dad and his second wife. Julie's half-brother.

I'd killed him. I'd killed Julie's brother. I'd killed him as surely as if I'd held Brandon's dad's gun to his head and pulled the trigger. Jesus, it was *me*. *I* made her sister run away. *I* made her father turn his back on her. *I* etched those deep lines of pain into her forehead. Every frown, every stab of pain, every tear—all because of *me*. The truth churned and swelled and darkened all other thoughts, all other questions in my mind. I didn't care if neighbors took up torches and pitchforks and burned us out of town. I was broken. Done.

A touch registered on my arm. I dragged my head up, opened my eyes, saw the gold light of Julie's hair. An angel, I thought, choking up again. *Julie*, Kenny said at the same time.

I straightened up, pushed past her, and fled.

CHAPTER 23

Can't Forget, Can't Forgive

The granite block gleamed under the late afternoon sun. I stared at the waves and seagulls etched in the stone, wondering how I got to the beach, to the airplane crash memorial, and how long I'd been there. I shivered, but I wasn't cold. I ached, though I hadn't fought. Somewhere, a radio played a classic rock station and the Police reminded me I'd always be the king of pain. I sat on a bench facing the huge sculpture and wished—just for a minute—that I'd been on the flight that crashed. An end. Why was there never an end?

Beside me, Kenny sat, knees hugged to his chest, quietly crying.

I don't understand. We're not Hitler. We didn't kill thousands of people in skyscrapers with airplanes. I'm sorry! There. Are you happy? I said it. How many times do we have to apologize? How much torture do we have to take? Just make it stop. Make it go away. Please.

I wish I could, I thought at him and pressed my hands to my face, squeezing my eyes shut, impatiently swiping at the tears that pushed from them anyway. The signs were all there, but I'd ignored them.

God, I *am* an ass.

So consumed by my retrospective, I hardly noticed the presence of anyone else until two hands grabbed my face.

"Dan."

I jerked at the sound of that voice, her voice, and saw her standing in front of me, her presence felt like a slash to my gut. "No." I shook my head and squeezed my eyes tightly shut. "Please go. I can't do this, Julie. I can't."

"Dan." She took my face in her hands. "Look at me. Look at me, Ken!"

My real name from her lips forced me to obey. How could I not look at her? She took my breath away every time I did.

"Please don't hate me. Please. Tell me you don't hate me."

We don't hate you! Kenny shouted through the tears.

Oh God, I wanted to. Tears dripped down her face, plopped onto my arm, and I couldn't stand it. Even over the dozens of questions in my mind, I couldn't handle it and twisted free.

"Is it true?" I didn't know why I'd asked. I already knew that it was.

"Please. You have to listen to me. I never wanted you to know. I'm so sorry you found out like this." Again, she took my face in her hands, forced me to look at her, at the years-old pain in those blue eyes.

No. No. No! Kenny's cries echoed in my mind.

The earth tilted on its axis, and my stomach pitched again. I pulled away from her touch, sinking, waiting for the weight of my guilt and shame to finally, hopefully suffocate me. "I knew it wasn't real. I *knew* it." I laughed out a harsh sound. "I'm on this…this staircase to hell. Every lie I told, every *single* one, it just brought me another step down, another lie closer to hell. But you—" I waved a hand at her, disgust tinting my vision. "You were on your own staircase, telling your own lies."

I leaned over my knees, buried my face in my hands. Laughter, hysterical and raw, burst from my lips.

"They say, 'It takes one to know one,' but I never knew! I asked you—I *begged* you to tell me your brother's name, but you swore it wasn't him. You kissed me." The words were like a blade, cutting me, bleeding me. "You *slept* with me. You told me you *loved* me, but it was all a fucking lie." I pressed my hands to my ears to silence the sound of that blade coming again. And again. And again.

I jumped to my feet, ready to run.

"No! No, Dan, that part wasn't a lie. I swear I love you. I admit what Jeff said was true, but then it all changed, Dan. *I* changed."

"Oh, you changed, huh?" I sneered. "When did all this change happen? 'Cause you didn't say anything on the first day of school. Or the day after that. Or the fucking day after that," I shouted. "So what was the plan, Julie? You wanted revenge? When were you gonna take it?" I taunted.

"No!" She pressed hands to her ears. "Not revenge. I swear I didn't want to hurt you." She sobbed. "I never wanted that."

That stunned me into silence.

"I just wanted my dad to like me again. He's been looking for you for years, and I thought…I thought I could give you to him. I could be, like, a hero instead of just the spare girl."

I got into a lot of trouble intentionally. For attention.

Julie's words, cued up like a favorite song, kicked my ass. All the crap she'd done to get attention—I was nothing more than the latest piece of it.

Somehow, that seemed fitting.

My face twisted, but she rushed on, “Since I was thirteen, I’ve had this picture of you in my mind. The big bad bully who teased Liam so badly he had to kill himself to escape. I *hated* that boy. And I hate my dad more.” She paused on a sob. “But it’s not who you are. You weren’t supposed to be so…so…*good*! Standing up for Brandon, kissing that baby’s boo-boos, always doing the right thing. I never expected to love you,” she finished and grabbed my shoulders.

“Don’t.” I pushed out through clenched teeth. “Don’t you *dare* tell me you love me.” I shook her hands off me.

Julie recoiled as if I’d slapped her, and my heart squeezed in my chest. My hand shot out to steady her, apologies hanging from my lips. When, when would I learn words could cut? Hadn’t I just felt their sting?

“Dan, please. Listen to me.” She clasped her hands together like a prayer. “I’ve been doing my best to keep my dad away from you. Making excuses, blowing him off, picking fights, anything to stop him from showing up and seeing you. I know he’s mad, but he won’t really hurt you—”

“Jesus, Julie! What the hell else do you think he’s gonna do?” I flung my arms up, striding back and forth on waves of rage. “Pat me on the back with a ‘Nice to see you paid your debt to society’ speech? He tried to strangle me right in the courtroom! He showed up at our house with a goddamn baseball bat.”

I paced, fury surging in my veins, until I saw Kenny. He was still curled up, crying. I sank down to the bench beside him, scrubbing my hands over my face. “I just want to know when you were gonna spring the big reveal on me.” I twisted my lips into a sorry excuse for a smile.

She jerked again.

Cut it out, man. Kenny lifted his head to snarl, but I ignored him.

"I was never going to tell you."

My jaw dropped. "How—"

"I know! It was dumb. As soon as I knew the kind of person you really are, I swore I would never tell you. All I had to do was keep my dad away from you, and I could have pulled it off. I hardly ever see him." She sobbed out loud, hiding her face in her hands. "But then he figured out something was up and just wouldn't stay away."

A surge of bitterness speared through me, and I started a slow round of applause. "Congratulations. I thought I was an incredibly gifted actor, but you have me beat by light-years. Every time you called me *Dan*, I had to swallow back the puke from the lies while you're telling lies just to get your daddy to look at you." My voice was a shrill screech by the end of my tirade. "You know what's seriously messed up? I have my grandmother's engagement ring in a box in my room. My folks gave it to me on Christmas Eve. I was gonna give it to you someday. Guess the joke's on me."

I said cut it out, dick! Kenny's mental punch to my gut made me gasp.

My rage evaporated as suddenly as it had formed, and I hung my head over my knees. "Why didn't you just tell me the truth?"

"The truth?" She twisted her mouth into the same mocking jeer I remembered from the first day of school. "Why bother? You don't believe it even when I do tell it."

Sucker punch. I jerked up with a flinch. "What…what the hell does that mean?"

Julie flung up her hands. "It means you believe what you want to believe. Poor Dan, he has all this guilt and thinks he's so bad," she mocked. "I fell in love with you, but that isn't good enough."

I stared at her, wished I could believe her.

Abruptly, Julie's fury faded to disappointment. "Oh God." She folded her arms around her middle. "What do I have to do to convince you? I know what you did. I've always known. And still, I hung out with you. I forgave you. That's why I gave you that medal for Christmas. I wanted to be with you so much. I even told my father I didn't want to see him again. Why can't you believe it?"

She's right, you ass. Think about it. She's done a lot for you. What have you done for her?

My hand flitted to the chain around my neck. I loved her, I wanted to scream at Kenny. But his question burned in my head. What *had* I ever done to show it? She'd pull away from me, but I pushed her, demanded to know why. And all this time, she was trying to protect me from her father. I went back over it all, back to the first day when I squinted, concussed and bleeding, into denim blue eyes. I'd gotten into her face, dredged up a ton of old pain, forced her to confront the ugliest truth about herself, embarrassed her in front of the entire student body, and even though I didn't know about her actions behind the scenes, she'd turned her back on her father for me. I pulled shaking hands through my hair, wishing I could rip it out by the roots as the realization, the *certainty* that I'd done nothing that deserved forgiveness or love or the truth about everything hit me like a steel boot to the head.

"Because," I murmured. "Because you can never forget. Every time you look at me, all you will ever see is the boy you hate, the boy who killed your brother. How can you really forgive me if you can't ever forget?"

She blew out a long, loud breath and collapsed beside me on the bench, stared up at the granite sculpture. "Are you kidding me? That's what this is about? You really buy into that forgive-and-forget crap?"

I laughed once because it was hopeless and I knew it, and if I didn't laugh, I'd throw myself into the surf and let the tide take me.

She made a sound of disgust. "You're right. I can't forget. I thought loving you in spite of that was enough."

She said that now, but what about a year from now? We stared at each other for a long moment, both afraid to say out loud what we knew to be true. It would always be there, like the scars on my chest. What I did tied us together only to keep us apart. An unbreakable bond. An unforgivable sin.

She sobbed, a hollow, sad sound. "I hope someday you'll believe me." With that, she stood and ran, and I let her go, listening to the scream inside my head as she ran, the low-slung sun turning her hair a flaming gold. She faded, moving farther away, stretching that bond until I was sure it would tear me in half.

I let out a groan, a guttural sound scraping from the depths of the soul I'd blackened the day I clicked Send. With my hands fisted and my eyes focused on the only light my life had seen in five years, a sudden white-hot pain between my shoulders sent me to my knees.

A pair of boots moved into my peripheral vision, and while I gasped on the ground, a hand grabbed my hair, forced my head back. What was left of my air whooshed out when I recognized the demented face haloed by the setting sun.

Jack Murphy had finally found me.

CHAPTER 24
Not Like This

"Kenneth Mele. I've been looking for you for years."

He stood over me in a cloud of body odor and boozy breath, the man whose son I teased to death five years ago but whose grief still boiled as violently as if it happened yesterday.

Jack Murphy.

Jesus, bro!

He was a bear of a man wearing torn jeans and a windbreaker zipped to his neck. Untidy dark hair framed the bitter pain frozen in his eyes. Julie's eyes.

Head in the game. Come on! Fight.

I shut my eyes. Julie forgot to mention she'd invited her dad to my beach. Suddenly, Brandon popped into my mind. I finally understood the desperation he must have been feeling to take that gun to school.

Game over, Kenny.

You can't just stand there and let him beat you.

Yes, I can. I will.

Kenny's eyes closed. He braced himself.

So I waited. There was no point in running. Let's just get it over with. One way or another.

"You remember me?" His voice was like gravel.

I nodded…or tried to with his solid grip on my hair.

"You took my son. I won't let you take my daughter too. I came here to save her before she makes the biggest mistake of her life."

I laughed, but the sound held no joy. "Yeah, well, I wouldn't worry about that. She dropped the act."

His eyebrows shot up, and he relaxed his grip on my hair. "So she's not going to college with you?"

His words made no sense. "College?" I laughed once. "Right. Wasn't your plan to break me? Well, congratulations. It worked." I twisted out of his grip only to slide back to the bench. "She's quite an actress. Willing to go as far as it takes to get the right emotion—up to and including sleeping with the enemy. You should be proud."

Blood colored his face. A muscle twitched in his jaw. I saw him pull back his fist, watched it come at me. I could have blocked it, but what would have been the point?

The blow knocked me off the bench, and the pain was blinding. I landed on my hands and knees, dizzy, when he delivered a savage kick to my gut. I folded in half, gasping. I should have been screaming in agony, but there was no time. Murphy's heavy boot collided with my face hard enough to flip me onto my back. I lay sprawled on the ground in front of him, Kenny screaming in my mind. My brain shut down. There was nothing, only the pain. Another kick—this time to my groin—and the air whooshed from my lungs.

For one short, beautiful moment, I felt nothing at all. No guilt. No heartache. No worry. Nothing but the cold white numb spreading over me, consuming everything, and I knew in that moment, I would have to die. Nothing I'd done, nothing I would ever do, could make up for Liam.

A life for a life.

No! Kenny's sobs leaked through the white and the pain. *Get up. Fight back. I don't want to die. Don't let him kill us.*

It wasn't up to him. It wasn't up to either of us. I clawed my way to my hands and knees, sucking wind and spitting blood—and, Jesus, a tooth—to the ground and laughed. Not because I thought this was funny. I didn't think that at all. But I figured *someone* had a hell of a sense of humor. Of all the towns, all the schools, all the girls in the world, it was not enough for me to meet the sister of my own victim. Falling in love with her wasn't enough either. No, I have to watch her tear the beating heart out of my chest and hold it up to her father like a fucking trophy. This *had* to be some kind of cosmic joke, right? Was God really this sick and twisted? So, are you laughing yet, God? I am. Look at me laugh!

When I could catch my breath, I blinked through my tears at Jack Murphy, who watched me with cold, dead eyes. I was rolling around the ground and knew he was waiting for me to climb to my feet just so he could knock me right back off them. It was real. It wasn't just a nightmare. It was real, and it was happening. Jack Murphy had to kill me. I stopped laughing then. It was all part of God's plan. It had to be. It *has to be* like this, Kenny.

No! he screamed at me, and my skull vibrated. *Not now. Not after everything that's happened. Not like this! We were happy. For the first time in five years, you let us be happy. We had friends! Stuff to look forward to! We have to make him hear us. Make him see the truth. This isn't only our fault! We don't deserve this. Think about Mom. Dad. Pop. They worked so hard to save us.*

I considered Kenny's words, already shaking my head to dismiss them. The motion sent another lash of agony through my chest. Every breath I took scorched my lungs.

Rib. Kenny offered, and I nodded once, in too much pain to care.

"Get up, you self-righteous son of a bitch." Murphy dragged me up by my collar. "You piece of shit. She wasn't acting. She's in love with you and done nothing but tell me how cruel I am for doing what I have to do. I couldn't count on her, couldn't count on my own flesh and blood. She said she didn't want to see me ever again. Because of you! She wouldn't even tell me where you were. I had to follow her!" The tendons in his neck strained as he half-carried, half-dragged me along the path to the water.

"Julie doesn't understand," he said. "Losing a son—" He squeezed his eyes shut for a moment, and when he turned them on me, they were full of anguish. "Why did you do it?"

Something rose in me, something bitter, black and years old, Kenny's words riding its crest. *We*.

Kenny had said we.

Don't let him kill us!

I felt Kenny's energy fading while Murphy ranted.

"Why did you take my boy? Tell me why!"

Us. Kenny's words echoed in my ringing head, playing on a loop.

We. Our. Us.

"Enough!" I screamed and surged to my feet despite the pain. "I did not kill him. He killed himself. You want to be angry? Be angry at *him.* Be angry at yourself for not seeing that he needed help. Be angry at everyone else who knew and never said anything. He was twelve years old, for God's sake. How did you not know your own kid was in that much agony?" My hands shook with the years of bottled-up rage. "I made fun of him, yes. I hurt his feelings, yes. But I. Did. Not. *Kill. Him.*"

"Shut up, shut up, *shut up.*"

Block right! Fight the pain, Kenny directed. My arm shot up to deflect the punch coming at my face. *Open middle!* I buried my left fist in his soft gut, shoved him back when he doubled over with a grunt.

"Don't you dare put this on me. It's your fault. Yours! Why should you get to live and he doesn't?" he raged with his hands on his knees.

I laughed, a maniacal sound. "You think what I do is *living*? He *haunts* me. Every day for the past five years, I see your son's face. It's the first thing I see in the morning and the last thing I see at night."

"Good!" Wheezing, he shoved a hand into his pocket and pulled out a gun.

I froze.

Don't run! Kenny warned.

I couldn't. I didn't have the strength.

"Walk." He jammed the gun against the rib he'd broken, and the pain clawed through the feeble surge of adrenalin I'd managed to stir up. My eyes crossed, and my knees buckled.

He grabbed my arm and hustled me down the path. "This is between you and me. I'm not out to hurt anybody else."

Gee, that's comforting.

We walked down to the sand, my chest burning with every step. My vision blurred. My head and face screamed. The early crowd was gone. Only a few fishermen remained. If these were going to be my last minutes on Earth, I was glad they were on a beach. He marched me behind a dune and stopped.

"On your knees."

Kenny, I'm out of ideas.

Don't give up. Just don't give up. Please.

I have nothing left, Kenny. I can barely breathe.

No! We have to fight!

There it was again. *We.*

"I said on your knees!"

He kicked at my knee, and I dropped, gasping against the fire in my chest.

"I waited so long for this. But Julie…she thinks I'm bitter and broken. She doesn't understand. I'm gonna send you to hell, where you belong. For Liam. I'm doing this for him."

I braced for the pain, but I had a few things to say first. "I'm sorry. I know you don't believe it, but I never meant for your son to die." One more crush of misery when I thought of Julie. "For years, I hated me too. Until I met Julie. I'm in love with her in spite of, well, everything. Please. Please don't do this to her. Let me go."

I stared down the black barrel of the gun Murphy pointed at my face, my eyes calm and steady. Everybody always said that your life flashes before your eyes in situations like these, but mine didn't. There was only the deluge of regrets, an endless parade of them. Teasing Liam to death. Hurting Julie.

Forcing my parents into a life of running. Getting branded a sex offender, carved up like a museum sculpture, and thrown in jail.

The regrets ebbed. All that was left was my relentless guilt, and if there was a merciful God, that was about to end. I watched Murphy's fingers with dread or maybe anticipation, I wasn't sure. His thumb released the safety. His index finger slowly moved for the trigger.

No! Kenny screamed.

Kenny. It's done. I lifted my head, found him sitting opposite me, his face screwed up as he sobbed, looking every bit the petrified little boy I used to be.

No! Please! I'm scared.

I know. Kenny, I have to tell you something. Look at me. I have to tell you something before he—I gulped hard. Kenny swiped at the tears falling from his eyes—our eyes. I said the words I needed to hear.

It's okay, Kenny. It'll be okay. I forgive you. You have to believe it. I'm sorry.

He gasped, and I swear I heard him out loud.

He nodded once. *Will it…hurt?* he whispered.

I shook my head. Only for a second. Don't be scared. Sing. It will help.

Liar. He managed his trademark smirk for a second, and I had to smile, and then he started singing "Zzyzx Rd.," my favorite Stone Sour song.

Suddenly, he was right there with me, arms wrapped around me, crying, and I didn't just sense him, I *felt* him—felt him as real and as solid as the sand under me. My arms circled him as he sang.

"Daddy!"

Julie?

My dead heart restarted. Kenny's astonished face lifted.

"Julie, get out of here!" Murphy shouted.

"No, you can't do this, Daddy. I won't let you."

With her eyes pinned to mine, she stepped between her father's gun and the convicted sex offender who'd bullied her brother to death.

"What the hell are you doing?" I struggled to my feet, moved to her, but the words came from the three of us—her father, Kenny, and me, the notes of disbelief distinguished only by what prompted the question. Fury from her father, shock from me, total elation from Kenny.

"Don't talk to her. Don't even look at her!" Murphy dragged Julie out of his way so he could backhand me with the gun. I hit the sand, my face exploding, ears ringing with Julie's scream.

"Stop, Daddy! Leave him alone!" She fell to her knees in front of me, brushed the hair from my eyes, and I moaned.

"Julie, get the hell out of here!" I spit the words out, bloodied the sand.

"No, I'm not going anywhere," Julie said. "Daddy. Daddy, listen to me. This is wrong. I know his heart, and it's good. It's so good."

And my heart gave such a leap at her words that it nearly cracked another rib.

"Liam would be so ashamed of you."

Jack Murphy staggered back a step, lowered the gun.

"Julie, I…I'm doing this for him, for us." His face twisted.

"No!" she screamed. "You're doing this for yourself. It's always been about you. Mom, Christine, me…we didn't matter! We never did. You married Erica, and even she wasn't enough. All you cared about was having a son, but he's gone now. You can't bring him back."

The gun swung my way again. "Because of him!"

The line in her forehead deepened when she shook her head. "No, not just him. All of us let Liam down, Daddy. All of us. Me. Even you."

"I loved him!" Murphy thumped his chest. "Just like I loved you."

Julie's face crumpled. "You left. You got yourself another baby to love."

Murphy swiped a hand across his nose. "No. No, baby. I always loved you. Always."

Julie shrugged. "Maybe. But you loved Liam more, and even you didn't know he was sad. I only saw him twice a month, and I *knew*. How come you didn't?"

A sob strangled in Murphy's throat. Tears poured from his eyes. "I was working, baby. I worked hard so you kids had a life."

"I didn't need another video game, Dad! I needed my father. More than just a couple of times a month. Liam needed you too. He lived with you, and you still didn't know the kind of pain he was in. Do you even know what he wanted to be when he grew up?"

"He loved baseball."

"No. No, Daddy. He hated sports. He told me that every time I visited. He wanted to be a guidance counselor so he could help other confused kids. I used to ask him what he was confused about. He said "Everything." He disappointed you. He knew it, Daddy. He *knew* it."

"You're blaming me," Murphy said. "It's not my fault. It's his!" The gun rose again. "He killed my boy. Get out of here so I can make him pay."

"No!" She stood to get right in her father's face. "He never meant to hurt Liam, Daddy, but you're standing here with blood on your hands, and that makes you so much worse."

I managed to roll until I was back on my knees but couldn't make it past my heels, dizzy from pain, fear, and…Julie.

He was crying, staring at my blood on his hands. "He has to pay. For Liam."

"He *has* paid, Dad. You have to believe me. I know him. I see the guilt he lives with. You have to let it go now."

Murphy was still shaking his head. I watched the hand holding the gun slowly come back up.

I dragged myself to my feet. My body quivered, and my knees could just barely support me. Gray spots danced in my vision. Blood ran in rivers from my face, and I knew I only had moments left.

"I'm sorry, Julie. I *have* to." Murphy grabbed Julie by her arm, hauled her out of the way and with his other hand, took aim, but Julie was determined to stop that bullet no matter what it took. She bucked, twisted, dropped, and finally succeeded in breaking her father's grasp just as he pulled the trigger.

God. Oh God, no.

CHAPTER 25
My Name Is Ken

I was floating.

Gauzy images danced along the edges of my mind. Julie smiling at me, kissing me, telling me she loved me. I burrowed deeper into the soft warmth.

Julie.

Her name, just thinking about her name zapped my hazy dreams into nightmares. Julie lying. Julie standing between her father and me.

Screaming.

Falling.

Bleeding.

I snapped back to consciousness. Pain pierced every cell in my body when I raised my hands to my head to fight the images and then to fight the hands that held me down.

"Shh, you're okay. It's okay. It's me. Pop."

Pop?

I wrestled my heavy eyelids open. My eyes wouldn't focus, and I squinted until I finally recognized my grandfather. My hands stopped fighting and pulled him closer. "Pop."

My throat felt like it had been sandblasted. My face throbbed. Pushing out that single word was like bench-pressing a few hundred pounds, and it was still no more than a hoarse croak.

"I had to kick your parents out for coffee before they collapsed. They've been sitting here since you were admitted."

Admitted?

I blinked some more and looked around. I was in a hospital bed, an IV plugged into a vein, some monitor vised onto my finger, and a tube strapped to my face pumping ice-cold air up my nose. Julie, I thought with a gasp that brought on another belt of pain. Oh God, Julie.

"Easy. No deep breaths. Your chest is taped. Bastard broke a rib, punctured your lung. It collapsed. You collapsed, been unconscious ever since."

Oh. "Is that all?"

"They say you have a concussion and a fractured jaw too. They want to wire your jaw. Left eye socket is cracked."

Made sense. I felt like I played a few hockey games—as the puck.

Pop's eyes squeezed shut. His hands tightened on mine. "Thought we'd lost you for good this time, Kenny."

The sound of my real name bounced around in my head. I didn't hear another word he said after that until he sat on the bed beside me.

"Really thought it was all over." He gulped.

"This is…what it takes…to get you in…same room as me." Talking was like running an uphill mile.

"I was wrong. I'm sorry."

The drugs they're pumping into my veins must have been incredibly powerful hallucinogens. I was certain my grandfather just apologized. I stared, my brain muddy. I shook my head once—damn, that hurt—and Pop's face fell. "Tell me…what the hell I did…to make you hate me so much."

He shook his head violently. "No. Never hated you. You—" He moved from my bed to the chair beside it. "You ran away from what you did instead of facing it like a man."

My hands clenched. "Never *ran*. Was punished by the law." I had to shove the words out through the swelling in my jaw.

"You changed your name. You changed *my* name." Pop pounded the arm of his chair.

I swallowed, my chest heaving in heavy, painful waves. "Changed it to keep everyone safe."

"Bullshit. You changed your name so you could *hide*." Pop stood up in a rush of fury, paced around my bed. "Ken Mele does. Not. Hide." He thumped his chest to punctuate every word.

"Maybe Kenneth Walter Mele doesn't hide, but Kenneth *James* Mele *does* because his parents asked him to. Kenneth *James* Mele does whatever it takes to protect his family instead of turning his back because of his goddamn pride." My rage eclipsed the pain for that one moment.

We glared at each other for a long moment, our faces red. Suddenly, I didn't care that much about the old man's reasons. All I cared about was Julie.

"Pop." I tugged on the bed rails, tried to sit up. "Julie. Need to see Julie."

"Uh-uh." He pushed me back and left his hands on my shoulders.

Bracing me.

"Julie's gone."

Something exploded inside me. My head spun, my vision lost color. I sucked air but couldn't breathe. Pop's hands tightened when the panic gripped me in powerful jaws and thrashed me from side to side.

"Easy! Easy! She was transferred to a hospital in Manhattan for special surgery."

Special surgery. She was alive? God, she had to be in bad shape. I brought a hand to my face, tried to rub away the throbbing. Jesus. I took in another deep breath, almost on a first-name basis with the pain now. "How long was I out?"

"Um. Two days."

"How bad is she hurt?"

Pop moved back to his chair. "Shoulder's tore up. Eventually, she'll be fine...physically. Emotionally, she has a long road ahead. Your mom called her mother, but she—" A dark cloud passed over his face. "She asked that you please stay away."

The heart behind the taped ribs and collapsed lung gave a sick twist at those words.

"No!" I clenched, my eyes crossing at another peak of pain. "No, they can't keep us apart."

"Kenny, you have to. It's what she wants."

"No!" I fought to sit up. "She said she loves me. She...oh God, I didn't believe her. She got shot to save my life, and I wouldn't believe her." My words slurred together.

"She watched her father nearly kill you, son."

I flinched away like he'd branded me.

"Where's he?"

"Cops arrested him, but he already made bail."

Great. I shut my eyes, abruptly exhausted. So I guess as soon as I'm sprung from the hospital, we'd be moving. Again.

"Don't think he'll be bothering us again though."

My eyes popped open again.

"Your parents had a little discussion with Mr. Murphy. Told him about your time in juvie. Your scars. Your nightmares. Your drinking. He…he likes the idea that you're suffering, so killing you is no longer his life's greatest ambition. Plus, he's grateful you helped him save Julie. Says you threw yourself over her, wouldn't move until he dropped the gun." Pop finished with a snort.

I didn't remember that. The gun went off. Julie fell. There was so much blood. It stained the sand. I kept trying, but I couldn't stop it. I put pressure on it. I kept calling her name, and the blood turned gray. Everything turned gray.

"Pop, I need to see her."

"I know, son. Do you really love her?"

"Yes." I did not hesitate.

"Then you give her anything she needs." He shifted, grabbed an envelope from the table over my bed. "She left you a note."

Great.

I took it, struggled to open the envelope, and cursed the vision that refused to sharpen so I could read the shaky, messy handwriting. Pop took the sheet of notebook paper out of my hands, put on his glasses, and read.

Dear Dan,

You probably totally hate me. But I never lied about loving you.

Pop looked up. "Stop or keep going?"

"Go." I swallowed down the bile that wanted to choke me. He stared at me for a moment and finally nodded.

I should have told you. I didn't want it always hanging over our heads. But it was there. It always will be. And now it's worse. I wish things were different.

Fuck. I didn't want to hear this.

I loved you. But love wasn't enough. I even forgave you. But it's not my forgiveness you need.

Good-bye.

J.

My hand automatically lifted to my neck, but the chain was gone. Pop folded the note, stuffed it back into the envelope, and tossed it on the table. I reached out for it, the pain peaking.

Pop took something from the table, pressed it into my hand. "Here. You've been looking for this, even in your sleep."

I opened my hand, found my forgiveness medallion. I clutched it and her note in a fist that shook. Dad said I'd know when I couldn't live without her, that would be when I'd know I really loved her.

I couldn't let her go. Damn it, I would not let her go.

We have to. Kenny's voice was a dull, faint echo in my throbbing head.

"No, Kenny! You were the one who wanted her in the first place."

Doesn't matter now. This is how she wants it.

I couldn't see Kenny. I could barely hear him. I hadn't heard him in days.

You were unconscious, you idiot.

"Where are you? Are you okay?" I shut my eyes, tried to find him.

Oh, I'm just awesome. And how are you?

"Ken? What's wrong?" Pop's voice was miles away.

"I thought you were gone."

Yeah, well, sorry to disappoint you.

"No, I didn't mean it like that."

I know. I'm glad you fought back. Did you mean what you said?

"Kenny—"

It's okay. It's okay now. His voice echoed inside of my skull. I covered my ears and moaned.

"Dan! Look at me, son. Look at me."

A hand tapped my face. I blinked past the blinding pain, gasping and panting, and saw not Pop but my father. When did he get here? One look at Dad's worried expression and I realized I'd been talking to Kenny out loud. My face burned, but the idea of trying to squeeze out an explanation for my momentary lapse of sanity felt hopeless. I sank back against the pillows, saying nothing.

Uh-oh, Kenny said.

"He's out of his goddamn mind." Pop was across the room. With Mom. Her eyes bulged. No. No more. I couldn't keep hurting them.

Dad sat wearily on the bed next to me and scrubbed a hand over his face.

"Dan, what the hell's going on? You're not just talking to…to yourself. You're having *conversations*?"

I wasn't crazy. What the hell could I say to convince them of that?

News flash, moron. You are. *Man up and tell them.*

If I tell them, you…you know what'll happen.

Yeah, I know.

I frantically tried to pull a convincing lie together, but the note still gripped in my fist derailed my plan. It's not my forgiveness you need, she'd said. I shifted my gaze from Dad to Mom to Pop and back again, tried not to wince at their expressions. I sucked in another shaky breath and closed my eyes.

"Dan, answer me."

"Yeah," I whispered.

"For how long?"

"Since I was thirteen."

He was silent for so long that I opened my eyes to see if he was still there.

"Why didn't you tell us?"

"Dad. I…God, I'm so sorry…I'm *broken*." I blurted and braced for the argument. He'd probably deny it, try to explain it in some perfectly logical way.

"Then we'll fix you," he said simply.

I blinked. His arms came around me and held me.

Damn it. Goddamn it. The fight in me dissolved. I squeezed my eyes shut, but the tears leaked out anyway. My dad's arms tightened around me as I cried in great gulping sobs. I cried for Liam, for Kenny, for Julie, for her parents and for my parents and for Pop. I cried because I hurt all over, because I was alive, because I had no more secrets to keep.

For days, I cried.

I sat alone in our family room, staring at the computer screen. Mom was in the kitchen, making potato salad. She'd invited Brandon's family over for a July Fourth picnic. She walked toward me, holding a glass of water. Pop and Dad were out…somewhere. I forgot where.

"Here you go, honey."

I took the pill she held out in her palm and swallowed it dry. After a few seconds, she put the water glass down next to the computer. She ran her eyes over the clothes that were now too big for my skinny frame.

"You must be hungry. I can make you a sandwich before everyone gets here."

"No, thanks." I wasn't hungry anymore.

"You sure? The potato salad's done. You love my potato salad."

I nodded. "I'm sure." The wires that held my jaw together had come out, but it still hurt to open my mouth wide enough to chew.

Mom stared at me for a long moment and then handed me a thick envelope that she had tucked under her arm. I didn't even notice it until she held it out. "This came in the mail yesterday."

I opened the envelope. It was my diploma. I'd missed graduation. I tossed it on the desk next to the water glass.

"Can I see?"

I shrugged. Mom opened the vinyl case and gasped.

"Oh, honey." She pressed a hand to her mouth. "You used your real name? Pop is going to *bust* with pride."

I didn't say anything. It didn't matter.

Nothing did.

After a moment, she closed the case and put it back where I'd tossed it.

"So what are you up to?"

I shrugged again. "Email."

"Anything interesting come in?"

"USC sent my dorm room assignment."

Mom's eyes dimmed. "You sure you want to do that?"

I rolled my eyes. "Mom."

"I know. I know. It's just…California is so far."

That was the whole idea. Pop said I was still running. Guess he was right. "I'll take the meds. Dr. Philips already found me a new shrink. I'll be fine."

She ran a hand over my hair, unconvinced. "Why don't you go out for a run? I can't remember the last time you ran. You haven't even been out of the house in days."

"I'm good, Mom." I turned back to the computer screen. A few seconds later, she sighed and walked back into the kitchen.

I scanned the email list. Brandon had been sending me a message every day since that day on the beach. I think he visited me in the hospital a few times, but I couldn't remember. He was bringing a new Xbox game over later. I even got a long apology from Jeff. Paul and Lisa emailed prom pictures. They went together. I missed that too. I would have taken Julie.

Julie.

My chest ached, a dull throb whenever I thought about her. My fingers drifted to the medallion I still wore around my neck. I waited for Kenny to say something snarky. But my head was so quiet that my thoughts echoed. I took a quick peek into his room. He was there on the bed, eyes closed, hands under his head, legs stacked one on top of the other.

Silent.

I opened a new email message and started writing.

Dear Julie,

I know you said to stay away, but it's so hard. I miss you all the time. I am so sorry—for everything. I know that doesn't fix anything, but it's the truth.

I drummed my fingers on the desk, thinking of everything I had to say. It all felt so…inadequate now.

I just got an email from Brandon. He said he's doing really well and that he and Jeff are cool. And Lisa and Paul went to the prom together. I got my room assignment from USC. I leave in, like, three weeks.

I slouched in the chair and blew my hair out of my eyes. This was lame. Fuck it. Time to lay it all on the table.

I am so, so sorry. I don't want to lose you. Not now, not after everything that happened. I'm getting help. We'll find a way to get past everything. You forgave me once. Please. Please let me see you before I leave, just once.

I love you, Julie. I always will.

Well, what do you think? I prodded Kenny, lying still on the bed in his room deep inside my mind.

I waited for myself to answer, my finger on the Send button.

Send Discussion Guide

Questions about Send:

1. The character of Kenny plays an important role in Dan's story. Why do you think Kenny exists? Do you think Dan loves Kenny?

2. Throughout the story, Dan acts to protect others. First, he protects Brandon from getting beaten up. Later, he aids an injured baby. Why do you think Dan does nothing to protect Kenny from Jack Murphy at the end of the story?

3. Laws are only now being written to address cyberbullying. Because no law existed for what Dan did, he was found guilty of distributing child pornography, sentenced to time in juvenile detention, and forced to register as a sex offender. Do you think his sentence was a fair and appropriate response to his crime? What would you have done if you were Dan's judge? How would you rewrite laws to address cyber-bullying?

4. Discuss the role Dan's family—Mom, Dad, and Pop—play in this story. How have they influenced Dan's decisions? How do they support him?

5. Discuss the old saying "Forgive and forget." Do you believe the key people in Dan's life truly forgave him? Whose forgiveness does Dan need the most?

6. Dan says often that he killed Liam Murphy, but his therapist suggests that Liam was deeply troubled and Dan's Internet picture added to his burden. What do you think led to Liam's suicide? Could it have been prevented?

7. Do you think Dan and Julie reunite after the book ended? Would it be possible for them to leave the past in the past?

Questions about You:

1. *Send* opens with Dan facing a difficult choice—risk calling attention to himself to protect a stranger or walk away. What would you do in Dan's situation?

2. Can you describe a time in your life when you felt like you were unfairly judged? What skills did you use to cope?

3. Technology—and its dangers—is one of *Send*'s major themes. Consider the role of technology in your life. How does it help? How does it hurt?

4. Another important theme in *Send* is forgiveness. Is it possible for someone you love to do something truly *bad* and still be forgiven? Why or why not?

5. When someone is being bullied, who is more at fault—the bully or the observers who watch but do nothing?

6. Consider a time when someone called you a name. How did it affect you? Several times throughout the story, Dan says he feels like he's been branded. Compare your experience to Dan's. How do the various names he uses to describe himself affect him?

Acknowledgments

Writing may be a solo activity, but Dan and I have never been alone on this journey. Big hugs and kisses to all of my friends and family for putting up with my obsession, especially my guys, Fred, Robert, and Christopher. Thank you for enduring all the hours of nagging ("What do you think of this idea?"), for playing what-if games with me, for reading draft after draft of the manuscript, and for not rolling your eyes every time I said things like, "Julie would totally love this bag." You've cheered with me after every up and cheered me up after every down. I love you all so very much.

To my day job colleagues, thanks for the wealth of material you give me each day. (Yes, I do take notes.) Extra helping of thanks to Don K., whose directive to incorporate social networking into my work planted the story seeds for what eventually became *Send*. Thanks also to Kristen Deutsch and Andrea Leelike for your feedback on that first draft.

Galactic thanks to Aubrey Poole and the entire Sourcebooks team for believing in *Send* enough to take this chance on me and for truly getting Kenny! Enormous thanks to Evan Gregory, my agent, for your wisdom, your humor, and especially your patience while you guided me through the publication process. You rock!

To all the incredibly talented members of my local RWA chapter, Long Island Romance Writers, thank you for all that you do, especially Jeannie Moon, who invited me to my first meeting. Sincerest thanks to Mrs. Kliphuis and the faculty at Smithtown High School East for organizing the best and brightest group of teen beta readers an author ever had. Maria Zollo, Demetrius Colaites, Casey Saslawsky, and Brianna Muschitiello as well as Jillian Buckley, your candor and detailed feedback—with color coding!—helped Dan find his voice. XOXO.

Tons of chocolate kisses to my Twitter, YAlitchat, and Book Hungry pals for your guidance, support, and advice. From you, I learned everything from how to write a query letter to what it feels like to be kicked in the nether regions. (Matt Delman and Julio Vazquez, I'm looking at you.) A bottle of whiskey-soaked thanks (and rainbow cookies!) to author Jeff Somers for the laughs, support, and especially, your encouragement—and to Sean Ferrell for the wisdom you shared. Colossal thanks to author Bill Cameron for reading an early draft and patiently helping me tackle the flaws that led to a *yes!* Bill, it is my fondest wish to thank you in person one day soon. I will bring bacon.

Send literally would not have happened without Kelly Breakey. In a dark moment of profound insecurity, with my finger hovering over the Delete key, you said, "Patty, this is good." Because you were the first person not related to me to say that, I said, "Surely you're not serious," to which you responded, "I am serious. And don't call me Shirley." *giggles* To you, I send a bottomless well of gratitude for being the light that guided me down off the metaphorical ledge. Dan sends his own thanks for shifting my finger off the Delete key and onto Send. *big, big grin*

Last but never least, I send deep and heartfelt sympathies to all who have lost a Liam of their own.

About the Author

Native New Yorker Patty Blount writes software instructions by day and novels by night. On a dare by her oldest son, Patty wrote her first novel in an ice rink during his hockey practice. Though never published, the *Penalty Killer* manuscript was the subject of so many seventh-grade book reports, the English teacher requested a copy and later returned it, covered in red ink. Powered by a serious chocolate obsession, Patty is always looking for great story ideas. Her boss suggested she learn about social media, so Patty began researching Twitter, LinkedIn, and other networks, and she had bad dreams about pictures going viral. She wrote her debut novel, *Send*, when she woke up. (Okay, not really.)

Patty lives on Long Island with her family, a fish, and lots of books. Visit www.pattyblount.com for more information.